A Choice of Vows

M. M. Liles

Table of Contents

Table of Contents

Chapter 1 To Wait... Or Not

Grinning, Talus rolled over in bed. He sat up. Finally, it was today. For today he would join the Border Guard. Today he would no longer be a Learner. Today he became an Adventurer. However, with this giddy feeling inside him, he felt more like a child becoming a Learner than a Learner becoming an adult. Actually, he had felt just like this on that day. He glanced over to where his mentor, Jornus, slept. Slept! How could he? On a day like this. Sure, it was still rather early, but... it was a big day today! Then again Jornus had rarely become excited since his sister had been killed last year, as she hunted a Tongath alligator. Talus laid back down, what would he do for the next hour? Four bells had only just rung, Jornus would not be up until five bells. Despite the ability to see in the dark, he could not read or study because the words in the dark would strain his eyes.

Jornus always counted to a hundred in all seven, wait eight, known languages to pass the time. Talus would have to make do with six. In five he was fluent and the sixth..., well, a few more months should do the trick. Hmm, if he counted through all six twice, Jornus should be awake.

Talus did so, some four times, in fact. After the fourth time he was utterly sick of numbers. Time for a new strategy, like waking him up. Hmm, he could throw a knife into the wall just above his head, that always got him up in a hurry. He grinned. The picture flashed through his mind, Jornus leaping out of bed sword drawn, only to realize it was Talus. Except, that never failed to put him in a sullen mood, and Talus did not want that, not today. Something else would have to do, something a little more mellow. Well, he could knock a chair over, that ought to do it.

Talus slipped out of bed and on silent feet walked to the table, which was in the back corner of the cabin nearer to Jornus' bed. Talus tipped a chair. As it crashed to the ground, Jornus jerked, but then laid still. Talus waited, but Jornus did not move again. Talus frowned. Was Jornus playing games with him?

He inspected Jornus. His breath was slow and steady. His eyes looked completely closed. His face was in a natural sleeping position. Talus did not touch him in case he was asleep. He had only made that mistake once, and nearly paid for it with his life. Do not wake a warrior.

"Come on, I know you are awake." Talus tried, but Jornus did not so much as stir. He sighed, running his hand through his jet-black hair, and tried again, "I'm not a fool. I KNOW you are awake." No answer, maybe Jornus really did still sleep.

Talus picked up the chair and dropped it again. Nothing. He tried another dozen times. No response. His shoulders slumped. How could Jornus sleep through all that? He went to the cupboard to find two tin plates, maybe if he banged- his eye snagged on the butter container. His master could not even pretend to sleep if a small ball of butter hit him! Finally, a plan. He took the lid off the butter container and scooped some out. He balled it, took aim, and threw. It bounced off Jornus' nose and rolled across the floor. Jornus scooped up the ball and threw it, rolling smoothly out of bed. "Fi-" The butter landed fully in Talus' mouth. Worse, it was covered in dirt from the floor. He really should have swept last night. Tasty, eh? Talus gagged and ran for the door. Once outside he spit it out. Yuck!! Butter covered in dirt is gross! Yet worse was the laughter that followed him from the cabin. An idea popped into his head. Yes! This would be great! Talus sent a hurt look at the cabin and ran to the well which was hidden from view by trees.

Once there, he filled the bucket with water. With a ladle-full, he rinsed most of the butter out of his mouth. After hanging the ladle back up, he untied the rope from the bucket. Talus grinned mischievously. Time to pay back Jornus for laughing.

Actually, he was quite glad Jornus was laughing. In the past year, he had barely smiled let alone laughed. That was the reason Talus played, usually, innocent tricks on him. He wanted him to smile and laugh like he had before his sister's death. This would also be one of the last pranks he could play on Jornus.

This would be fun. Besides, who could pass up on an idea like this? With the bucket in one hand, he slipped through the forest to the back door. On the way he had carefully checked to make sure Jornus was still standing by the open front door.

Talus slowly opened the back door, scared it would squeak. It did not, thank Theos. He walked silently across the floor, avoiding any boards that creaked. Stopping a yard behind Jornus, Talus heard him mutter.

"I got that young rascal good this time. Ha. He probably is still scrubbing butter out of his mouth." He was still chuckling.

"Or is he?"

Jornus spun, knife drawn, just as Talus splashed the whole contents of the bucket, catching him right in the face. Jornus splattered while Talus nearly died of laughter. Jornus' shocked expression and the water dripping off him was too much.

"Talus."

The stern tone evident in his mentor's voice caused him to look up.

6

"Shame on you!"

Talus laughed harder than before. Jornus had slipped on the word "on" and grinned. Jornus gave in and laughed too. Finally, he spoke again.

"Well, Talus, are we even? Or shall I look for hot peppers in my oatmeal? By the way, that was an impressive sneak attack. 'Tis no easy thing to keep water quiet. I should know."

Talus grinned, again, but noticed the faraway look that had come into Jornus' eyes on the last couple sentences. For a moment Talus wondered what games he had played with his brother and sister as children or Learners. He did not ask, however. Those kinds of questions tended to make Jornus quiet. Talus decided just to answer the questions put to him, causing Jornus to refocus on him.

"I guess we will say we are even. As for the pepper trick your reaction has never been as good as the first time, master. And... thanks."

Jornus smiled slightly. "In that case, I shall, um, dry off, change, and head up to the village for my coffee. While I am gone, you can clean up and make breakfast..." a hint of sadness entered his voice. "...one last time."

They both changed out of their nightshirts, which were made of the well-tanned, yellowish skin of a Tongath alligator's underside. Their day clothes consisted of a shirt of the same skin section, and a jerkin and a pair of knee length pants made of the greenish dark tan skin of a Tongath's side. The Elerins had long ago discovered that the side of Tongath could withstand arrows and, to some extent, the impact of a sword. Five bells rang, and Jornus headed to the village, leaving Talus with the mess to clean up and breakfast to make. However, Talus' mind kept drifting to what would happen in seven hours

Chapter 2 Ceremonies

Look, master, I see them." Talus declared.

About a quarter mile in front of them two other Elerins were walking, also headed to Elnola, the capital city, for the same event.

With a sly glance at Jornus, he added, "Race ya."

Talus focused on running as fast as possible, since Jornus was a fast silent runner, and maybe a half step behind. Every ounce of energy he had he used to push his legs faster. Jornus had never been beaten, *now* sounded like a good time to change that. Suddenly, Dalus, the younger Elerin, appeared directly in front of him. He could not stop. He could not turn. Hurling right into him, he took them both to the ground. A half second later, Jornus landed hard on his back near them. *Ouch, that had to hurt.* But Jornus just laughed. Then he stood up and winced. *So, it did hurt.*

"That, brother, was an old trick well pulled." Jornus paused. "I must be getting old; I shall feel that for a while." Jornus felt his back, grimacing.

"Ha, Jornus, tell the elders that. That would be a sweet lecture to listen in on. On second thought you must be getting old; losing to a Learner *and* falling for an old trick." Korus, Jornus' younger triplet brother, smirked.

Jornus tried to look insulted for a moment but gave up. "We should be going ere these Learners miss their own ceremony."

Talus, grinning, glanced over to Dalus as the group set off at a quick pace. "Aren't you excited?"

"About...?" Dalus began innocently. Talus shot him an exasperated look and started to speak, but Dalus did not let him.

"About becoming an Adventurer, joining the Border Guard, or having to put up with you for the next fourteen years. The first two, of course, but the third...."

"Hey!!!"

Talus shoved him, but Dalus kept his balance, grinning impetuously. Talus tried to jump on him. Dalus sidestepped, preferring to let Talus jump on the ground. He kept walking, calling over his shoulder.

"You coming? You're going to miss it if you lie on the road all day."

Talus, not bothering with retaliation, caught up. They talked about other things. Well, mostly talked, now and then one or the other would find himself on the ground.

"I, Dalus, son of Havus, swear to..."

Finally, they were entering the next stage of life. Dalus and he were kneeling before the Belon lord in a coliseum of sorts. The surrounding seats were full of witnesses to this event, including both of their families. Talus, Dalus, and the Belon lord were in the center, the captain of the Border Guard and the three judges of Belon flanked the lord, two to a side. On either side of the Learners were Jornus and Korus, who had testified Talus and Dalus were ready to become Adventurers.

As Dalus finished his vows, the Belon lord spoke.

"Dalus, I and all those gathered here will hold you to these vows you have spoken. Now, by the power vested in me by Theos and all Elerinkind, I hereby announce you an Adventurer, bound by the customs of our ancestors."

He reached down and pulled Dalus to his feet. As the onlookers cheered, Dalus went to stand by Korus. The Belon lord turned to Talus.

"Talus, son of Valnis, is it your wish to become an Adventurer?"

"It is."

"Do you swear to follow the laws of our forefathers, to speak the truth in all matters, and to protect the innocent even with your life?"

Talus drew a breath, focused on speaking slowly and clearly. "I, Talus, son of Valnis, swears to follow the laws of our forefathers, to speak the truth in all matters, and to protect the innocent with my life."

"Talus, I and all those gathered here will hold you to these vows you have spoken. Now, by the power vested in me by Theos and all Elerinkind, I hereby announce you an Adventurer, bound by the customs of our ancestors."

The Belon lord pulled Talus to his feet. The newly sworn Adventurer moved to stand by Jornus while the crowd cheered once again.

The captain of the Border Guard stepped forward, stilling the crowd with a hand. "Dalus, Talus, it has come to my ears that it is your wish to join the Border Guard. This body of men and women protects our borders so that those here on Hangnol are free to live untroubled lives. Because of the importance of this duty, I now require the Guards Oath of you."

They stood before him, placing their right fist over their heart when they spoke. "I, Dalus, swear to willingly give my life in defense of our borders, to never question an order given unless it goes against the faith, and to always stand with my brothers in life until death." Dalus replied confidently. Talus repeated the words in his own name.

"I will hold you to your oaths, as will these good people." The captain waved toward the audience. "Report to me at three bells for your new duties."

Talus and Dalus gave the captain an Elerin salute: right fist over heart with a slight inclination of the head. The Belon lord dismissed everyone.

People rushed down to offer congratulations, generally swamping the new Adventurers. They thanked strangers, chatted with friends, and sometimes listened to elders go on and on about things they should do while they are Adventurers.

"Talus!!"

He spun around to find his father directly behind him. His father immediately pulled him into a bear hug. A few seconds later his father stepped back and looked him over. "Congratulations, son."

He just grinned.

"Whenever you are stationed here you should have some wild tales to tell. At least I know I did some crazy things while on the Border Guard."

"I doubt I will have half the adventures you had."

"You never know. Remember though," his father continued more seriously, "the swamp is not a safe place."

Talus snickered. "Only when one startles Jornus."

"I believe I heard something about that. Didn't he fall off a branch and land on a Tongath's snout?"

"Yep, though none of us Learners intended for *that* to happen. We did help him kill it. Then he gave us a long lecture on paying attention to one's surroundings."

Valnis smiled. "You deserved that."

Talus merely shrugged. His mother entered, demanding a hug, then remarked how much he had grown up. Jornus, who overheard, teasingly disagreed, saying that he was still the same rascally Learner simply with a new title. Talus scowled at him, then shrugged. He spoke with several other Elerins that morning.

Just before three bells, Talus and Dalus headed to the Captain's quarters.

Chapter 3 Family and Friends

Anna glanced back at the hill that blocked her view of her home, her parents, and her little brother. Everything about her old life: gone. Gone because King Hissin had summoned three hundred of the fairest maidens of his realm to serve him in his palace. Gone because Baron Wilfred had chosen her to be one of the fifteen from his fief.

Anna looked about the wagon; three girls from her village sat against the sides. None of them were exactly friends... but they were all they would have. Perhaps it was time to start becoming friends. Everyone looked sad and were quiet. Maybe she ought to start a conversation. That could not be too hard since they were all thinking the same thing.

"Why do you suppose we're being taken to the king?"

The response was rather dismal. Cat just said, "Wish I knew." Mara and Violet stared at her, unseeing. Maybe they needed something different.

"Remember, we are not alone."

Three pairs of eyes widened in fear, then calmed as understanding brought peace. Violet smiled sweetly, but Cat and Mara glanced apprehensively at the driver of the wagon. Anna beckoned for them to join her in the back of the wagon.

Drawing close together, they spoke in a whisper, drowned out by the wind. Anna spoke. "We will need to stick together, after all, the palace is not the safest place in Alvar. Especially for the likes of us."

"Not just that, we will have to protect each other. We can't have anyone finding out who we are." Mara said, looking each of them in the eye.

"Unless it was a choice between revealing who we are and doing something wrong. Then we will have to take a stand and... die." Cat sounded decided as she laid out this fact. They let that sink in. If they did not die on a whim of the king, a likely possibility, then they would die because of Who they followed.

After a moment, Violet sighed. "If we are questioned before... that. We cannot say anything. It would not be hard to get our families, the Baron, and everyone else in Rocklin Valley killed."

"Aye, do you think we will ever see any of them again?" Cat wondered.

They decided they might see the Baron. They discussed other things. The wagon stopped at more villages and, as the wagon filled, they grew quieter.

Talus and Dalus were leaving the Captain's office. The meeting had gone well. At dawn the next day, they were to set out for the eighth outpost along the Colmea-Belon border. The assignment was unlikely to bring much excitement since the Elerins and Fumins were friends and Tongaths were not plentiful in that region. However, as the Captain had pointed out when he noted their hidden disappointment, "It is better that you learn your duty somewhere semi-safe as to someplace where danger lurks. Besides, you two have some fourteen years plus to have harrowing adventures." The last part had been said with the usual Elerin grin.

"Well, I'll see you at dawn. My family insisted that I stay with them one last time before we leave the city. Not that I mind, of course." Dalus added quickly, seeing a smirk starting on Talus' face.

"Mine does too. It will be *nice* though; I haven't seen much of my little sister since I was apprenticed to Jornus. I have only seen my little brother, maybe, a dozen times. See ya."

"See ya."

They parted ways, each heading to his parents' home. As much as Talus wanted to hurry, that was near impossible. The streets of Elnola were always somewhat busy, but this was rush hour. The streets were crammed with schoolchildren and with Elerins finishing last minute shopping before everything closed for the night.

It had taken Talus fifteen minutes to go a block. Time for a new plan. Maybe the side streets were less busy, anything would be better than trying to swim through this Elerin-sea. Of course, he still had to cross the main streets every two blocks. After picking his way north across three main streets and east across two main streets, he stood at the gate of his father's house.

Talus pushed the gate open and walked towards the house. He did not make it inside. With a squeal of "Talus!" Kellia, his little sister, raced across the yard and launched herself at him. Talus put a foot back to brace himself and caught her in his arms. He squeezed her, then let her sit back so he could look at her.

"Did you grow? You look taller."

Kellia put a hand on her hip. "Of course, it has been ages and *ages* since you last visited."

Marcus, their little brother, arrived at that moment. He stared shyly up at his brother, "Tawus?"

Talus set Kellia down and knelt in front of Marcus. "Hello, Marcus."

"Hi." With that word said, he stuck his thumb in his mouth, sat down, and found his toes with his other hand.

Talus stood and looked at Kellia. "Did you see the ceremony?"

"Yeah." She made a pouty face. "But then Mommy took me right back to school. She said I would see you later. Which, I guess *was* true."

Talus laughed. "Yes, well, you can see me now."

Kellia grinned and seemed about to reply when their father's voice broke in. "Talus, there you are. I was beginning to wonder if you had gotten lost. Kellia, why don't you convince your brothers to come inside."

"Sure, Daddy."

She placed Marcus on her hip and grabbed Talus by the hand, pulling him after her.

<<<<<<<<<<<<<<<>>>>>>>>>>>>>

Anna stretched, glad to be out of the wagon. When it had just been the four of them it had not been bad, but once all fifteen girls had been picked up.... That was a little much for the six-foot by six-foot back of the wagon.

The place they had stopped at seemed to be a large camp. Tents, fires, girls, more tents, drivers, wagons, more tents, and soldiers littered the area. *Soldiers!* Why were there soldiers?

Maybe some of the girls or their fathers had been stubborn. Or perhaps trouble was expected? Hmm, no escaping tonight, should they have wanted such a thing. After all, what the king did to girls was... blood chilling. And after tonight escape would be near impossible. A nearby sergeant's bored voice broke into Anna's thoughts.

"Girls, break into groups of four, to determine your sleeping arrangements." Quickly, Anna and the girls from her village moved a little farther away from the rest of the girls. When all the girls had broken into groups, the sergeant had guards show each group to a tent. Almost immediately, different guards called them out again for supper.

<<<<<<<<<<<<<<<>>>>>>>>>>>>>

Anna glanced up as Cat ducked back into the tent.

"I couldn't get past the guards, not even when I told them it was *very* urgent." Cat sighed. "I guess we are stuck with the king."

13

Anna cupped her chin and stared into space.

Mara looked up, a determined expression coming across her face. She pushed a strand of waist-length, dark red hair behind her ear.

"Maybe we shouldn't look at it that way. After all, is it not our duty as Followers to obey the king that Theos has placed in authority over us and as Garians to obey him as the king of Garia even if the duty required of us is most unpleasant?"

Anna winced. Why hadn't she thought of that?

Cat had also turned red, even Violet looked a little pink. Anna took a deep breath. "You are right, Mara."

Mara's words had emboldened Violet who added almost eagerly.

"And we should do it to the best of our ability with joy."

Anna felt the blood creeping back into her cheeks. That would be so easy for Violet. She was always so perfect. She pushed the envious thought away. Violet was right and she could do it, with Theos' help.

Cat must have realized her embarrassment.

"Now that we have got that figured out, do you remember the story about the cat that got loose into the royal dining room?"

The mere mention of that lightened the conversation immediately. Laughter echoed through the tent.

<<<<<<<<<<<<<>>>>>>>>>>>>>

Anna woke with a start, a scream cutting across her consciousness. She sat up suddenly and the scream came again, along with a voice. Mara's voice.

Anna jumped to her feet and ran out of the tent. One of the guards was holding her new friend with a knife to her throat. Anna grabbed the first thing she saw, a chunk of firewood and hit him over the head with it, until the man dropped like a stone.

Mara collapsed with him, the knife drawing a thin line on her neck. Thank Theos, it had not cut more than skin. Anna helped Mara sit up and put an arm around her.

Mara sobbed for a long time.

"What happened?" Anna asked gently after what must have been a half an hour.

"He wanted me, and I refused, so he decided to kill me first." Mara touched the line on her neck, her voice trembling.

"That was really brave of you." Anna tried to comfort her.

"And now I-I hate him!" She started to cry.

"Of course, you do. He's horrible and he hurt you." Anna glanced at the downed figure, her own anger building up.

"But we're supposed to love people. Hate the sin, love people."

Anna stared at her. "Well, yes. But...." She could not think of anything to say. She mostly couldn't believe Mara's mind had come to this conclusion at the moment. Right or not.

"Mara, he almost killed you, among other things; he's a monster!"

"True." Mara nodded. In the moonlight, it looked like a weight had settled in her face. "I suppose I ought to forgive him."

The words hung in the air, and Mara started crying again. "I can't, you're right, he's a monster!"

Anna rubbed Mara's shoulder, staring east as a faint light grew.

The man stirred and Anna jumped up. "Mara, he's waking up, let's go!"

Mara let Anna pull her up. She stared at the man as the light increased.

"He doesn't care about it." Anna tugged on her arm.

"But I do." Mara said, resolve building in her voice. "I forgive you."

The man groaned and Mara let Anna lead her back to the tent. They lay down, and Anna stared up at the cloth, thinking.

Talus sat cross-legged atop the Hangnolin Wall, the long wall surrounding Hangnol Isle. All the Elerins of Belon lived on the Isle except the Border Guards, Wood Cutters, and the Tongath Hunters. The sun's first rays lit the eastern sky, making Dalus officially late. Talus grinned, imagining how fun it would be to torture Dalus over the fact.

His thoughts drifted back to the night before. At nine, Kellia was much more grown up than she had been four years ago when he had been apprenticed. And there was Marcus. He had been shy at first, until he found that Talus was more fun to sit on than Mommy or Daddy. That was after Talus had captured him and given him horsey or "alligator" rides. His ear caught the sound of heavy breathing. Seconds later, Dalus swung himself on to the wall.

Talus grinned. "You're late!"

Dalus shook his head gravely. "Certainly not. The sun simply rose early this morning."

"I see."

They stared at each other trying not to show a hint of laughter. Slowly Talus' grin resurfaced.

"We should be going, or the sun will declare us late, when, in fact, we are yet early."

"I'm sure there is no rush. Commander Valoris is sure to know if the sun rose early. Besides, we cannot really be late since we're only expected sometime this evening."

"Oh, we could be quite late with your speed. It will probably be dawn," He paused. "Tomorrow!"

"You!!!"

Dalus lunged for him. Talus, however, had leapt from the wall, catching the top branches of an Oklmar tree some twenty feet below. He raced off through the trees with Dalus hot on his trail

Chapter 4 New Lives

Anna stared around in wonder. She had never seen anything that compared with Ketlin. Her village, the Baron's castle, even the town they had passed through on the way there; they all seemed like playthings to the city that lay before her.

The main part of Ketlin lay on an island in the Kointh River. The city was heavily populated as was most of Garia. Even with the beggars and pickpockets that lined the streets, Ketlin was a beautiful place. The buildings were of white cut stone, with carvings inlaid with precious stones and metals, and covered in ivy. In some places, however, it could be seen that those things were from a different age. Here a figure was missing its eye. There a building crumbled. In stark contrast to the white and green of the older buildings, the newer buildings were painted deep red, a twisted black and silver dragon over their doors.

Just inside the castle, Anna saw something that made her shiver and look away. A grim reminder of the real Garia: a platform stained crimson.

<<<<<<<<<<<<<>>>>>>>>>>>>>

Once inside Ketlin Castle the wagons were directed to stop by the kitchen door. A stern-faced woman greeted the girls.

"Good afternoon, girls. I am Helena Crage. You will address me either as Miss Crage or Mistress. Obey your betters promptly and do *not* get in the king's way, do this and you will live longer. Should the king ever notice and require you, you will go with him immediately."

She divided them into groups of twenty, showed each group to a bunk room, and dismissed them to chores.

Anna, Mara, Cat, and Violet were assigned kitchen duty, to Anna's joy and to Mara's chagrin.

The kitchen was busy, and the cook could have been a little nicer. Violet thought that tasting the food was an essential part of kitchen duty. The cook did not agree. Whenever he caught her, which was quite often, he would rap her over the head with his ladle. Violet told the others later that all the food was wonderful. Indeed, it was fit for a king's table!

<<<<<<<<<<<<>>>>>>>>>>>>

Despite Talus' previous prediction, Dalus and he arrived fairly early that evening. Of course, both were breathless, the result of having chased each other most of the last hour. They were now standing on the porch of an outpost in a tree. In front of them was Commander Valoris, who studied them for a second before he asked.

"Did Tongaths start climbing trees, chasing you about?"

Dalus shook his head. "No sir. You see Talus here told me a fish could walk faster than I could. I...um...you see...simply wished to prove him wrong."

Talus feigned offended innocence. Valoris, who was already smiling, laughed. He motioned for them to follow him.

They followed their commander across the porch to a door. The door led into a large room. To the right sat the kitchen and dinner table. To the left lay two rows of nine beds. In the back corner two walls separated Commander Valoris' and Lieutenant Rhemus' chamber from the main room.

"Warriors of Belon," Valoris began. The men scattered across the room stood and came to attention. "Elnola has sent us a couple of young rascals. That being the case, they should mix well with you lot. This is Dalus, son of Havus, and Talus, son of Valnis."

That said, Valoris crossed the room and disappeared through a door, leaving Talus and Dalus at the mercy of the strangers. One of them, Alavis, gestured toward two beds at the nearer end of the two rows.

"You can have those ones."

As Talus and Dalus put their stuff on their beds, Alavis spoke again, a wicked grin playing across his face.

"Let's see how good you are."

Confusion played across both their faces and Talus asked, "Good at what?"

"Hmm, blades, bows, or knives, Taevus?"

Taevus, who was sitting on a bed some five down, stroked his beard then slowly grinned.

"All three."

"Shall we start with blades?"

Still grinning wickedly, Alavis walked to the wooden weapon rack. He picked out four wooden blades: one he threw to Talus, one to Dalus, one to Taevus and one he kept for himself. As he and Taevus faced down Talus and Dalus, Alavis called to the other Elerins.

"Get some blades, mates, and let's see what these green hands are made of."

As they armed, Talus decided two to twelve was going to be a bit... difficult. Apparently Dalus was thinking along the same lines.

"Six each. A little steep, eh, Talus?"

Yes, but time had run out to answer. Their opponents rushed them. They stood back-to-back parrying the blades seeking to get them. They searched for an opening in the enemy defense. Although they disarmed four of their opponents, the fight was short. Elerins, ninety-nine out of one hundred, are amazing swordsmen. And none of the last percentile were to be found here.

Two minutes after the fight began, Talus failed to parry one of the blades seeking him and was knocked to the ground. Dalus did not last long alone. Their new comrades pulled them up.

"Well, they are good swordsmen, especially for graduated Learners." Taevus said to no one in particular.

"Yeah," Alavis grinned again, "shall we go outside to see their bow skills?"

Talus swallowed, hard. *This would not be good.*

<<<<<<<<<<<<<>>>>>>>>>>>>

The next morning, Anna and her friends woke to the headmistress' grim voice.

"Up, all of you. The king has ordered all the staff to the courtyard. You newbies get to witness the real Ketlin on your first day."

She swept from the room, leaving the sleepy girls to decide what that meant. Mara, being a bit more of a morning person than the rest, asked.

"So.., how exactly do we get to the courtyard?"

The other nineteen girls gave her blank stares. After a moment, Anna found the answer.

"We could just follow the crowd. I mean, if everyone is called to the courtyard, we can follow them, right?"

The others agreed. Cat practically suggested they change, or they would miss the crowd.

<<<<<<<<<<<<<>>>>>>>>>>>>

As they entered the courtyard, Anna's eyes widened at the sight that met them. In the center of the courtyard a man was bound to a pole, surrounded by sticks. The man's face seemed familiar. Who was he? A small cry escaped Violet. Anna studied her. Her usually cheerful face had gone deathly pale and shock had frozen her. Anna looked up into Mara's eyes. Mara answered her unspoken question.

"He is her oldest brother."

That broke a quiet sob from Violet. Anna put her arm about her.

Anna looked back to Violet's brother; she watched his eyes widen as he found his sister in the crowd. He bowed his head for a second, looking up again when a pair of doors opened. The gray-haired king entered surrounded by his guards, two of whom bore torches. King Hissin made his way to the center and raised his hand. Instant silence fell.

"My dear subjects, this man is one of those few remaining Followers of Iasos. These people are dangerous, outdated, and disobedient. This man disobeyed a direct order from me. Why? Because of his *beliefs*. These people are treacherous, if my loyal guards had not taken this man in hand, he would have slain me and everyone else in the room!" The king turned to Violet's brother.

"Any last words, before we make you a living sacrifice to Althon?"

"You cannot win, Your Majesty, for those who follow Iasos are never alone."

King Hissin laughed and all the courtyard with him. But Anna watched Violet straighten and hold up her head. His last words were for his sister, and perhaps for any other Followers in that courtyard. The king's voice burned into her thoughts.

"Light him up!"

The guards were only too glad. The torches landed in oiled sticks, and he was gone in fire and smoke. In the shout and applause that followed, few noticed Violet's strangled sobs as she fought tears.

How could King Hissin kill so callously? And how could people applaud that? Anna wanted to cry, but she didn't. She just pulled Violet into a hug.

Chapter 5 The Danger of Bubbles

C at had gone ahead to ensure they avoided all people. After all, as Mara had pointed out, if Violet was seen in tears, she would be arrested and killed for supposed sympathy for the Followers of Iasos. Poor girl, she was trying to be strong, but she was still pale, and tears occasionally slid down her face. In fact, they were all pale after that ordeal. However, Violet's tears would betray her, thus they did not want to encounter any people.

After slipping into a side room-or pretending to be doing something- several times, they reached their room. *Now*, Anna thought, *they were safe*. Mara quickly dispelled that idea.

"You know, we are supposed to be in the kitchen in around three minutes. She can't go like this."

That was certainly true. When they had entered the room, the tide of tears Violet had been holding back had broken free. Even now, her quiet sobs reached them from where Cat held her across the room. Anna frowned.

"We could say she is not well...."

Mara shook her head. "Maybe but someone would probably be sent to see what she has. Besides, that is not true, or at least it's not in the way they would take it."

"Yeah. Hmm... perhaps if we wait a little bit she will be okay."

"I doubt it."

"No, I'll be alright." Violet's weak voice entered their conversation. They must have looked uncertain, because Cat reassured them.

"Really, I pinched her cheeks to bring some color back. Then we used her cold fingers to draw the redness from her eyes. After all she'll attract less notice if we are not late."

"We will be hard pressed to not be late at this point." Anna said grimly.

"What are we waiting for then?" Violet gave a weak little smile as she made for the door.

"Violet, wait!" Anna called as they hurried after her.

<<<<<<<<<<<<>>>>>>>>>>>>

"Oh, Talus! You would never guess what Alavis told me."

That was Ramis. He had been on duty the day before when Talus and Dalus had shown their bow skills. One of Talus' arrows had completely missed the target, a feat nearly unheard of in Belon.

Talus winced slightly but called back. "Was it that if you ate much more you would be as round as an Oklmar tree?" Oklmars grew to be four to six feet around.

"Oh no. I heard something unbelievable about your bow skills."

"If it is unbelievable, then don't believe it."

"Oh, Alavis assured me it is true. In fact, speaking of Oklmars, you probably couldn't hit one if it was right in front of you."

"That's not true." Dalus broke in. "His first shots were better."

"Better!! Alavis said they were six inches off. SIX INCHES!!!"

Dalus snickered. "I believe someone said your knife throwing skills are worse."

"Ramis! Dalus! Enough." Commander Valoris' voice was stern. They looked up into his icy gaze, then looked away, ashamed. Silence descended.

Valoris had been showing Talus and Dalus the area they would participate in patrolling for the rest of the week. They had arrived near the end of the patrol's duration at that outpost.

A little way off the path to the left, something was causing a large amount of bubbling in the swamp water. Talus' curiosity ended the silence.

"Commander, what is the source of the bubbling, yonder?"

Valoris' eyes widened as memory flitted across his face. "Trust me, Talus, you do *not* want to know." Turning to encompass all of them, he added. "No one is to go near that place."

As hard as Talus tried, he could not stop thinking about it.

<<<<<<<<<<<<>>>>>>>>>>>>

"Dalus, what do you suppose Valoris is so keen on keeping us away from?" Talus asked softly.

They were sitting on Talus' bed, so that their backs rested against the wall. Dalus stared blankly at him for a moment.

"Oh..., you're talking about that bubbly thing, right?"

"Yeah, of course. What do you think causes it?"

"How should I know? Maybe a large Tongath or a large...hmm... something?"

"Tongaths tend to float. And-"

"There are two ways you can find out." A new voice broke in. It was Ramis.

"And what are those?" Dalus asked guardedly.

"The first is that you could ask Valoris, but I would not- the subject seems closed."

Talus murmured in agreement, while Dalus asked for the second option.

"The second way is to simply go investigate."

Ramis said that casually, but both Talus and Dalus leapt to their feet.

"Are you CRAZY? That would be direct disobedience to our commander!" Talus sounded horrified.

Ramis shrugged dismissively. "Valoris is losing it. He is *always* misplacing his sharpening stone. Also, a couple weeks ago he completely forgot Lieutenant Rhemus' name."

"Even so it would be wrong!" Dalus maintained fiercely.

"Hardly. Didn't you see the wild look in his eyes right before he gave the order? He was not in his right mind. Besides, who is afraid of a few bubbles?"

"Still, I do not think-" Dalus began.

"Valoris will never know. He won't be back from his patrol for a while. Not to mention *everyone* is counting on you finding out what is under those bubbles. You would not want to disappoint them, would you?"

"I don't-"

"Come on, Dalus," Talus broke in. "We don't have to get very close. We can just throw a stick or something at it and see what happens. Then we will come back. Nothing wrong about that."

"Are you sure?"

"Aye."

"All right." Dalus sounded reluctant.

After about ten minutes, they arrived at the place on the path from which the bubbles could be seen. They climbed through the trees to a branch some ten feet from and twenty feet above it. Because of the Elerin trait of nocturnal vision, the bubbles were perfectly visible in the center of a small pool. The trees parted enough to allow the moonlight to cast a haunting brilliance on the water. Everything was silent and still, until Talus tossed a small log into the bubbles.

Silence remained for half a second before an eerie screech shattered it. Water flew everywhere. It smashed into Talus, knocking him backwards. Talus reached desperately for a lower branch. His fingers snatched the rough bark. He hung for a second before pulling himself on to the branch. He looked back to the pool and froze, horrified at the sight that met him.

It was a huge octopus-like creature, only with dozens of arms. It had wrinkled gray-brown skin matching the water in which it lived. But Talus saw only the eyes: huge, calculating, bulging like a fly's, but solid with small black pupils.

Slowly, a scream registered in Talus' mind. Whose scream? Dalus! Where was he? He was not on any of the branches around Talus.

His gaze caught on something. A tentacle of the thing was moving towards its mouth. And trapped in its coils was Dalus! The top part of the creature's head tipped back, revealing a huge, gaping throat: no teeth, no tongue, just a throat.

Talus grabbed his bow and checked the string, a little damp. Well, it would have to do. He put an arrow on the string. The creature had Dalus almost to its mouth! He rushed the shot. Thankfully, the arrow still landed in the creature's eye, just a little to the side. The thing screamed in rage. Talus tried a second shot and utterly missed, nearly hitting Dalus. So much for the legendary Elerin skill.

The creature moved toward him, annoyed. Talus saw his chance. Drawing a knife, he jumped. He landed on the coils surrounding Dalus. He sliced into them. The thing screeched and ripped Talus off. Coils encircled him. Talus pushed against them, trying to free himself. It was so slimy. The coils grew tighter, locking his hands in place. Before him yawned the throat. Talus frantically tried to move, to escape. He did not want to die like this. The coils tightened. He could not breathe.

A wordless shout filled his sleepy senses. The creature screamed, hurting Talus' ears, and dropped him. He floundered attempting to breathe and get away from the creature. A voice roared.

"Dalus! Talus! Get in the trees and on the path... NOW!!!"

Talus moved without thinking, shock had taken hold. He swam to the nearest tree and scrambled up it. He hurried to the path. Dalus was there, but he did not truly notice. Another scream. In a different state of mind, Talus would have recognized the thrum of a bow string right before it. But he heard nothing. Silence filled the swamp.

Valoris appeared on the path before Talus and Dalus.

"What were you think-"

What was he going to do to them? The fierce anger in his eyes frightened Talus. In his shocked state, he slunk back, scared of more pain. For some reason, Valoris' eyes softened.

"Are you hurt?" The commander asked.

Talus stared at him blankly, not registering the question as a question.

Valoris sighed.

"Let's get you two home." Gently, he guided them down the path toward the outpost.

<<<<<<<<<<<<>>>>>>>>>>>>

Valoris pushed the outpost door open and stepped inside, followed by Talus and Dalus. Rhemus, who had been sitting against the wall separating the mess room, jumped to his feet and spoke.

"Valoris, there you are. Did you get lost- what happened to them?"

Talus and Dalus were no longer dazed, but their eyes were shadowed, and bruises were appearing on their arms and legs. Talus noted the tired smile Valoris gave Rhemus.

"No, these two decided to go play with a multapus."

Rhemus' eyes widened. "And all three of you survived? Surely you warned them?" Talus and Dalus turned red. Talus stared at the ground. Why had he not listened? And why had he dragged Dalus into it?

Valoris glanced at them. "I did, but it may be that I misjudged them, and they will be trouble."

Why had he been so foolish? He had killed Valoris' trust right at the beginning.

Someone moved among the other Elerins, all of whom were pretending to sleep. Ramis rolled out of bed and stood.

"They are not the trouble, Commander. I am. I, uh, encouraged them to go."

Valoris studied him with an unreadable expression, but he remained silent. Ramis swallowed and took a breath.

"You see, Commander, when I first suggested the idea, they were completely shocked. Then I pressured them until they were convinced and left. I do not believe they would have done it without me."

"They made the choice, Ramis." Valoris said softly.

"Yes, but I am the reason they made that choice."

Valoris regarded him for a minute. "Let's continue this conversation in private." Valoris motioned toward his bedroom door. He turned to Rhemus. "Get them in bed, they have had a long evening, but this night will be longer."

"I'll take care of them, Valoris." Rhemus answered. "You should get some rest soon as well."

Valoris waved the comment aside and followed Ramis. Rhemus frowned at his back, before turning to Talus and Dalus with a soft smile.

"What happened?"

Talus and Dalus exchanged a look. Surely, he did not want to know. The throat loomed in Talus' mind. His breath stuttered.

"It will be easier to sleep if you tell us about it." Rhemus added.

"Well, okay," Dalus started then stopped. "You should tell them, Talus. I do not remember much after I fell from that branch." Talus nodded slowly.

He spoke, fear evident in his voice. Occasionally, Dalus added something. Very little made much sense, especially when they attempted to describe the creature, which they learned in the process that only Rhemus had seen. After a while, the lieutenant stopped them and sent everyone to bed.

Talus paused and looked back at the lieutenant.

"Sir?"

"It's Rhemus, Talus." He answered gently.

"Sorry, Rhemus, I um... Ramis said Valoris forgot your name, why was that?" Should he really be asking? He was already in so much trouble.

Rhemus winced. "The courtesy of a shadow man's club. He was only semi-conscious at the time. Now try and get some rest, Talus."

"I will.

Chapter 6 Carrots

Talus changed position for the one hundredth time in the last five minutes. He muffled a gasp as a bruised rib took too much weight. Every time he closed his eyes, he could see it. The creature's gaping throat and bulging eyes filled his vision. His heart started beating wildly and terror clouded his mind. It was always there. However, eventually exhaustion overwhelmed his desire to remain awake.

He crouched on that branch; the creature was staring at him. The eyes filled his vision, enticing him. "Come, come to me," they called. He tried to move, to escape. His feet were glued to the branch. No! Please! Move! It was hopeless. Its tentacles rose out of the water, swarming toward him. They encircled him. It ripped him off. The dark wet throat appeared. Terror filled him. He screamed.

His eyes popped open. At least a dozen Elerins leapt to their feet, weapons drawn. One looked at him and spoke quietly.

"Go back to sleep, Talus. It cannot get you here."

Some other Elerin muttered. "I just got to sleep too!"

Talus laid still for a while, thinking through the adventures of the day. After a little while, his thoughts turned to what the next day might bring. Valoris would undoubtedly speak to them at some point. The day before Taevus had warned him and Dalus that such interviews were almost always painful, even if it was not physically. He sighed softly, three days as an Adventurer and already in trouble.

The door to Valoris and Rhemus' quarters opened, letting Ramis out. He walked carefully to avoid waking his sleeping comrades. Long shadows painted under his eyes and a hint of blood escaped his shirt, suggesting the intensity of what the Elerin had been through. Talus suddenly realized how he could get answers to his thoughts, indirectly of course. He got up and crossed the room to Ramis.

"You still alive?"

Ramis looked up and let something resembling a smile show. "No, I am dead."

"Really?"

"No, not quite." Ramis paused, and resolve settled on his face. "Listen, Talus. I'm sorry I pushed you, I should not have said what I did. I've been undermining Valoris like that for a while, and I did not even think of it being wrong until you and Dalus almost died. Will you forgive me?"

Talus looked into Ramis' troubled expression. "I forgive you. Dalus and I are the only ones to blame for what we actually did. You just, as you said, pushed us."

For a long moment, neither spoke. Talus drew a slow breath and asked hesitantly. "Do you mind if I ask what it was like?"

Ramis studied him a second then answered.

"Wondering about tomorrow? Valoris is a good leader. Everything he does, he does for our betterment. But you might as well know the same thing happened to Valoris and Rhemus several years ago, so he understands everything you went through perfectly."

"Oh, no wonder the order, at that memory...." Talus shivered, the monster's eyes again passing through his brain.

Ramis put his hand on his shoulder.

"I don't know exactly what you saw but give up what happened to Theos. He is stronger."

"Thanks, you're right." Talus smiled a little bit and added. "Perhaps I should let you get some sleep, so you are no longer 'not quite dead.' Though you might not get much." Talus added rather apologetic.

Ramis raised an eyebrow. "Why not?"

"Well, you see, some of them have this habit of screaming in their sleep. Bad habit, I know."

"Ahh, well, good night."

They made their way to their respective beds. They slept with only a few interruptions until five bells.

<<<<<<<<<<<<>>>>>>>>>>>>

Anna and her friends walked to the kitchen. They were all in good spirits, even Violet; courtesy of waking up on the right side of the bed, or maybe just good camaraderie.

On reaching the kitchen, the cook set them to work on kneading bread. After a half minute, Cat smiled.

"Let's race!"

They kneaded as hard and fast as possible. Finally, Anna stopped, panting, "Mine's done." Half a second later, Mara shouted, "Finished!" Cat and Violet finished seconds afterwards.

They put the dough on to rise and were talked into flipping sausage patties. Well, 'talked into' is a bit of a loose term, 'ordered' might have been better. It went a little like this, "Oh, you're done. Now you can flip sausages."

Once breakfast for the king, his lords, his knights, the guards, and the rest of the staff was cooked and eaten, the kitchen staff ate. The food was good. After all, it was leftovers from the king's table.

For supper that night the cook decided to make three stews- beef stew, chicken stew, and vegetable stew. This meant that half the kitchen had to chop meats and vegetables. Anna and Cat were put to work cutting carrots. Anna was chopping away thoughtlessly, when Cat grinned.

"Don't you feel sorry for the poor carrots?"

Anna gave her an odd look but said nothing.

"You ought to comfort them. Tell them that being eaten isn't too bad."

"They don't have feelings, you know." Anna replied dryly, as she reached for another couple carrots. Cat snagged them, making them walk away and speak.

"Oow, she has a knife, run away, run away!"

Anna set her knife down and grabbed at them. The carrots ran, taking Cat with them. They called back.

"Oh no! She's coming, she wants to kill us!"

Anna chased them all over the kitchen. She and Cat were both laughing, until they ran full into the cook. He glared at them.

"What are you doing?!! The carrots will not cut themselves!" He roared, hitting them over their heads with his ladle.

They hurried back to their counter, still suppressing giggles. Anna beckoned the carrots.

"Come here, little carrots. It won't hurt very much."

The carrots came tentatively. Anna picked them up, and she and Cat returned to work.

<<<<<<<<<<<<<>>>>>>>>>>>>

Eirin, king of Alcasa, strode down the halls of Aubin castle. An Elerin, at least a foot shorter, jogged to keep up with him.

"Eirin, you should not do these things. It is not fair to them, or to yourself for that matter. Think, would your father have approved?"

Eirin stopped, turning on him. His face was red with barely contained anger.

"I am supposed to be nice to people, Lentus! Would you like it if I was always mean to people? So what if I enjoy talking to them."

"My lord, you can talk to them all you want. However, it is once you go past talking and often even the way you talk to them that is not kingly and ought not be done. You are the example to your people." Lentus' voice was calm and quiet.

Whatever constrained Eirin's anger broke.

"I am the king! I decide what is kingly! I say there is nothing wrong with it! So SHUT UP!!!"

Eirin stormed down the hall, leaving Lentus alone. Eirin turned a corner and found the guards King Hissin of Garia had sent as a gift some weeks ago. The accompanying letter had said they would do anything for him. He approached them and spoke quietly.

"You two, can you get rid of that Elerin, Lentus. Do not kill him, just get rid of him. He is driving me crazy."

They bowed. One spoke, voice sinister.

"With pleasure, my lord."

They departed, and King Eirin headed to his chambers.

Chapter 7 Friends

The morning following the incident with the swamp monster, Talus and Dalus had seen Valoris. The meeting was thankfully brief. Valoris' ending words were, "So do you understand that when I give an order, I give it for a reason?" They had replied in the affirmative, and it became the forgotten but remembered past.

Four days after that, the company had moved from the outpost on the Colmea-Belon to one on the Alcasan-Belon border. It was still a relatively safe place. After all, not everyone could be on the Tritha-Belon border!

Strange rumors were afoot among the Alcasan farmers. Rumors said that Lentus, the translator to King Eirin of Alcasa, had disappeared. Those rumors made the Elerins uneasy. Elerins do not usually disappear. They *never* run away from duty. Lentus had been in the Alcasan court for some thirty years, why would he vanish now? Many Elerins thought he had been killed, and King Eirin was hiding the fact. So far it was all talk, and normal life continued.

Talus and Dalus were out patrolling three days into the duration at the new outpost. That is to say they were looking for cows, sheep, or angry farmers stuck in the mire at the edge of the swamp.

They rounded a tree and stopped. A little beyond the swamp, not a hundred feet away, was a party of nobles and ladies on horseback. Talus, who was in the lead, glanced back at Dalus.

"Do you suppose they lost a boar or a stag?"

Dalus grinned. "Perhaps. Let's see who they are and what they want. If it is too important, you can run for Commander Valoris."

"Why me?"

"Because you are younger."

Talus made an annoyed face.

They dropped down to a branch from which the noble company could see them. Dalus spoke.

"Lords, ladies, and horses of Alcasa, what brings you to our border?"

Two men urged their horses forward a few paces. The herald spoke, motioning to the other rider.

"You are speaking to his majesty, Eirin, King of Alcasa. His majesty has a request to make of the Belon lord."

Dalus grinned at Talus and asked softly so that his voice could not carried to the group on horseback.

"Do you suppose he meant that the horse or the man is the king?"

"Oh... Probably the man. After all, what king allows someone to sit on them?"

Dalus grinned, then called to King Eirin. "Would you like my friend here to fetch our commander?"

Talus glared at Dalus.

The king nodded and the herald replied.

"His Majesty wishes that you would do so quickly."

Talus muttered, "I'll be back." Dalus smirked.

Talus ran along the branch to near the trunk, then leapt to another branch. In six minutes, he arrived at the outpost. He hurried inside and explained matters quickly to Valoris, who called Alavis and Taevus to follow them.

Fourteen minutes after Talus had left, they met up with Dalus, who was still watching King Eirin's party. Valoris nodded to Alavis and Taevus.

"Stay here and unseen, if he tries anything funny put an arrow by his horse, with Lentus' disappearance I don't want to take any chances."

"Will you ask him about that, commander?" Alavis questioned.

"No, if he's innocent in the matter, he'll tell me." Valoris replied shortly. "Besides, I can't just ask a king that, he'd think I was accusing him."

"We are!" Taevus muttered.

Valoris shot him a glance but nodded to Talus and Dalus. "You two come with me. I will handle the talking, keep your faces neutral."

Valoris leapt from the branch over the mire to the hard ground beyond without waiting for an answer, giving Talus the brief impression that the commander was nervous. He pushed the idea away as Dalus and he jumped. Each rolled to break his fall. Valoris approached the king and saluted.

"Your Majesty, I am Valoris, son of Hangis. What can I do for Your Majesty?"

King Eirin dismounted. "I need a message taken to the Belon lord. I assume you can arrange that."

"Yes, Your Majesty. What will the message be?"

"I find myself without an interpreter, Commander. As I soon leave for Garia, this is quite a problem. Therefore, in accordance with the old agreement, I request an interpreter. I would prefer the youngest Adventurer they will give me."

32

Valoris raised an eyebrow. "Your Majesty is aware that younger Adventurers have not completed their full linguistic training?"

"Yes, yes." King Eirin waved the question aside impatiently. "All he needs to know is Alcasan, Garian, and Fumin."

"As you wish. If you will return in a week-"

"Four days."

Valoris shook his head. "Too short, Your Majesty. The messenger would barely get there and back. The Council of Elders will need time to deliberate."

"Fine! Five days. Is that long enough?"

Valoris raised an eyebrow again.

"Yes. I will meet you on your return, Your Majesty." He saluted.

The king remounted and called to his lords that they were returning to the castle.

Valoris watched them ride away, then turned to Talus and Dalus, studying them. After a moment he directed his gaze on Talus.

"Talus, how long have you been sixteen?"

Talus sighed. "A month in three days."

Valoris nodded. "I see. I want the two of you to deliver this message to the Belon lord and his Council. You will need to hurry." He paused then added. "You two seem to like running, considering that whenever you arrive at the outpost you are out of breath...."

Dalus grinned, but Talus was thinking of Eirin's request. Valoris continued speaking.

"Off you go. Grab anything you need as you pass the outpost. Farewell."

"Farewell, Commander." Dalus responded and Talus echoed him. They ran lightly across the beginning of the swamp. Reaching the trees, they climbed and soon disappeared into the swamp.

<<<<<<<<<<<<>>>>>>>>>>>>

They ran. For almost four hours, they had been running along one branch and jumping to the next. Their legs burned, not that they would have admitted it.... They had often insulted each other, resulting in a chase; then left off; then, of course, repeated the pattern. They were determined to push through the exhaustion. The truth was they had been moving as fast as possible, which was much different from the run-stop 'chase' pace.

Talus jumped. He missed the branch, barely managing to catch it with his hands. He struggled, trying to pull himself up. He was too tired. An agonizing moment passed before Dalus realized what happened. He hurried back and helped Talus up. They studied each other for a long minute through clouded vision. Dalus spoke lightly, or such it would have been if he could have breathed properly.

33

"I... think you... falling into the... swamp might de... delay us a bit."

"Really?" Talus paused. "Dalus, you think we need to keep up this sprint? Because we are both going to slip and drown at this rate."

"Then the message would never be delivered. We probably don't, it's just the urgency makes it feel so necessary. Maybe we should walk for a bit. Then perhaps we should pace ourselves, like Korus used to say."

A tired smile played across Talus' face. "Or Jornus."

"No one said Learners were good at taking their masters at their word." Dalus half-heartedly punched Talus on the shoulder.

Talus almost fell again. "Seriously, man?"

But full grins appeared on both faces. They set off at a slow walk which gradually grew faster. Eventually it became a run, but not the neck-breaking speed of before. This was the pace they had chosen when Jornus or Korus had made them run long distances.

<<<<<<<<<<<<<<>>>>>>>>>>>>>

Anna was homesick. Sure Violet, Mara, and Cat were wonderful friends; but her parents and brother, they were family. It had been eleven days since she had been taken from them.

Those kinds of thoughts drifted through her head as she chopped raw meat into steaks. Mara's voice broke into her lonesome thoughts.

"Anna, are you okay?"

Anna looked up at her. She had not realized that tears were streaming down her face. She replied in a choke voice.

"Fine."

"Well, that is certainly not true. Do you want to talk about it?"

Anna shrugged. "I don't know."

"Come on, what's up? You didn't cut your finger, did you?"

Anna looked into Mara's deep hazel eyes. Love filled them.

"I guess I am a little homesick. My parents," Her voice broke, "my brother, I miss them." In a small voice, she added. "It seems like it has been forever."

Tears welled up in force. Mara drew her into an embrace. When they parted, Mara spoke softly.

"I know how you feel. The best way I have found is-" She looked around to make sure that no one was near. "To pray, and to think through passages you memorized in the Logos. It helps."

Anna smiled weakly. "Aye, I will do that. Thanks."

"Anytime. It's what friends do." Mara returned to her work, pushing a stray dark red strand of hair behind her ear.

Chapter 8 Changing Life

Talus was exhausted. He and Dalus had run for two days straight, except for an eight hour stop the night before to sleep. It had not been a restful eight hours either for Talus. His mind had been mulling over King Eirin's request. A week and a half ago, he had been so excited because few Learners became Adventurers as young as he had. Finally, he had told himself that the council would probably look for someone a little older than his sixteen.

It was evening when they arrived in Elnola. They hurried through the darkening street to the small castle in the center, the home of the Belon lord. Once at the castle, a guard check their identity, then sent them to the Secretary of Belon.

He sat behind a large desk filled with drawers in a chestnut-brown antechamber. He peered over the desk at them as they approached, looking tired.

"Why do you wish to see the Belon lord?" He inquired in a bored tone, before continuing without allowing them to reply. "Unless it is quite important, please come back tomorrow." The Secretary looked back down at whatever he was working on.

Dalus glanced at Talus, who shrugged. How was he supposed to know what to do? Dalus gave a slight cough. The Elerin looked back up.

"I apologize for the hour, my father, but we are carriers of a message from King Eirin."

The older man stared at them for a long minute, before he gestured to a couple chairs along the wall opposite the desk. "Please sit." He wandered off to find the Belon lord.

"Now what?" Talus asked, sitting down.

"We wait and then talk to the Belon lord." Dalus folded his hands in his lap and then unfolded them.

"No, actually you talk to the Belon lord." Talus managed a smirk.

"Why me?" Dalus stared at him.

"Because you're older."

"Very funny." Dalus sighed, but a half-smiled appeared on his face anyway.

They waited for what felt like a century. Finally, the Secretary reappeared and told them to follow him. They entered a large room completely encircled by the empty seats of the Council.

They approached the Belon lord and saluted. He greeted them.

"Dalus, son of Havus, and Talus, son of Valnis, greetings. Good Urasus here, tells me you are the bearers of a message from King Eirin."

Dalus replied. "It is true, my lord. King Eirin of Alcasa wishes for a new interpreter, seeing as something has happened to Lentus. Also, he has a request concerning this matter. He would like, well, the youngest Adventurer you will give him."

The Belon lord's eyebrows shot up. "Is that so."

A pained expression crossed Dalus' face. "Yes, my lord."

"Hmm, I do not know how the Council will take this. I will summon the Council in the morning. When do you need your answer?"

"Preferably by tomorrow evening or the following morning, my lord." Dalus offered.

"Then I will see that you have your answer by the end of the day tomorrow. Good evening, young Adventurers."

"Evening, father." Dalus and Talus returned, using the term of respect for Elerin Elders.

Once outside, they parted ways, to surprise their families and get some supper.

Kellia had run all the way home the next day for lunch, in order to spend more time with Talus. The family was in the middle of the meal when someone knocked on the front door. Valnis, Talus' father, looked around puzzled and shrugged.

"I guess I had better see who it is."

He left the room and opened the door. Talus heard Valnis asked the obvious.

"Greetings, I am Valnis, son of Patrus. What brings you here?"

"Corus, son of Sethis. Is your son, Talus, here? He is summoned by the council."

"I see. Please, come inside. Talus is in the dining room."

"Thank you, but I need to keep going. Please inform your son that he is to be in the antechamber of the Council room by first bells."

When his father returned, he didn't repeat the message, probably guessing correctly that Talus had heard everything. He simply told Talus he had some ten minutes before he needed to be going. Talus suddenly did not feel hungry. Was Dalus also summoned? Had the Council finished early? Or was this summons only for him?

He tried to focus on what Kellia was saying. Shocking how much a nine-year-old had to tell you when you have only been gone a week.

<<<<<<<<<<<<<>>>>>>>>>>>>>

Talus was sitting in the antechamber of the Council. No Dalus. Would he come? First bells rang and hope died. Dalus was not coming.

Talus was nearly sick when he was finally called into the Council Chambers. Terrible thing, nerves.

He entered the Council Chambers and walked to about the center. Almost every seat was filled today. Talus saluted.

"My fathers, you wished to see me?"

Talus was caught by surprise when, instead of the Belon lord answering, one of the older Elders to his right stood and approached him.

"Talus, son of Valnis, undoubtedly you are aware that Learners are rarely made Adventurers as young as you were yourself. We have considered many of your peers for the position of translator to Alcasa. However, you were the most qualified, primarily because of your linguistic ability. Most Elerins your age are finishing their fifth, not sixth, language. Now, young Talus, the Council's choice is you. Will you accept this charge of honor, and of our trust in you? If you wish you can refuse, this is a lifelong commitment."

Time stood still as thoughts flew through Talus' mind. Did he want this? What would it be like? He could refuse and go on with his life, but the Council had chosen him.... Talus looked up.

"Why did you pick me?"

The Elder appeared amused. "Well, you are the most qualified of the young Adventurers for this position. You are also finishing your sixth language while most of your age group is only on their fifth language. Will you accept?"

Talus suddenly realized he had already said that. He thought for another second before replying slowly.

"I... accept, my fathers. I hope I will gratify your confidence in me."

The Elder placed his hand on Talus' shoulder. "We are sure you will." He paused then added. "Tomorrow, you and Dalus should return to the border. This afternoon, I would suggest you visit Thatus, son of Albanus, who, as you should know, was translator to the Alcasan court before Lentus, son of Cifbus. He will be able to give you some hints on your position as well as on the Alcasan culture, if you can keep him awake that is." The Elder grinned.

Talus nodded and thanked him. After saluting the Elder and the Council, he began to leave the room. He stopped and turned.

"Uh, so where do I find Elder Thatus?"

The Elder Talus had been talking to answered. "Good question. His sister's son's house is at 29 eltha 5 sitha, you should find him there."

Talus thanked him, saluted again, and left.

Dalus would not be stuck with him for years after all. He, Talus, son of Valnis, would spend his life serving King Eirin. What would it be like? Humans were... so different from Elerins. They wanted to be rich and pampered, right? Did they care about each other like Elerins did? What were they like? How strange would living among them be?

As Talus hurried through the crowd, he noticed someone familiar.

"Jornus!"

Jornus nearly lost his balance when Talus crashed into him. Sure it was customary for family and close friends to greet each other with a hug, but this bordered on painful. Jornus untangled himself.

"Talus, Talus, what's up? I was not aware you were in town."

"Everything."

Talus' reply was not the most enthusiastic answer and had something of a bewildered note to it. Jornus raised his eyebrows.

"Really? Did your parents die, your older sister marry, Dalus drown, Kellia and Marcus go missing-"

"No, no, nothing like that. I am going to Alcasa."

"Alcasa? What are you doing there? Or is it a secret?"

"Have you heard about Lentus?"

"Yes, what does- You are not serious?"

Talus looked away. Jornus reached out and gripped his shoulder, drawing Talus' eyes up to his.

"Do not worry over this, just be yourself. After all, that grin of yours is irresistible." Talus let a slight smile show. Jornus continued. "You are a smart young man. You can figure this out. Just always try to do the right thing and remember, our King is with you."

"I will. Thanks, Jornus." Talus' grin emerged.

As Talus turned away, Jornus added one more thing.

"And Talus... sneaking hot peppers into the king's oatmeal is probably not a good idea."

Talus laughed. "See- Farewell, Jornus."

"Farewell, Talus."

Talus stared after the retreating form. Would he ever see him again?

According to the Council's instructions, Elder Thatus should live in the house in front of him. Talus pushed the gate open and followed the path leading to the door. He knocked. As he waited his nerves kicked up again. Silly nerves, it was only a one armed Elder. The door opened to reveal an Elerin in his seventies. He spoke.

"Greetings, friend. I am Darcus, son of Fritus. How may I serve you?"

"Good afternoon, Darcus, son of Fritus. I am Talus, son of Valnis. May I speak to Thatus, son of Albanus?"

"I expect so. Will you come in?"

Talus entered. Good, right house.

Darcus led Talus down a long hallway to a sitting room on the right. In the far-left corner of the room, an Elder sat asleep in a rocking chair. A book lay open in the Elerin's lap. Darcus shook him gently. The Elder opened his eyes.

"What? Supper already? I have yet to finish my book."

"No, uncle. A young man wishes to speak with you."

"Oh? Where is he? Ah, come here my son."

Talus crossed the room and saluted.

"My father. I am Talus, son of Valnis. The Council said you could give me advice on the Alcasan culture and the position of translator."

Thatus frowned, puzzled. "How did a lad like you get that position?"

Talus winced. "King Eirin requested a young translator."

"Hmm, odd, very odd. Any idea why?"

Talus shook his head. "Only guesses."

"Is that so?" Thatus mused. "Well, I would advise you to be careful, lad. Now, you have questions?"

"Yep. What is Alcasa like? How are humans different from Elerins? How do they interact? Do they enjoy sparring-"

"Whoa, whoa, one at a time." Thatus grinned at him.

Talus grinned back, a little contritely. "Sorry. What is Alcasa like?"

"Alcasa is a flat grassland from Belon to the sea. You can see forever, unless you are in a dip, of course. It boasts a couple rivers and many castles. The majority of the people are farmers, making Alcasa thinly populated. Outside of temperament, the major differences between Elerin culture and Alcasan culture is their inability to climb and the role of women. Their women typically do not fight with weapons...." As Thatus spoke a light lit in his eyes. Almost like he missed it.

Thatus frequently switched languages to test Talus. Talus still had questions when suppertime came, so the wife of Thatus' nephew invited him to remain for dinner. They continued to talk late into the night. When Talus finally went home, he had gained a new level of confidence about his position.

<<<<<<<<<<<<>>>>>>>>>>>

39

Anna climbed quietly out of bed. She grimaced. Why could they not put a pot in the servant quarters? She walked carefully from the room and down the hall to a door that led to the side courtyard. She slipped outside, finding herself in the long shadows of the keep.

Movement by the main gate caught her eye. She froze. The gate opened slowly. Five figures entered. The fifth, a foot shorter than the other, staggered. One of the other men shoved him. He hit the ground without using his hands to break his fall. He was bound. His guards snickered. One kicked him in the back.

"Get up, filth. Or I'll beat you until you can't see your own skin."

For a horrible moment, Anna feared the man could not rise. But slowly he pushed himself to his knees and stood. The guard cackled.

"Too cowardly to want a beating, old man?"

The man did not rise to the insult but bowed his head. The guard struck him.

"Your God won't save you, wretch. You are King Hissin's now."

"Do not speak of what you do not understand, Meves."

Anna was surprised by the quiet authority in his voice. The guard did nothing but growled.

"Move. It is time you never saw the light of day again."

The man gave no reaction. The guards hurried him inside the keep.

Anna, having lost the urge, returned to her room, deep in thought.

Violet was exploring. Sure, night was not the safest time, but she could go to different parts of the castle than during the day.

She slipped through countless halls and rooms, often stopping to admire a painting or statue. She turned another corner and was confronted by a heavy iron-studded door. She studied it. What would be beyond it? Dungeons? Secrets? Could she open it? The key was in the lock. She twisted it and tried the doorknob. The door swung inward, revealing a dimly lit stairwell.

Common sense told her not to go, that the door was locked for a reason. But... she had already defied common sense by leaving bed. She pushed the doubt away and took the first step down.

The steps were steep, but who cared? It was an adventure. Silence enveloped the stairs. Every step echoed.

An angry voice filled the air.

"Who left the door open?!!"

"How should I know, Meves?" Another man answered. "Maybe discipline has gotten lax since we were deployed."

Meves growled. "Let's rid ourselves of this fellow. The sooner he is locked away, the sooner we can get to the ales and foods."

Violet froze. Where could she hide? Theos, help her. Wait, a black doorway invited her. She slid into it, praying the shadows hid her. Their footsteps grow nearer. Five men appeared around the corner. Four of them were prodding the fifth. Violet did not breathe. They were almost on her. As they passed the captive looked up. Violet stared into the violet-blue eyes. His eyes held so much sorrow. He bowed his head and did not look at her again. If only she could help him, do something, anything.

After some time, her mind returned to her predicament. She hurried up the stairs.

As she reached her room, she was still wondering about the man. What race was he? Who was he? What had he done?

Chapter 9 Meeting Horses and Kings

Talus rolled over. Light filtered in through his window. Wait? Light? He was supposed to meet Dalus on the Wall at dawn! He was never going to hear the end of this.

Talus dressed and hurried down to the kitchen. His mother stood at the counter kneading.

"Mom, do you have something I can take with me? I was supposed to meet Dalus half an hour ago."

His mother smiled. "Anyone would think you were up half the night talking to the former translator of Alcasa.... There is bread in the box and apples in the basket. If you can spare a few minutes, you can eat some oatmeal while I pack you lunch."

Talus, like any young man, could not turn down the offer of food. Even with his hurry, he readily agreed to his mother's scheme. He made a four-minute meal of oatmeal, a slice of bread, and an apple. As he finished, his mother placed a cloth bag with his lunch next to him.

Talus looked up at her; she appeared to be struggling to hold back tears. A lump formed in Talus' throat. When would he see his family again?

He stood and hugged her. Stepping back, he tried to keep his voice calm.

"Theos be with you, Mom."

"And with you, Talus."

He grabbed his lunch and turned away, before his emotion grew too strong. In the hall, he took a deep breath. This should not be so hard. It had been four years since he had lived at home. But this was different somehow.

Following a sudden urge, he ran back upstairs. He stopped at Marcus' and then Kellia's rooms. He peeked inside watching his little sister breathe in and out. Would she be all grown up next time he saw her? Would there be a next time? Forcing himself to lock those thoughts away, he turned away and climbed back downstairs.

Talus took another breath and stepped into the living-room. "Farewell, Dad."

Valnis looked up from his weekly paper. He set it down and stood. "Off on an adventure? Theos go with you, my son."

Talus hugged him. "And you, Dad."

He left hurriedly. Outside, Talus glanced back once. He pushed farewells from his mind, trying to focus on the task at hand.

<<<<<<<<<<<<<<>>>>>>>>>>>>>

The next day, darkness crept across the sky as Talus and Dalus dropped on to the outpost's porch. They were, predictably, out of breath. On reaching familiar territory, Dalus had declared a race.

Commander Valoris and Lieutenant Rhemus, who had been sparring, paused. Valoris studied them, amused.

"Good to see you back. What did the Council think?"

Talus and Dalus exchanged a look. What did the Council think, indeed? Talus replied between breaths.

"Good... to... see... you... too, Commander." He stopped for a long second. "The Council has appointed me translator."

Valoris nodded slowly. "Ahh. Let me congratulate you. The Council chose well." Talus reddened.

Dalus grinned. "I agree, but perhaps we should put the new translator to bed. He seems to be coming down with a bad case of red fever."

Valoris furrowed his brow. "Red fever?"

"Aye, just look at him. Bad, don't you think?"

Talus and Valoris rolled their eyes while Dalus and Rhemus laughed. Valoris answered.

"Hmm, I think you both better go to bed."

Dalus looked dejected. "But what about supper?"

Valoris' face was stern. "Talus' is inside, but Elerins who pull their Commander's legs do not eat supper."

Dalus made a sad puppy face. "I'm hungry though."

Valoris laughed. "Inside, inside. Go eat but give me some peace."

Talus and Dalus fled inside. Talus glanced back out to see Rhemus finish the sparring match. Valoris dissented.

"Hey, I was not ready."

Rhemus grinned fiendishly. "I'm sure all the enemies you meet will wait until you are ready."

Valoris rolled his eyes and muttered something about everyone picking on him that day. Talus chuckled and headed to the food.

Talus woke the next morning and his stomach tightened. Today was the day he swore to serve the king of Alcasa. This treaty was the last standing of three such commitments of goodwill with the human countries, Melotha, Garia, and Alcasa. They had been made in an effort by the Belon lord of the time to restore Elerins to respectable society after an era of violence in their history. Of course, that was centuries ago now.

Alcasa would become his home until he was old and senile or dead. He took a deep breath and tried to push the apprehension away. He closed his eyes and focused on things Thatus, his parents, and even Kellia had told him. Nothing seemed to ease his stomach. Why did nothing help? Then he remembered one phrase Jornus had said, "Our King is with you."

He repeated the phrase through breakfast. He found when he focused on its meaning, his stomach calmed somewhat. After breakfast, Talus slipped outside. It was quiet. He could think. Why was he so nervous? He should not be. He knew what would happen.

Trying to push it from his mind, he consciously focused on other things.

His branch shook. Dalus stared down at him.

"Hey, Talus. You want to spar once more before you leave?"

Leave? Talus swallowed and repeated his phrase. At least sword fighting would force his mind off it.

"Sure."

He hopped up and drew his twin blades from their sheathes across his back. He checked the area for branches within jumping distance. He enjoyed the thrill of fighting with the impending possibility of a fall into the swamp... for Dalus of course.

Dalus charged savagely. Talus parried and launched a series of quick cuts, forcing Dalus to give ground. Dalus leapt to a new branch and delivered a sweeping blow towards Talus' neck.

Several minutes passed. Talus had a little skill on Dalus, but Dalus had more strength. They bounced from branch to branch, trading heavy blows in attempts to unbalance each other.

Talus jumped to the next branch. He crossed his swords, one strengthening the other, to block an overhead shot from Dalus. A sharp clang filled the air. A flaw presented itself in Dalus' plan. He leapt with his blow and body slammed into Talus, knocking both of them into the air. They hurled their swords into a rotting tree trunk.

They hit the water. On resurfacing, they struck out for the nearest tree. Elerins cared little for swimming and thus were not particularly good at it.

Once safely back in the trees, they retrieved their blades. Dalus glanced at the sun.

"We should head back 'cause you may want to change before meeting up with that bossy little king you get to hang out with."

Talus smiled briefly. A thought struck him. The King was with him. Who was a bossy little king compared to him?

<<<<<<<<<<<<<<>>>>>>>>>>>>>

Talus forced a grin. This was it. This was goodbye. Well, sort of, Dalus was going to visit him weekly until it was certain that Talus was safe. He faced Dalus. Dalus was not fooled by his grin.

"Hey, Talus, this isn't goodbye, I'll see you in a few days. Don't worry, you will do great. You are a quick learner. I reckon you will know the remaining languages before you are seventeen. Theos goes with you."

Talus smiled a little. "Thanks, Dalus. Uh... see you."

"See you."

Talus stared at him searching for something to make this longer.

Valoris called and Talus turned away. Dalus grabbed Talus by his shoulder, spinning him back. Dalus grinned.

"Go get those humans, Talus."

Talus grinned back a bit. He jumped from the tree and rolled to a stand beside Valoris. King Eirin and his men neared. As they reached the Elerins, King Eirin dismounted and approached them.

"Commander Valoris, a pleasure to see you. You and your men are well?"

"Yes, Your Majesty."

"Good. How did things go with the Council?"

"The Council has chosen Talus here in response to your request."

The king smiled good naturedly at Talus and bowed in greeting.

"A pleasure to make your acquaintance, Talus, son of...."

Talus saluted. "Son of Valnis, Your Majesty. I hope to be of service."

The king nodded a bit impatiently. "Of course." He looked back to Valoris. "I believe vows are required? We need to leave shortly. A ball is held tonight in Talus' honor."

Valoris smiled, amused. "A ball? Of course. Talus, place your right fist over your heart."

He paused then continued.

"Son of Belon, do you swear to obey the lord of Plains in all matters, unless it goes against the faith, until your death or your lord releases you?"

45

Talus took a breath. His answer would plunge him into a life he had never even dreamed of.

"I, Talus, son of Valnis, swear to obey the lord of Plains in all matters, unless it goes against the faith, until my death or my lord releases me." It was done. He was bound to the king of Alcasa.

Valoris spoke to King Eirin.

"Lord of Plains, do you swear to protect this son of Belon as it is within your power?"

"I, Eirin, king of Alcasa, swear to protect this son of Belon as it is within my power."

The king nodded to a brown and white paint horse.

"Your horse, Talus. We ride immediately."

The king mounted his horse. Talus stared at the horse, then the king. King Eirin motioned towards the horse again. Talus looked helplessly at Valoris, who shrugged.

"I don't know. Just sit on it like they are, can't be too hard. I believe you use that piece of leather rope to change direction."

Talus nodded tentatively and analyzed the situation. The horse's back was only a little shorter than he was tall. No way that he could mount like King Eirin. He would have to jump. He took a running leap. Grabbing the saddle horn and the back of the saddle, he swung one leg over to the other side, plopping on to the horse. For a second, he sat there. He had made it.

Or not. The horse was unused to Elerins mounting. It reared. Horrified, Talus tightened his death grip on the saddle horn. He gripped the horse's body with his legs the best he could. He hung on. Finding Talus still on it, the horse bolted... straight towards the swamp.

It wouldn't run right into the swamp, would it? No idea. No point risking it. He had to make it turn. Turn. Valoris had said a leather rope. There, sitting a little in front of the saddle horn. How was he supposed to grab it and not fall off?

They would hit the swamp in seconds, he had to do something. Talus snagged the reins with one hand. He tilted backwards as they climbed a small knoll, inevitably pulling the reins. The horse reared a second time. Talus screamed as he dangled, holding only the saddle horn and reins. He let go of the reins as the leather cut into his fingers.

The horse spun and raced back towards the king. Talus felt his fingers slipping from the saddle horn.

A shadow crossed his peripheral vision. A voice spoke softly but strongly.

"Whoa, Altros, whoa...."

Altros slowed then stopped. Talus released what was left of his hold and slumped to the ground. He looked up at his rescuer, who smiled down at him sympathetically. The man dismounted and helped him up.

"Well, that was an exciting first ride. Shall I assume you have never ridden before?"

Talus shrugged. "Horses are not particularly useful in the swamp."

"Hmm, probably not. Would you care to ride beside me while I explain the elementary points of riding? After we teach you to mount a horse, that is."

"Sure. Thanks, um...."

"Lord Kalrick Rodan of Seaworth, but just Kalrick will do."

"Thanks, Kalrick. Should I guess you don't, uh, mount by jumping?"

Kalrick grinned. "You can mount quickly, but not exactly like that. First you should introduce yourself to Altros...."

Talus glanced from side to side. Everything was different. The plains rolled away into the sky. Not a single tree rose on the horizon. Farmhouses, however, dotted the landscape. Single horned bulls and their cows grazed contentedly.

"This, Talus, is home." Kalrick nodded in front of them.

Talus wondered how, with all his training in observation, he had missed the fortified city before them. As they neared, Talus guessed the wall rose about eighty feet. The city, Aubin, sat on a peninsula formed when the Rock Stream separated from the Scarlet River. Those rivers flowed through canyons some fifteen feet deep. All in all, Aubin was a fairly defensible place.

As they approached the drawbridge, the peasants hurriedly finished crossing the bridge and arranged themselves on either side of the road. Except for one elderly woman pulling a small handcart; she looked up as the king's party reached the bridge. She tried to hurry but the cart repeatedly stuck in the dips between the boards.

King Eirin called the party to a halt and, after a moment's hesitation, dismounted, handing the reins to the soldier riding next to him. Kalrick drew a sharp intake of breath. He released a small sigh of relief as the king spoke.

"Good afternoon, mother. Would you care for some help with that cart? I am afraid this bridge was built to make cart crossing difficult."

"Um, if you wish, Your Majesty. I, uh, am sorry to be in your way."

"Think nothing of it, mother."

King Eirin stepped forward and took the cart from the woman. He rolled it a few divots, before picking it up and carrying it off the bridge.

"There you are, mother. The going should be much easier from here."

"Thank you so much, Your Majesty. You're too kind."

King Eirin bowed slightly.

"An honor, mother."

He nodded to the crowd and remounted his horse.

As they crossed, Kalrick urged his horse next to the king.

"That was gracious."

King Eirin grinned. "A good political move, too."

Talus furrowed his brow. Was that his motive?

Inside the city, the buildings progressed from small, cramped shacks to spacious mansions. The castle loomed up before the party. The castle itself was smaller than would be expected for the royal residence. Still, it would defy a force for some time.

They entered the courtyard. To the right of the keep, several men-at-arms sparred. To the left, a beautiful garden bloomed with summer flowers.

The king dismounted and handed his horse to, presumably, his page. King Eirin turned to Talus who was sliding cautiously down from Altros.

"Talus, son of Valnis, welcome to Aubin, the throne of all my fore-bearers." The king paused. "Lord Kalrick will show you to your chambers, then I would like to see you in my office immediately following."

Talus nodded as the king began to walk away. He looked at Kalrick.

"So...."

Kalrick glanced at him and added to his page.

"And, John, would you take Talus' horse? You do not have to care for him, feel free to have the stable hands do that."

A boy, probably about thirteen, slipped around Kalrick's horse into view.

"Of course, my lord." He bowed to Talus. "I'll take your horse, my lord."

Talus saluted. "Sure, thanks."

John stroked Altros gently then led both horses away.

Talus looked up at Kalrick.

"Now what?"

Kalrick grinned. "We follow His Majesty to the end of the third floor. We hurry up the stairs to your room, the first on the fourth floor. You drop your things. Then we head back to His Majesty's chamber."

Talus furrowed his brow, confused. "What's the hurry? The king did not sound that urgent."

"Oh, with kings, you always have to hurry."

"Ahh."

<<<<<<<<<<<<<>>>>>>>>>>>>>

Life in Ketlin did not change. Now that lunch was cleaned up, supper preparations began. Or continued; Anna and the rest of the staff had put several small deer on the fire that morning.

"You, girl," Anna glanced away from the dough she was kneading. "Put that dough on to bake and fetch me some more water. Move lively!" The cook shook his ladle at her.

Anna placed her dough in one of the empty ovens in the wall of the fireplace. She picked up the bucket and turned towards the kitchen door. Her steps slowed almost of their own accord. Her stomach muscles clenched. Too many horror stories happened on trips to the well. As she passed, she shared a glance with Mara, who gave her an encouraging smile.

When she reached the door, she scanned the courtyard for guards, knights, and unoccupied male servants. No one in sight but the old gardener.

After another quick scan, she raced across the yard to the well. She lowered the well bucket, wincing every time it hit the side and cut into the unnatural silence. It sank into the water far below. Anna glanced around the courtyard. The gardener was gone.

It took an eternity to draw the bucket back up. Her gaze flitted around the courtyard. The bucket arrived at the top. She dumped the water into her bucket.

Two men came around the corner of the keep. Anna lifted the bucket, her heart accelerating. The water splashed against her skirt, forcing her to slow. She watched the men. They stopped talking and continued toward her. She concentrated on the door.

"Where ya going, sweetheart?" The men laughed.

On the edge of panicking, she glanced at them. She turned her head away.

The door. It was in front of her. She had made it. She stepped inside and shut the door. She slumped against the wall. Her adrenaline drained.

"Anna? Are you alright? You look pale." Mara's voice broke through the cloud.

Anna shrugged, stating the obvious. "I went to the well."

Mara nodded slowly. "But you made it safely back, thank Theos."

"There were some men out there, and they seemed to be coming at me." Anna drew a calming breath, trying to dispel the rest of her fear.

"I'm so sorry, Anna."

The memory of that night before they had reached Ketlin passed between them.

Mara gave her a weak smile to cheer her up. "Theos definitely protected you, then."

Theos.... All the terror had distracted her. He had promised to never leave her or forsake her. She thought back through the last few minutes, ashamed.

Chapter 10 The Ball

Talus knocked on the king's door. It opened, revealing the fourteen-year-old page from the courtyard. The boy studied him.

"You are Talus, my lord?"

"Yes."

"Come in, my lord. His Majesty awaits you."

The page let Talus into a small entry chamber. Two guards stood at each of the two doors leading from that room. A squire lounged in one of the light blue cushioned chairs against the walls of the room. The page opened the door to the left.

"Talus is here, my lord." The boy announced.

King Eirin looked up from his desk.

"Thank you, Matt. Talus, please come in and have a seat."

Talus saluted and took the indicated seat in front of the desk.

"How do you find your chambers, Talus?"

"Very... comfortable, my lord."

King Eirin frowned. "Is something wrong?"

Talus shook his head. "I was going to say 'large,' but determined 'comfortable' would be better suited."

The king smiled. "What? Do Elerins prefer small rooms?"

Talus shrugged. "Eighteen of us shared a room in the Border Guard." Talus grinned. "Imagine an outpost with twenty castle chambers. It only might fall out of the tree!... my lord."

King Eirin nodded, apparently trying not to smile too hard. "On that arrow, to business. I need you to translate these two replies. One is a letter in answer to Hissin's invitation and the other is to Colmea to send with the payment for a supply of swords. I also need this letter to Carna translated to whatever they speak. You know that language?" He asked, uncertain.

"Carnish? Yes, my lord. The only languages I have yet to learn are Talrin and Weetin. Would you like the letters done in that order, my lord?"

"That would be best. Talrin is hardly important, but Alcasa does have dealings with Saxa. Thus when you have time, learning Weetin would be good."

"Then I'll bend my mind to Weetin as soon as I finish the last of Zofish grammar. I will start on the letters as soon as I finish unpacking, my lord."

"Good. Do you have any questions concerning the ball tonight?"

Talus thought for a moment.

"Yes, do I have to dance with all the girls or just some?"

King Eirin laughed. "I am afraid the song list is far too short. No, you will have to dance with a couple because it is expected. But other than them, you may just dance with the pretty ones. Anything else?"

A touch of color dusted Talus' light brown skin. "My lord, um, what do Alcasans talk about? At dances in Belon we swap adventures and discuss weapons, little siblings, food, and the like."

"Hmm, the men are the same here as there, I reckon. However, the women here do not fight. They are always talking, though. Thus, if you let them, they will talk your entire dance. If they do look for a reply, just agree, actually exaggerate. Also, compliment them. They *always* love compliments."

"Thank you, Your Majesty. I'll keep your advice in mind. I suppose I should start with these." Talus indicated the letters. "If you will excuse me."

The king sighed. "I also have things requiring my attention. You may go."

Talus saluted and left the room.

<<<<<<<<<<<<<<>>>>>>>>>>>>>

Talus and Kalrick stopped as the stairs escaped into the Great Hall. The floor was an array of colors. Tables offering food lined the walls. The king stood surrounded by nobles on a dais against the wall opposite the main doors. To the right, a small door led to the garden.

Kalrick grinned at Talus.

"Since I am babysitting tonight, the first thing we do is inform the king we are here."

Talus raised an eyebrow. "Babysitting?"

Kalrick nodded, grinning harder.

"Babysitting?!!" Talus repeated.

"Yep! Shall we see the king?"

Kalrick turned, headed for the dais.

Talus followed Kalrick. This was not exactly babysitting. Kalrick was just showing him around. That's all. Talus shook his head. Why was he still thinking about this?

51

"Ah, Lord Kalrick, Adventurer Talus, welcome." The king greeted them. Kalrick bowed as Talus saluted. Kalrick replied.

"Your Majesty."

King Eirin widened his gaze to include the nobles.

"My lords, may I present Talus, son of Valnis, my new translator."

A few of the lords greeted him, most bowed, and the rest simply nodded.

The king smiled. "Lord Kalrick, I will trust you to see that Talus enjoys himself. Now to the floor, my lords." The nobles bowed and the king led the girl on his arm out onto the floor.

Kalrick grinned at him. "See anyone you would like to give your first dance to?"

Talus paused and looked around. Almost a hundred girls danced or fanned themselves as they chatted with friends. And he had to pick one to dance with. It was overwhelming.

"Maybe I should just walk up to a random girl and ask her to dance."

Kalrick laughed. "You could. Or if you don't want to dance with any *random* girl, I could introduce you to one, which might be slightly more polite, or you could simply dance with my little sister. I am sure she would love it." Kalrick added with a smirk.

"Very well." Talus agreed guardedly, eyeing the smirk.

Kalrick guided Talus to a group of fifteen-year-old girls. As they approached, Kalrick called out.

"Katrina, I have someone you may wish to meet."

Katrina excused herself from her friends and skipped over to her brother. A smile lit her face.

"Is this Talus? I love Elerins, Kalrick. They are so handsome."

As Talus reddened, Kalrick laughed. Katrina put her hands on her hips and glared at him.

"Don't laugh."

Her order only served to strengthen Kalrick's amusement.

The red in his cheeks having receded, Talus saluted.

"Thank you, Lady Katrina, my race is flattered. You will excuse me for addressing you without introduction, but I am afraid your brother is a bit indisposed to do so. Be that as it may, would you care to dance?"

Katrina squealed. "I would love to!"

This would be interesting.

The dance was similar to a swing taught in Belon. Of course, with Talus as lead, Katrina encountered a few moves she had never done. Still, she only stumbled once. Talus enjoyed their dance. Katrina was well mannered and well informed, and quickly put Talus at ease. When the song ended, Talus returned Katrina to her friends. Kalrick scouted out another lady.

After his seventh partner, Talus searched the sides in vain for Kalrick. He had disappeared.

Talus sighed. How should he do this? He spotted one of his former partners sitting next to a young woman with black hair and wide blue eyes. She was watching him. He thought for a second. How had Kalrick done this?

He approached them.

"Excuse me, ladies. Lady Lydia, might I ask who your friend is?"

She smiled flirtatiously up at him.

"Oh, of course, Adventurer Talus. May I introduce Lady Veral, the daughter of Earl Domin of Hartford. Lady Veral, the new official translator, Talus."

Talus saluted. "Thank you, Lady Lydia. Lady Veral, would you care to dance?"

She rose and curtsied.

"I would love to dance with someone as handsome as yourself."

Great, another one of these.

"I am flattered, my lady."

He offered his arm and led her on to the floor. It was a group dance that Talus did not know. *Hmm, what are the other men doing?* Lady Veral had fallen silent. Talus searched for something to say. He remembered the king's advice. Compliment them.

"Your eyes are a beautiful shade of blue, Lady Veral."

She met his eyes for a moment. Talus saw through to a broken child. Or maybe he had imagined it. She flashed a loose smile.

"Do you really think so? That is a compliment, indeed, coming from one of a race known for stunning eye color."

Silence returned. Talus noticed Veral's breath was growing short. At last, he asked.

"Are you okay, Lady Veral?"

She turned wide innocent eyes up to him.

"Oh, Talus, it is terribly hot in here. Would... would you be awfully annoyed if we stepped outside for a moment?"

How could Talus ignore such a plea? Besides, the cool fresh air beckoned his wild self.

"'Tis no trouble, lady."

Veral smiled and Talus led them from the floor. Mensis had just risen in the north, while Luna and Pusilla could almost touch in the western sky. The moons cast strange shadows in the garden.

Veral drew in a breath.

"It was so romantic of you to bring me out here."

Talus glanced at her. This had been her idea. Girls are weird, not that he could say that.

"It is pretty."

"Oh, yes. It is gorgeous, especially walking next to you!"

Talus glanced at her again. Why bring him in?

"We could run or climb instead." Talus added sarcastically. Sarcasm which she either completely missed or ignored.

Her eyes widened.

"Wouldn't it be scary to climb something tall like the keep?"

Talus looked up and shook his head.

"No, it appears to be a little less than sixty cat's tails."

"My, you must be so brave. What if you fall?"

"Little possibility of that. My nine-year-old sister could climb this."

"Really? Could... you teach me?" She turned vivid blue eyes up to him.

Talus paused. She wanted to learn to climb. Cool!

"Sure."

He helped her over some bushes to the side of the wall. As soon as Veral stepped off the smooth paving stones of the path, a peculiar thing happened. She grew about four inches shorter. It seemed the spikes of her heels enjoyed the soft garden dirt surrounding them.

Talus barely hid his grin. He did have the good sense not to comment, however. At least, not on that.

"You may wish to remove your, uh, shoes. Climbing is easier barefoot."

Veral glared at him. "I cannot move my feet, stupid."

Talus was confused. "So? Don't you slide them off?"

"No, stupid, you unbuckle them!"

Talus raised his eyebrows. "Right, right. No sense in getting upset."

"I am not upset! I am stuck!"

"Why don't you unbuckle your shoes and step out of them?" Talus inquired calmly.

"I, I." She spluttered. "It's not proper for a lady to bend down, stupid."

Hmm, she certainly liked that adjective. Talus shrugged.

"Okay, sit down and if you want, I'll unbuckle your shoes."

"Sit down? IN THE DIRT?"

"Um, yes.... The dirt won't hurt you."

"Of course, it doesn't hurt. It's... it's dirty!"

Talus sighed. "You need to take your shoes off if you wish to learn to climb, if you don't we can go back inside."

"Fine." She growled. "I'll sit in the dirt, but if I wreck my dress, it is your fault!"

Talus rolled his eyes. He knelt and undid her shoes. As he pulled her up, she gave him a wide smile.

"Oh, thank you! You are such a gentleman!"

Talus barely managed not to give her an odd look. Why the sudden change?

"Now that your shoes are off, lady, shall we proceed to the wall?"

"Okay!"

She ran eagerly up to the wall and stopped.

"How do you climb a wall? Walls go straight up."

"Of course, but the wall is covered with finger and foot holds. See this stone, it comes out farther than the stone above it." Talus pointed to a stone on the wall about five feet up. It jutted out a half inch.

She stared at the stone then at Talus.

"How will I ever hold on to *that*?"

What did she mean? Was it not obvious?

"With your fingers and eventually with your foot. Now can you locate another hold a bit to the right as high as you can comfortably reach, another two cat's tails up to the right, and one other one cat's tail up to the left." A cat's tail was an old measurement that originates from the Legend of Dracin the Builder and His Cat. It is the equivalent of a little more than twelve inches.

Veral took a minute, but she found the required stones.

"Now what?"

Talus grinned. "You climb."

She grabbed the handholds, then tentatively put her left foot on the lower foothold.

"Stand up on that foot as you place the other." Talus suggested.

She did so.

"Now what?" She asked, her voice strained.

"Reach up with your left hand. Good. Stand up on your right. There you go. You got the idea."

Talus watched her crawl slowly up the wall. Once she was a little more than five feet up, she let out a screech. She had slipped. Talus instinctively caught her. She stared up at him wide eyed. She beamed.

"Oh, Talus, you saved my life!"

To Talus' horror, she moved her face towards his face, to kiss him. He jerked backwards and quickly set her on her feet. A hurt expression crossed her eyes.

"Dear Talus, you must let me thank you. You saved my life."

"No, not really," Talus began. "If you had landed-"

Veral lunged at him. Talus hastily placed the bushes in between them.

"Lady, surely you can find another way."

She smiled, almost fiendishly. "Oh-"

Talus suddenly felt compelled to run. He met her eyes for a second and fled. A cry of "Wait, Talus," echoed in his ears. He did not look back. Something was wrong. He had to get away.

His course led him back to the wall. He climbed. He had to get away. He did not even know why.

He entered his fourth-story bedroom window in minutes. Talus flopped into a chair. What had happened? What was wrong with her?

He sat still for a long time. Finally, he stood. He should head back downstairs, Kalrick was probably wondering where he had disappeared to.

It took Talus about six times as long to walk the halls and steps as it had to climb straight up. Mainly because each stairway was on the opposite side of the castle from the previous one.

Once back in the Great Hall, Talus scanned the room for Kalrick. Hmm, he must be in that sea of dancers. Now what? Well, he could visit the refreshments tables. Kalrick might see him, because it was less crowded than the rest of the room. Talus crossed the hall to the wall opposite the garden door. He approached the first table. Little pastries covered it. Sconces, finger pies, and mini muffins revealed themselves in intense variety. Which one should he try first?

Pie? Tentatively he reached out and picked up a little pie. He broke it open. Cherry filling oozed onto his fingers. That definitely belonged in his mouth. He had not had cherries in some time.

He chewed slowly, enjoying the flavor. So good. He started to raise his hand to lick his fingers. He stopped. Sadly, this was public. Hmm, napkins. They must be piled or in a container somewhere. He examined the table he was at, none. Perhaps some other table?

He turned intent on his quest, slamming full into Kalrick. Talus stepped back.

"Oh, Kalrick! Sorry, I did not see you." He really needed to pay better attention to his surroundings.

"No worries. I was attempting to sneak up on you." Kalrick admitted, grinning. "Where have you been? I have not seen you in ages."

Talus shuddered.

"I danced with a Lady Veral. She was warm so we went out to the garden. She started acting... weird and I... ran away. After a few minutes in my room, I came back down here."

Kalrick winced.

"Sorry, I should have warned you about her. She has quite a reputation. How did you get to your room, out of curiosity? I do not remember you crossing the Great Hall."

Talus paused then grinned.

"I, my friend, am an Elerin. We do not need stairs."

"Oh yeah, right. I forgot about that."

Talus feigned a hurt expression.

"You forgot I am an Elerin? Isn't it obvious?"

"No-" Kalrick began.

"Then what do you mean?" Talus demanded, interrupting.

"I *forgot* Elerins can climb."

Talus crossed his arms.

"Well, I guess you may do that."

Kalrick bowed.

"Thank you for the permission, kind sir." Kalrick replied dryly.

Talus could not prevent the grin that forced its way onto his face. Maybe he would like Alcasa after all.

"So," Kalrick broke into his thoughts. "Shall we find you another partner?"

Talus almost agreed, before remembering his sticky hands.

"Um, well." He began sheepishly. "Do you Alcasans believe in napkins? I cracked one of this pies open and got filling on my hands."

Kalrick laughed.

"Why would you open a pie?"

"To see what is inside." Talus answered, trying to avoid sounding like a child.

A mischievous glint appeared in Kalrick's eyes.

"Why not read the labels?"

Labels? He had not noticed labels.

"What labels? Er, why would one read labels?"

"To see what is inside." Kalrick mimicked.

He was not going to get the best of this conversation, was he? Perhaps it would be better to return to the original question.

"Where are the napkins?"

Kalrick grinned at him. He pointed down the table.

"In a basket on the last table."

"Thank you."

Talus hurried in that direction. Talus drew out one and wiped the tasty syrup off his fingers. He tossed the napkin on the pile of dirty ones. Kalrick had followed him so Talus inquired.

"Pick someone for me yet?"

Kalrick rubbed his beard.

"Hmm, a lady who won't mind sticky fingers."

"They are not *that* sticky."

"No, but still, you want a calm lady after dancing with Lady Veral."

Talus looked up at his new friend. He pushed the awkward moments in the garden from his mind.

"Aye, that would be nice. Thanks."

Kalrick glanced at him.

"No problem. Ah, perfect. Countess May, Lady Duoaquae. She is my mother's friend and married to Earl Duoaquae."

"Won't the earl wish to dance with her?"

Kalrick smiled a touch.

"The earl is not in attendance. Even if he was, he wouldn't mind you dancing with her, considering you are half her age, and this is a social event."

"Ah."

Talus followed Kalrick up to a middle-aged woman with gray flecking her dark brown hair. She smiled as they approached.

"Kalrick, good evening. Why I believe you have broadened a bit in the last three years." She paused and Kalrick just grinned. She continued. "Kalrick, where are your manners? Introduce me to Adventurer Talus."

Kalrick grinned impudently. "Why? You already know who he is."

Lady May raised her eyebrows.

"Um, I meant: Lady May, this is Adventurer Talus. Talus, Lady May." Kalrick quickly amended.

"Better." Lady May smiled and addressed Talus. "A pleasure to meet you, sir Adventurer. How do you find Alcasa?"

"The pleasure is mine, Lady May. It is pretty, but it is so..." How to say this? "Empty."

"Empty?"

"Flat grasslands spreading in every direction. I grew up with trees, so it is so different and incomparable."

Lady May studied him for a few seconds.

"True enough. And humans, what do you think of us?"

Talus noted the twinkle in her eyes.

"Well, humans are certainly interesting."

"Interesting. Neither good nor bad, I suppose you may get away with that."

Talus grinned and saluted. "Will you dance with me, my lady?"

She curtsied and answered gravely.

"I would be honored."

He offered his hand to her and they mingled into the other dancers. Talus was surprised by her first question as no one else had inquired on the subject.

"What is Belon like?"

"What exactly do you mean, my lady?"

She paused.

"Mayhap it is better to ask in pieces. Your style is different but you dance well. What are Elerin dances like?"

"Most often we dance under the leaves of Catha Forest, in small glades illuminated by colored lanterns. Our dances are far less formal, a few families together."

She smiled softly.

"That sounds beautiful."

Before Talus could reply, some woman called out.

"Lady May, when is the baby due? Let me congratulate you."

She was spun away, leaving Lady May in shock.

"I am not pregnant. Does my stomach look that big?"

Talus furrowed his brow. How had his mother appeared when she was pregnant with Marcus? Um, bigger? He did not clearly remember. The king's voice popped into his head. "If they do look for a reply, just agree, actually exaggerate." King Eirin had lived in Alcasa, so he must know best.

"My lady, you have one of the biggest stomachs I have ever seen!"

Lady May stared at him, stricken, for a long moment. Tears formed in her eyes. She slapped him and disappeared among the dancers.

Talus rubbed his face. What had he said wrong? According to the king, she should have loved that response. After a space of time, he realized he never would have said that to a lady in Belon. Common sense apparently needed to be coupled with the king's advice. Still, where had she gone? He wanted to talk to her to find out for sure, or at least apologize for upsetting her with his words.

Ah, there. He approached her from behind. He drew a deep breath.

"Countess Duoaquae?"

She turned and immediately her face darkened. Talus plunged in without giving her time to speak.

"Forgive me, Lady May. I did not mean to hurt you. Looking back, my words were a fool's. I was told to agree and to in answer exaggerate a woman's question. I now see this was faulted somewhere. I am sorry I caused you pain."

Talus held his breath waiting for her reply. Suddenly she smiled, a hint of laughter revealing itself in her voice.

"I forgive you. Whoever told you that meant in response to questions relating to beauty. I should not have asked you that question in the first place, but still use your brain. You are an intelligent young man, you will figure this out. One other thing, be kind, but do not exaggerate. It belittles the woman; such flattery is despicable."

Talus saluted.

"My thanks to you, my lady. I will not forget your advice. Your words remind me of my mother's saying, 'let not your heart lead you to speak that which is not completely true.' Perhaps Alcasan women are to be treated no differently than those of Belon."

Lady May covered her laughter.

"Is that unexpected, sir Adventurer?"

Talus smiled contritely.

"It shouldn't be, my lady. Forgive me."

"There is nothing to forgive. Cultures change, expectations change, but people are still people. You are as uncertain to our way of life as we are to our manners around you."

Talus saluted again.

"Thank you, lady. Though you need not be concerned, we Elerins are pretty laid back on manners."

Kalrick chose that time to find them, the dance having ended.

"How was the dance?"

Lady May laughed.

"Short."

Kalrick's expression took on an understandable confusion. The song had been a long one.

Lady May told him the tale, despite Talus' chagrin. Time passed into night and the castle fell into sleep.

Chapter 11 Kalrick and Celery

Anna and another kitchen servant, by the name of Kelly, raced through the halls of Castle Ketlin the next morning. The cook had needed more carrots five minutes before they left. Once they collected the carrots from the cellars, they were forced to slow slightly. Still, they made good speed.

"Almost there." Anna gasped.

Kelly nodded. "I'll beat ya."

She sped up.

"Won't," Anna protested.

Ahead of them, their hall crossed another. A knight stepped out into the intersection. Anna's eyes widened. She swerved, angling to reach the other side. She glanced back to see Kelly run full into the knight. Kelly stumbled backwards. The knight grabbed her arm and pulled her to him. He stared at her, eyes blazing. So soft Anna almost missed it, he spoke.

"Would you insult me by running away after slamming into me?"

Kelly's eyes widened. She wriggled, trying desperately to escape. A harsh light lit in the knight's eyes. He drew his dagger and traced her neck. She stilled.

"Foolish girl, pity you never learned to watch where you were going. And now, it is too late."

He buried his dagger in her chest and twisted it. Kelly gave a faint scream as her eyes clouded. Tears blurred Anna's vision. The knight laughed.

"See and be warned, girl."

He flung Kelly's body at her. She stared down into the face once so alive and warm, now fading as death crept over it.

Anna looked up at the knight who brandished his bloody dagger. She fled towards the kitchen, not caring if she dropped a carrot. The castle was not safe. Surely everything was hopeless. How could the world go on with the horror of this castle? How could one kill someone and laugh?

She pushed into the kitchen. Her face was deathly pale. She stumbled forward and dropped her remaining carrots on the counter beside the cook. He studied her.

"Anna, what's wrong? Where's Kelly?"

Tears flowed faster.

"He... he killed her."

The cook placed his hand on her shoulder and led her gently to an empty counter. He mixed some flour and water, and added a touch of oil.

"Knead, Anna. Sort your thoughts. It will be easier to come to grips with what you have seen if your hands are busy."

At first, she kneaded blankly. After some time passed, she began to pray and think.

The last rays of the sun had slipped from the western sky. Talus closed his eyes, trying to sleep, but the amount of Fumin grammar he had forgotten haunted him. Still, he had revived most of it, right? *Now, brain, go to sleep.*

His window creaked. Talus tensed. The window groaned and squealed, sliding up. Talus touched the knife under his pillow. A shape stepped through the curtains.

"Man, Talus, you keep it dark in here." Dalus' voice.

Talus grinned to the darkness and deepened his voice.

"Talus? Why would Talus be here?"

Dalus laughed.

"You had better work on that voice if you ever want to fool someone."

"Yeah, I guess." Talus rolled out of his bed and stood. "So what are you doing here?"

"Creeping around the castle and thought I would drop in." Dalus grinned.

"Really." Talus drew out the word.

"Yep. Actually, I am making an official report to Valoris and Jornus, concerning you." He made a show of looking Talus up and down, making notes on an invisible piece of paper.

"Ah," he said. "That should satisfy them. So...." He plopped into the chair by Talus' bed. "How's this weird place?"

"Fascinating and different. They have different intense emotions, I mean they have the same ones, but they stress different ones. Certain emotions are more acceptable here, too, than in Belon."

"Ah."

"And the customs and cultures are so... different. I do not think I can truly describe it yet."

"Hmm, then I will expect a full description next time." Dalus stood.

"Wait, you are not leaving already?" Talus asked almost desperately.

"No, no. I thought I would stay a little while." Dalus wandered around Talus' sleeping chambers. "You want to show me around your house inside a castle?"

Talus grinned. "Sure! Come see this."

Talus opened a door, revealing a near empty closet.

Dalus stepped inside. "It's kind of small. What is it?"

Talus shrugged. "I don't know. I found Lentus' clothes hanging from this bar, so I hung mine. It's odd. Maybe I'll ask Kalrick sometime."

Dalus eyed the hanging clothes distrustfully. "Do humans not believe in trunks?"

"Yes, and... no. There is one in my sitting room, but it is full of blankets and pillows. Here, I'll show ya." Talus ran out of the little room and opened one of the two other doors.

Two couches, a chair, and several stands surrounded a rug. The chest sat opposite the chair on their side of the room. Talus opened it to let his friend see.

Dalus shook his head. "Strange." He stretched out on a pale green couch. "Who's Kalrick?"

Talus glanced at him. "The one who helped me with the horse."

Dalus snickered. "You certainly needed a lot of help."

Talus raised his eyebrows. "Shall we adjourn to the stables?"

"Um... no thank you. I am quite comfortable here. You mind if I borrow this couch? I would like to take it with me."

Talus laughed.

"I'll bring it back next week." Dalus promised.

Talus grimaced.

"Oh, about that.... The king is leaving the morn after next. So I won't be here next week."

"Oh, right. Well, when do you get back?"

Talus furrowed his brow.

"It seems I neglected to inquire."

"Of course. Hurry back."

"I do not think I have much choice when I get back."

Dalus rolled his shoulders. "I suppose not. So...."

They talked late into the already late night, before Dalus left the way he had come. Talus was relieved that he did not take the couch, as that would have been awkward to explain to King Eirin.

<<<<<<<<<<<<<>>>>>>>>>>>>

Today, they left for Garia. Though part of him was not certain about leaving Belon so far behind, he would see so much of the world. Garia, mountains, the Hithlin Pass, the northern plains....

He had finally finished the letter for Carna, he really needed to extend his vocabulary. He jogged down the stairs separating his hallway from the king's. He knocked and pushed the door open to the king's entry room. The guards nodded to him. King Eirin had told him the day before to throw formality to the wind and enter. The gesture had caught Talus off guard, but he expected it must have been something Lentus had been allowed. Talus questioned the guards.

"Is the king in his sitting room or office, sirs?"

The guards managed stoic grins. The one to the left answered, with a shrewd glance to another.

"Uh, the sitting room, my lord."

Talus studied them. They were hiding something.

"Thank you."

Talus pushed the door open. He froze. A maid lay in Eirin's arms, giggling as he played in her hair and traced designs on her neck and shoulders. However, as Talus stepped in, awkward silence fell.

<<<<<<<<<<<<<<>>>>>>>>>>>>

Eirin tried desperately to keep the blood from rising to his face. Unsuccessfully. Something changed in Talus' eyes and his face turned to stone. What would he say? The last time Lentus had caught him.... Not something he wanted to remember. Finally, Talus spoke.

"Forgive me, my lord, I was not aware you were preoccupied. This is the letter to Carna."

Talus placed the correspondence on a table by the door. He saluted and closed the door.

The maid looked up at him.

"My lord, may I go? I should attend to my chores. Besides, you should see that Matt packed everything." She attempted to smile but it failed to reach her eyes.

Her voice held guilt, the same guilt Eirin struggled to press down. He was king. He could do whatever he wanted, right? After all, King Hissin messed with girls all the time. He shook away thoughts of justification.

"Of course, Maria. I will see you when I return."

Maria curtsied and hurriedly left the room.

Eirin watched her leave. Unbidden, part of Lentus' last lecture on the subject rose to mind. "You are the king, you must keep yourself above reproach for the sake of your people. Even if you were no one, you ought not bring shame on yourself and your father's memory." His father. He never would have dared touch a girl save in chivalry while his father lived. He banished his father's and Lentus' faces from his mind. He was a man, he could do as he pleased.

<<<<<<<<<<<<>>>>>>>>>>>>

Talus rode beside Kalrick, his mind still considering the scene on which he had walked in. Was that normal for Alcasans? But if it was, then why would the king be avoiding him? And he had appeared embarrassed.... Maybe Alcasans also looked down on it?

It was none of his business, so he dismissed the incident mostly from his mind. Still, what other secrets did the king hide?

"Hey, Talus." Kalrick broke in. "What's up? You have barely uttered a word since departure."

Talus noticed King Eirin, riding in front of them, turned his head slightly as if to hear what was said.

"Not much. Just thinking about something that happened this morning."

Kalrick's forehead creased, but he did not ask further. Silence lingered. Talus grinned, seeking to lighten the sudden heavy mood.

"When do we eat? I am starving!"

Kalrick laughed.

"Sure." He drew out the word.

Talus shrugged.

"Well, just hungry, but still...."

<<<<<<<<<<<<>>>>>>>>>>>>

Talus pushed aside the flap as he stepped into King Eirin's tent for supper. The king occupied a small rectangle table with Lord Kalrick to his left and Lord Henry, the king's uncle, to his right. King Eirin looked up as Talus entered.

"Ah, Talus, welcome. Are you still starving?" A twinkle in the king's eye showed he had overcome the awkwardness of the day.

"Definitely." Talus saluted, grinning.

"Well, well, can't have the report reaching Belon that I am starving you. Come, will you join us?" The king motioned to the end seat.

"I would be honored, Your Majesty." Talus answered with gravity at odds with the light mood. He took the indicated chair.

"Now, gentlemen," the king began, "we have a tasty beef stew for dinner."

"And..." Kalrick prompted.

"And rolls fresh from the fire."

"And...."

"And wine to ease the swallowing." The king speared Kalrick with a glare.

65

"And...." Kalrick grinned back.

"And sweet biscuits for after."

"And...."

"And a large amount of celery just for my dear lord Kalrick!" King Eirin drew twelve sticks of nearly round celery from under the table.

Lord Henry burst out laughing, while Kalrick edged away from King Eirin, a look of pure horror on his face. Talus was puzzled for a moment until he remembered something he had overheard a servant girl say. Kalrick avoided celery no matter what.

Kalrick stared at the stalks in distrust.

Talus grinned. "It won't bite if you bite first, you know."

Kalrick glared at him but did not touch the stuff.

King Eirin tried. "Come on, Kalrick. Let's see you eat it."

Kalrick's face grew pale in fear. "My lord, I pray you, do not make me."

King Eirin placed the celery on the table away from Kalrick and studied him. "Will you tell us why celery frightens you, my lord? 'Tis but a request."

Kalrick grew still as distant thoughts flitted across his face. He drew a breath.

"When I was about four, my elder brother Celblin gave me my first and only piece of celery. My memories are shrouded. It was a new food, so I put the end in my mouth and bit down tentatively. My brother neglected to inform me that the stalk was the home of a small green snake. The snake did... not care for the pressure. It bit my tongue. It hurt like mad, and I started crying and ran for the keep, my brother's laughter echoing in my ears. It turned out it was somewhat poisonous, and I am told I was sick for days."

"You poor lad." Lord Henry sympathized. "I remembered hearing of that, save, your family never gave out why you were sick."

"To protect reputation, I suppose." Kalrick mused. "Celblin rarely left my bedside while I was sick, my mother told me. A few years ago, Celblin and I were discussing it and he said watching me lay there was far worse than the retribution he received from Father for that prank."

Eirin snapped a piece of celery and held the larger half of the hollow stick up to his eye. "Well, no snake here if you are interested today, but if not, I understand."

Kalrick gingerly took the celery from Eirin's hand. He drew his dagger and slit the vegetable long wise on the table. Satisfied it was empty, he cut off a small piece and grasped it in his fingers. He stared at it for a length of time. Finally, he placed it in his mouth. A moment later, he shrugged.

"I guess it is not too bad."

Eirin smiled. "Better without snakes, my lord?"

Kalrick nodded. "It would seem, Your Majesty." Kalrick suddenly grinned. "Eirin, exactly how long were you plotting that?"

Eirin raised his brows. "Plotting? Plotting, Kalrick, why would I plot?"

Kalrick did not reply, he just grinned.

"Well, perhaps since yesterday, if you must know." Eirin confessed with a failed attempt not to smile.

"Ahh, what am I to do with you?"

"Hmm, a little respect now and then would not hurt...."

Kalrick stood and made an exaggerated bow. Eirin shook his head, laughing.

"I am all too lenient with my lords, Hissin would have had your head."

A bit of trouble spilled into Kalrick's eyes as he retook his seat.

"Aye, my king. But you are not King Hissin, and in some ways it would be better if you did not imitate him."

A dark shadow crossed Eirin's face as Kalrick held his eyes. Eirin breathed in and spoke in a soft voice, too soft.

"Kalrick, I would rather you did not push some lines."

A swirl of emotions played on Kalrick's face.

"You are my king and my friend."

King Eirin nodded. Yet, Talus noted Kalrick had not pledged himself not to push the lines.

Chapter 12 Fear and Forgiveness

Four days after Kelly's murder, the cook had left the whole kitchen making bread. A dangerous affair indeed. Two lads had gotten into a fight, with dough. Like leaven, it quickly spread to the whole kitchen.

Anna laughed, ducking Mara's ball of dough, and hurled a lump at Cat. It was the first time Anna could laugh since the awful day, and the laughter felt relieving. Cat, who had been busy torturing Violet, turned on Anna with a vicious grin. Cat scooped a pile of dough off the floor. She took a threatening step forward, tearing a piece off and examined it meticulously. She threw it. Anna dodged and ran. Cat pursued, pelting her mercilessly. Anna tripped. She curled on the ground, hiding her face.

"Stop, stop." She laughed.

The balls paused. Anna looked up cautiously. Cat dropped the rest of the dough on her face.

"Not fair." Anna attempted to glare at her.

Cat giggled helplessly. Anna smiled mischievously. Deftly, she pulled the dough off her face and threw it into Cat's. The other girl tugged the majority off and frowned at her.

"I thought you were done."

"Well, not quite." Anna grinned.

An angry voice resounded among the cupboards.

"What in all Alvar is going on?!!"

The cook was back. Everyone raced back to their counters, ducking the cook's ladle. They quickly started new bread, as they could not serve the dough they had been using for the game.

The cook glared at them the rest of the day. However, Anna thought he was secretly amused because, occasionally, when he thought no one was watching he would regard his staff with a smile.

<<<<<<<<<<<<>>>>>>>>>>>>

The sun burned hot on the fourth day of their journey. Talus was relieved when, on reaching a small stream around midday, the king called for a halt.

Once he had staked out his horse, he stepped into the water. He closed his eyes, enjoying the cool water rushing across his bare feet.

"That must be nice."

Talus looked up at Kalrick who crouched on the bank. Talus nodded.

"Aye, why don't you come in?"

"I am wearing boots." Kalrick said sadly.

Talus rolled his eyes. Did not these people believe in bare feet?

"Can't you take them off?"

Kalrick stood and stroked his beard.

"Well, it is not really proper etiquette, you know with servants and soldiers around. We nobles are supposed to appear dignified." Kalrick sounded wistful.

"Hmm, then I shall have to give the others a reason...." Talus splashed the water straight up into Kalrick's face.

"Hey!" Kalrick grinned. "Challenge accepted."

Talus laughed. Kalrick could not get his boots, socks, and weapons off fast enough. He slid down the bank. Talus gave him about half a second to recover before bombarding him with flying water. Soon discovering the hopelessness of a counterattack, Kalrick tried a new method. He ran through the water attack and knocked his shoulder into Talus. The Elerin stumbled back, but pushed Kalrick sideways. Kalrick hit the water with his most successful splash yet.

Kalrick pushed to his feet, wiping his chin length hair from his face.

"You know that actually felt good."

Talus laughed. "Probably."

He looked down at the beckoning water. Water hit him in the face.

"Hey-" River water filled his mouth. He spat most of it out.

"What are you two doing?" King Eirin questioned, creating a pause in Kalrick's barrage.

"Just a little challenge." Kalrick said innocently, right as he splashed Eirin.

"Hey!" Eirin stood in indecision.

He needed a little more help, Talus determined. He also dared a splash.

"What? Not two of you!" Eirin grinned. He called over his shoulder to his men. "Lord Kalrick and Adventurer Talus have taken it upon themselves to soak me, anyone care to give me a hand?"

More people than Talus thought Kalrick and he could handle took the king up on the offer. A minute later, everyone had their boots off and were in the water. Though Kalrick and he were supposed to be the targets, it quickly became everyone against everyone.

The fight lasted about ten minutes, until by universal agreement they all scrambled back up the slope and lay on the grass panting and laughing.

Talus leaned his head back and stared up at the passing clouds. Perhaps humans, at least in some regards, were truly not that different from Elerins.

"Think, Talus. You started all that." Kalrick drew his wandering thoughts back to the present.

Talus grinned.

"It depends on how you look at it. One could say you started it since you refused to remove your boots."

Kalrick's eyes widened. "What, you would try to blame me?"

Talus laughed. "No, since I splashed you first it is my fault."

"Hmm." Eirin rubbed his beard. "I shall have to complain to Belon, they sent me a mischievous rascal."

Talus let horror flood his features.

"Please don't, I'll be good. At least, most of the time." He pleaded.

Eirin and Kalrick laughed. The three of them settled into conversation for some time.

Suddenly the king looked at the sun.

"We have to go!" Eirin raised his voice. "Everyone, pack up! We leave in five."

Industry overtook the previous docile mood. By the time they mounted, grimness had overtaken the king's expression.

<<<<<<<<<<<<<>>>>>>>>>>>>

The color faded in the west. They were still riding. Night was upon them on the Northern Plains of Alcasa. This part of the plains was too close to Darqin Forest to be safe in daylight, never mind at night.

A faint howl reached Talus' ears. A normal wolf. At least, he hoped. However, this close to Darqin....

"Kalrick, did you hear that?"

Kalrick glanced at him. "Hear what?"

"I thought I heard-" Talus began, but a deep joyous howl interrupted his sentence. Darqin wolves.

In front of them, King Eirin straightened in his saddle and called calmly to those around him.

"Men, we need to ride hard and fast. Leave no man behind."

As the column urged their horses to a gallop, the howls thickened the air, growing ever closer and from all directions. The king spoke.

"Take courage, men. We only have a few miles left to Dunlong."

The wolves howled, ominously applauding King Eirin. Across the plains, still some ways distant, Talus spotted the dark forms of the wolves. Suddenly, a deathly silence descended.

His mount grew nervous beneath him. He touched her neck. "It will be alright." Or so he prayed. The silence deepened. It was as if he could feel breath on his neck.

A low growl sounded to the left. The men let the horses have their heads and they bolted. Deep baying began. A scream split the air behind Talus to the right.

Before him a huge shadow arched, knocking the king and his horse to the ground. The king screamed.

"Kalrick!" Talus shouted.

"Hopeless, Talus." Fear evident in his voice, he galloped away.

Talus called his horse to a stop, speaking in Zofish.

"Ahh... Ashom, Ashom, klecix Ashi." Altros heeded that musical tongue and, foreign to his kind, stopped in the middle of the wolf pack. The rest of the riders disappeared in a desperate attempt to gain safety.

A sword point appeared out of the head of the wolf who pinned the king to the ground. The wolf leapt back, loosing a terrible howl, and slumped in death. Immediately, the surrounding wolves ripped into the carcass. King Eirin rolled from the carnage, leaving his sword in the wolf, and lay unmoving.

"My lord! Over here!" Talus shouted.

Eirin stood slowly like a man in a dream, watching the blood fly above the wolves.

"King Eirin!" Talus called more forcefully.

The king jumped and snapped out of the horror. Eirin ran and swung himself up behind Talus. The Elerin leaned forward.

"Aclesa, Altos!" The horse took off at a run. Talus guided him toward the growing castle, his heart racing faster than the horse. After a moment, Eirin touched his shoulder.

"They are coming."

Talus drew a slow breath but kept his eyes ahead.

"Let me know when they are ten cat's tails back." Seconds passed.

"That would be now."

Talus spoke softly to Altos. Altos reared, turning, and smashed his hooves into the lead wolf. The wolf stumbled back, dazed. Two more wolves sprung toward them.

Talus dropped the reins and whipped out his twin blades, taking each wolf in the eye. Talus shouted for Altos to run; the horse needed no prodding. As the wolves behind tore into their dead comrades, Talus looked ahead. The wolves had circled and now cut them off from the castle.

"Ashom!" Talus screamed, destroying some of the musical quality, but still bringing Altos to a dead stop. The sea of wolves stared at them in dark silence, waiting. Eirin tapped him on the shoulder.

"Do you have a weapon to spare?"

Talus sheathed one short sword and drew his broadsword. He handed it to Eirin.

"Don't chop my head off, please."

Despite the danger, Eirin laughed. "Sorry, had other things in mind."

"Always good to hear." Talus grinned and leaned forward to whisper to Altros.

"Aglca, Altros!" Altros hesitated a second, before rearing and racing towards the wolves. The wolves were amused that these little creatures were actually charging them.

"Amazing what Zofish words do."

Talus nodded, not that Eirin could see. "Aye."

"Why not tell the wolves to leave?" Eirin queried.

"Many Elerins have died in that belief. The Darqin will only heed a Kazof." Talus paused, just before they crashed into the line of wolves. "Their eyes. I'll take the left side."

Talus buried his blades in both eyes and whipped them out again. And into the next. And the next.

A huge wolf farther in, released a long howl. The wolves leapt for Altros. As soon as he realized the intent, Talus scrambled for the reins. Talus yanked. "Ashom!"

Altros reared and came to a dead stop. The wolves ripped into those on the opposite side just in front of them. Too close. A stray claw found Altros' nose. The horse gave a guttural scream and fled. The opposite way from the castle. Talus could do nothing about it. He tried to swallow, his faulty grip was failing. He was going to fly off.

Eirin's left arm hooked around him grabbing the reins. Out of the corner of his eye, Talus watched Eirin pull steadily with his right. The horse followed a sweeping circle back toward the castle. The gates loomed large and inviting.

Behind Talus, Eirin screamed. Talus was thrown backwards off the horse, Eirin's arm caught on his jerkin. Talus flew free. He hit the ground winded, but he jumped up regardless.

Eirin rolled from the wolf. But not fast enough. The wolf planted a paw on Eirin's chest. The king screamed as its claws gored through his armor. Talus drew a knife and hurled it into its eye. It growled. Eirin screamed. Talus dropped one blade and dashed under the wolf on its now blind side. Talus used everything left to pierce the hide and slid it into the soft flesh. Blood poured from the wound, soaking Talus. The wolf gave an agonized howl and flung Eirin. At the gate, thank Theos.

Eirin collapsed in a heap. Talus raced to him, forcing his legs to move. He reached him as Eirin pushed himself up. Talus helped him stand and they stumbled through the gate.

The men of the company crowded them, inquiring after their health.

"Nothing that won't heal." The king forced a smile.

As Lord Henry embraced Eirin, uncaring of blood and grime, Talus missed Kalrick. Where was he? Talus scanned the courtyard. Kalrick stood alone in the shadows of the wall, watching. Talus tried to meet his eyes, but Kalrick turned away. What was up? The panicked moment after Eirin fell came back to Talus, and he thought he understood. However, he was left with no time for thought.

The Earl of Dunlong, Lord Stalton Stay, pushed through the crowd.

"Welcome to Dunlong, my lord. I was about to offer you and your noble friend supper, but perhaps you wish for a bath and the attention of a healer, first?"

"Certainly, Earl Dunlong, that would be most appreciated. Lend me a moment, however. I must see to my men."

"Of course, Your Majesty. I will order your baths and summon the healer." The middle-aged lord bowed.

King Eirin turned back to his men.

"Form ranks!"

The men quickly fell into a five by four formation, each man in his place. Three places were empty. Quietly, the king inquired after them.

"Have any of you seen your comrades since you entered Dunlong?"

Silence and grim faces were the only answers.

"Let those who have passed from this world find peace after such a death. You may move freely."

Eirin walked slowly to the keep. Talus followed, a thought darting through his mind. Had those men been in the position to find peace after death? He pushed it away, wondering if they had friends in the company, or families back in Aubin.

Suddenly Eirin turned to Talus, his face littered in pain.

"I should have ordered a stop when the day grew old. Then those men would still be alive. It is my fault, I should have stopped. Why did I continue? Now they are dead."

Talus met Eirin's eyes and answered calmly, though he struggled for the right words. "You did what you thought was best at the time, my lord. Did you not? Think not long on what you should have done; it will only bring despair. Learn from it and move on."

73

"Move on? Move on! They are dead, Talus! How could you tell me to move on?" The grief and shock mixed in the king's eyes.

"Remember it, grieve it, but leave it in the past. You, Your Majesty, are a lord of men. Your choices will cause the deaths of men. Even so, those men died because it was their time." Talus paused. "But consider, my lord, if we had camped and the Darqin had found us. Surely no amount of flame or valor could have saved us."

The hall grew silent. Tears slid unashamed into the young king's beard. His face grew grave and grim. He straightened.

"You are right. Even right choices have costs, but to death...." Eirin's voice clogged. "Even death. Well, be glad you don't have to make these kinds of choices. Now, our baths grow cold." The barest hint of a smile peeked out.

"Yeah, cold or hot, a bath sounds good. I have never been so filthy in my life!" Talus answered lightly, trying to match Eirin's hint of a smile.

<<<<<<<<<<<<>>>>>>>>>>>>

King Eirin, followed by Talus, entered a small hall, set as a private dining room. Earl Dunlong and Lord Henry stood as they approached. The earl bowed.

"Ah, my lord, there you are. I hope you found everything comfortable?"

"Indeed, I did, my good earl. Alas, I am afraid my appetite was sharpened by the bath." Eirin grinned.

"Now, what can I do about that, my lord? Please, please be seated. The food will be served momentarily."

Eirin sat down on Earl Dunlong's right across from Lord Henry, while Talus took the chair beside the king's uncle.

The earl continued. "Shall I ask Theos' blessing on it, or would you prefer?"

"You do it, Sir Earl." Eirin answered hastily.

Talus bowed his head and listened to the earl's prayer.

"Heavenly Father, we thank You for this food You have given us. We thank You for the protection with which You blessed the king among the wolves. Yet we mourn the loss of the fallen, Father. I pray that You would grant us the blessing of Your comfort. Bless our fellowship this evening. In the name of Iasos, let it be so."

The servants entered, placing dishes of food on the table. After they returned to the kitchen, Eirin inquired of Earl Dunlong.

"Where is Lady Dunlong, my lord?"

"She is feeling poorly and sends her regrets. Hopefully, she can join us in the morning." The earl's concern lingered in his eyes.

"We miss her company; I hope she recovers quickly for her sake." King Eirin replied quietly.

"As do I, as do I."

After a moment, Eirin frowned.

"Where is Lord Kalrick?"

Lord Henry answered, puzzled. "Last I saw, we were on the wall together, watching. His face was shadowed, but that was the scare you threw us for, I imagine."

"Yes, and he seemed subdued, I thought." Earl Dunlong agreed.

"I think I could honestly say the scare was not my fault. Was he back to himself after?"

"I lost track of him." Lord Henry responded.

"As did I," was the earl's answer. "I could send a servant to find him, if you wish, my lord."

Eirin shook his head. "No but thank you. He'll turn up or I'll search him out later."

"I am sure he will, my lord. Your Majesty, will you introduce me to your valiant new translator?"

A pained look crossed Eirin's face. "Forgive my lack of manners, Sir Earl. This is Talus, son of Valnis. Talus, the Earl Dunlong."

"Talus, son of Valnis, 'tis an honor to meet you. For after your deeds today in the service of the king, all who know will honor you. Your presence with the king gave many hope as it would not have been with another."

"Yes, you certainly saved my life, twice actually." The king was smiling. "Perhaps one day I can repay you."

A hint of red darkened Talus' face.

"You did, my lord. When I lost control of Altros."

Eirin rubbed his beard.

"That covers once I suppose. And twice?"

"Oh, right. Well, you are stuck with me for a while. I have no doubt you will. But, my lords, you honor me over much. Surely anyone would have done the same."

Lord Henry shook his head sadly.

"Were this the field of battle I would agree with you, but nothing lights terror in the heart of men as those dark wolves. Alas, many brave knights will cower and run in the face of those foul creatures, regardless of duty. Let men learn from you."

Talus met his eyes and, placing his fist over his heart, he saluted slowly.

"Though," Lord Henry smiled. "I must ask, is fear in the vocabulary of an Elerin?"

In Talus' mind, the eyes of the swamp monster glowed and the great throat opened. The tentacles tightened. The scene changed. Jornus loomed over him, grief and disappointment having combined into dark anger, after the Tongath incident. Talus shook his head clear, his remembered fear and shame and grief all too vivid.

"Yes," Talus replied, voice low. "Elerins fear, same as humans."

Silence lingered as thoughts overtook the party. Earl Dunlong looked up from his musing.

75

"Eat, my good sirs. Ere the food grows cold. 'As a smile nourishes the heart, so food the body,' as the poets say."

"Perhaps," Eirin grinned slyly. "The poets were referring to a lady's smile...."

Earl Dunlong smiled distantly, undoubtedly a particular lady on his mind, before refocusing.

"It is possible, though I believe the writer was referring to one's own or a companion's smile."

Eirin shrugged mischievously. "But it is not impossible for your companion to be a-"

The doors burst open. Lord Kalrick rushed in, his face pale and haunted. He dropped to his knees beside the king's chair.

"Slay me quickly, my lord. I am a dishonored knight; I cannot bear the shame. My vows are trampled underfoot. Fear took me and when I saw your need was dire, I fled. I beg you, slay me! My disgrace is too great!"

Shock and Kalrick's pain echoed in the hall. Nothing moved. King Eirin pushed his chair back and stood. Before him, Kalrick waited, head bowed. King Eirin knelt and lifted Kalrick's chin with his fingers. Tears flowed unrestricted down Kalrick's face and his eyes were alive with hurt. He stared at the floor, refusing to meet Eirin's gaze. When the king spoke, his voice was quiet and gentle.

"Kalrick? Look at me, Kalrick." Kalrick glanced up. "Few in all Alvar are as loyal to me as you are. Kalrick, look at me! The howls of the Darqin wolves drive fear into many a courageous heart. But 'today's fear is tomorrow's victory.' I know you, Kalrick. You are the closest thing I have to a brother. You failed today, but you will not again. It is not in your nature. If there ever is a next time, you would ride with me to the end. 'Mercy is the king's right.' I forgive you, Kalrick. Fear shame no more."

The king stood and pulled Kalrick up into his embrace. His tears still fell, but these were different. Tears of thankfulness and joy. A grimness settled in his features. When they parted, Eirin gave Kalrick a gentle smile. After a moment, Kalrick returned it. Eirin motioned to the chair next to him.

"How does supper sound, Kalrick?"

Chapter 13 Anna's Choice

Eirin paced next to his horse. One of the horses had thrown a shoe in last night's run. Earl Dunlong had offered the services of his blacksmith. Time was slipping away. The horse, of course, needed its shoe. Eirin was convinced the man could not go any slower. He really wanted to tell the smith to hurry up, but his father had made a point that he never said anything negative to a man doing his job. By the same teaching, he should thank the man afterwards.

Eirin glanced at the sun. So much time was passing. They were never going to reach the outpost in the Hithlin Pass. Shoved his frustration down, he forced himself to stop pacing. He walked over to where Kalrick and Talus were leaning against a wall laughing about something. He pushed a smile, far too conscious of how fake it looked.

"Now whatever is so funny?"

Kalrick began a children's singsong.

"Horses a-mulling

"Time's a-pulling

"Men a-jawning

"Kings...."

Kalrick stopped suddenly and looked contrite. The next line was "Kings a-frowning." Eirin sighed.

"I suppose that does describe the situation perfectly. Nice to see how much respect children have for their kings." Eirin regretted the jab almost immediately.

"Sorry, Eirin. We didn't mean disrespect."

"I know, Kal, I am just tired and frustrated. Sorry."

"Anything we could do to help?" Talus asked.

"No, not unless you can make the smith hurry up and push back time."

"Want to spar?" Kalrick asked. "I don't think you and Talus have crossed blades yet."

Eirin glanced over his shoulder. The blacksmith had finally finished.

"That would be fun, but we can leave now. Perhaps later, Talus?"

"Sure, my lord." Talus' grin peeked out.

Eirin paused for a second. "In private, Talus, my friends may call me 'Eirin'."

Talus nodded slowly. "Then I am honored to be counted among them, Eirin."

Eirin smiled. "Let's go." He turned and projected his voice. "Mount up, men!"

Eirin swung into his saddle. Finally, they could leave. He urged his horse toward the gate, waving to the earl. "Thanks, again for your hospitality, my lord."

Behind him, the men fell into travel formation, moving in pairs. The road rolled away beneath the horses' feet. Dunlong grew small. Eirin smiled, now that they were on the road, they were making good time.

"Your Majesty?" A tentative voice asked beside him.

Eirin nodded to the man-at-arms, beckoning him up beside him. "Yes?"

"I-I am really sorry, Your Majesty. I didn't mean to, honest. I am really sorry." The man stammered.

Eirin stifled a sigh. "Calm down, man. Didn't mean to what?"

The man raised his eyes. Fear, either this man had done something terribly wrong or Eirin had, he thought.

"I left my bow in Dunlong, Your Majesty. I really am sorry. Can I, maybe, retrieve it?"

Delay. Why now? This was ridiculous. How could a man-at-arms forget his weapons! Eirin swallowed this question.

"Of course, take someone with you. Be as quick as possible without hurting the horses. We will walk the horses until you get back."

The man nodded. "Thank you, Your Majesty. I am really sorry."

"Don't worry about it. Accidents happen." Why to him? Why now? And why did he have to be understanding and gracious? After the man turned away, Eirin let the smile slip from his face. He slowed his horse to a walk and the others followed his example. How long would it take for him to return?

"Your Majesty?" The same man.

"Yes? Find a partner?"

"No, my lord. I, no one will go with me."

Uncomplimentary words that should not be in his vocabulary rose to mind. However, before he could respond, Talus volunteered.

"I can go, my lord."

"Thank you, Talus. Be quick."

They nodded and Talus followed the man as they pushed their horses into a gallop.

They faded into the distance. Eirin looked at the sun, his frustration growing with each passing moment. How long would this take? Time was slipping away! Finally, after an hour that seemed like an eternity, Talus rode up beside him.

"All remedied, my lord."

Eirin nodded. "Good." He quickened the pace of his mount. So much time was lost. Would they even make it before dark? His uncle, who was riding to his right half a horse back, came alongside him.

"Eirin, pleasant midday, eh?"

His eyes slid closed. Lunch. He should have called for lunch while they were walking. Why was everything piling up against him? This was stupid.

"Sure. Thanks." He knew his voice sounded wooden and anything but thankful. He just didn't care. His uncle would understand.

"Let's have a quick lunch, men."

Grins broke out among the riders. Food was always welcome. Eirin dismounted and staked out his horse. He pulled his food out, cramming some meat in between two pieces of bread and joined his uncle, Kalrick, and Talus.

"Who will give thanks for the food?" Lord Henry asked as he prepared to raise his food.

"You do it." Eirin pushed.

"Sure. Heavenly Father, we thank You for this food You have given us...." Would he hurry it up? "...We pray You will guide the rest of our journey and protect us as we travel. Yours, Father, is all honor. In Iasos' name, let it be so."

Finally, he could eat. He paid little attention to the conversation. It was going to be dark at this rate before they got there tonight. That was the last thing he wanted. What if the Darqin found them again? Perhaps they could push the horses a little harder after lunch.

Eirin swallowed the last of his food. He looked around. Why was everyone eating with such agonizing slowness? He stood abruptly and repacked his things. The men didn't take the hint and continued at the same monotonous speed. Eirin sat back down, resting against a lump in the ground. He closed his eyes. Somehow, he had to wait. What was wrong with these people? What part of quick did they miss? The sun felt nice.

Eirin rolled over and sat up suddenly. Had he fallen asleep? How could he have? He looked at the sun. He had been asleep for almost an hour.

"You are awake." His uncle greeted him.

"Why didn't...." Eirin stopped; he couldn't blame anyone but himself. And conversation would take too much time. "Aye. Are the men ready to ride?"

Lord Henry nodded. "Yes."

Eirin called to his men. "Mount up. We leave now."

He took his horse off the picket and stuffed the rope and stake into his bag. He mounted and, checking to see that everyone else was mounted, urged his horse into a canter. They kept the pace for several minutes. Eirin spoke to no one. He simply had no desire to converse. They were never going to make it. Dread settled in his stomach. The column had caught the king's mood and silence reigned in the plains.

A snap followed by a crash and a shout of annoyance from one of the men. Eirin spun his horse around and galloped back to the disturbance. The man's things littered the ground. One of his saddle bags' straps had broken. He dismounted and stalked toward the poor man.

"Why didn't you think to replace your strap? Are you that stupid?" Eirin roared as he surveyed the mess. The man paled and wilted beneath the rebuke.

"Your Majesty." His uncle's voice failed to register.

"How dare you waste time like this?"

"Your Majesty!"

"You had better make it quick or I'll leave you to the Darqin tonight!!!"

"Eirin!"

Eirin jumped. His eyes closed, every word echoing in his brain. Stupid. If anyone was, it was him, not this man. And what kind of monster would make a threat like that? Eirin looked back to the man.

"Forgive me. Everything is piling up against me, and I allowed myself to take my anger out on you. It was wrong of me. I am sorry."

Eirin offered his arm. The man stared at him. How could Eirin have put his own soldier in such shame? He was such a fool.

The man stepped forward to close the gap and grasped his forearm. "I forgive you, Your Majesty. And I am sorry about this. You are right, I should check my equipment more often."

Eirin met his eyes. "We all live and learn. I thank you for your nobility." A smile touched the soldier's face. "Now, Graton, let's get your things together."

Eirin picked up the bag and handed it to the man. "Figure out a way to fasten this to your packs. I'll gather your things."

The man took it. "You don't have to, my lord. I can get them."

Eirin gave him a smile though regret made it hard. "I do not mind getting my hands a touch dirty."

The man grinned. "Then thanks, my lord." The soldier turned to his horse. Eirin knelt and gathered the spilled items. What would his uncle say or not say after this? A king taking his anger out on a subordinate. Sometimes he didn't think he learned much in the two years since his father's death. His father. Something similar had happened seven years ago when he was fifteen. The dread of following his father into his office. His father had ignored him for several minutes. Until he had said, "Do you think that was right? Anger is a grievous fault, my son. But it can be overcome through hard work. You will be king, Eirin. You must overcome this or shame yourself. I believe you can do this, Eirin." He pushed the image away. The quiet words had hurt that day and no less today.

Eirin stood and handed the things to the man-at-arms. "Here you are."

"Thank you, Your Majesty. Sorry for the inconvenience."

"No problem, Graton. Everything secured?"

"Yes, my lord." The man bowed.

Eirin bowed just enough for politeness. He remounted and rode to the beginning of the column. His friends followed him. Eirin did not look at them. He could imagine their faces. Lord Henry would be disappointed. Kalrick would wear that same mask he always used in these situations. And Talus. Talus' face would probably hold shock. After all, anger in Elerin culture was looked down upon, to put it mildly.

After a couple minutes, Eirin heard his uncle urge his horse up beside him. Eirin braced himself.

"Eirin, I am proud of you."

Eirin looked at him.

"What?"

"You handled your fault with humility and graciousness often forgotten by people in your position."

Eirin met his uncle's gaze. "Thanks, Uncle."

"And, Eirin, leave the past in the past. Do not tear yourself down about this. Learn and remember even so, you did well. You are a king your people can be proud to call their own."

Eirin shoved down emotion suddenly too strong.

"Thank you, that means a lot." His voice came out a little deeper than normal.

<<<<<<<<<<<<<>>>>>>>>>>>>

"You two!"

Anna turned to see the cook pointing at her and Violet.

"Yes sir?" She asked.

"We are nearly out of flour. Run down to the cellars and fetch some more. Lively now!"

"Come on." Violet grabbed her arm, eager to leave the heat of the kitchen.

They ran haphazardly to the door of the kitchen, where Anna stopped suddenly. Violet tugged on her.

"What are you waiting for?"

Anna looked into the silent hall, looming dark in her mind.

"Remember Kelly? I think we should stop at each corner and ensure no one is close enough to kill us."

Violet's smile faded and she shivered.

"You are right. Out of the kitchen, this place is so awful!"

"We will just be careful, and we should, Theos willing, be safe."

Violet nodded.

Cautiously they approached the first corner.

Nothing.

They darted to the next one.

Nothing.

A voice echoed from the next hallway.

"Why, my dear, you are a pretty little thing."

"No, please, help, don't hurt me."

"It won't be that horrid, my dear."

Anna peeked around the edge. The sight she expected met her eyes. She had seen it so many times, but it still made her sick.

"Could we help her?" Violet whispered, pain evident in her eyes.

"I don't know. If we distracted the knight holding her to the wall, she could run and then we would have to run as well."

"And if we have to separate, meet in the cellars? Once all is safe." Violet suggested.

"Sounds good. We'll bait him from a distance. Once she runs, we run. If he gets too close, we split. Avoid dead ends."

Violet grinned. "Was that supposed to be funny?"

"What? Oh, dead ends. Not really. Have any taunts in mind?"

Violet nodded mischievously. They leapt into the hall.

"Hey, you! You picked poorly; *I'm* the pretty one!" Violet shouted.

"Hey, big nose!" Anna added. "What's a great oaf like you doing harming a child?!!"

He turned, shoving the girl to the ground. He stalked toward them. The girl leapt to her feet and fled.

"What did you say?" He growled.

"Um, nothing." Anna stepped back.

They raced down the hall away from the kitchen.

"Get back here!" The knight screamed and charged.

They darted down every new hall that offered itself. But no matter how many twists and turns, the feet still pounded after them. Coming to an intersection, Violet glanced at Anna. They turned opposite ways. The feet went silent for a second behind Anna. Then they resumed, remaining constant in volume. He was following her.

They grew louder. Anna swallowed. He was going to catch her. Anna pushed her legs harder. She could hear his breathing.

She turned a sharp corner and took the immediate door to the cellars. Maybe the cellar keeper would protect her. She took the stairs as fast as she could.

"Help." She gasped as she reached the keeper.

He looked from her to the corridor leading to the stairs and back. Wordlessly he lifted her into a barrel and shut the lid. Anna found a peek hole and tried to calm her breathing. The knight stomped into the room.

"You there! Where's the girl?"

"Hav-ve a drink, man?" The keeper laughed uproariously.

Disgust laced the knight's mummer.

"Lowdown drunk. I will search for myself."

His footsteps softened. Anna breathed a soft sigh. He was gone.

The barrel rocked violently. Anna stifled a scream. She held her breath. Had she made too much noise?

Another fear crept into her thoughts. What if Violet came down with the knight around? She swallowed hard. What if she was caught? She drew a slow silent breath. Only one thing she could do. She prayed.

Eventually the footsteps returned.

"No luck for me, drunk. She must not have come down here, stupid girl." His steps echoed annoyance as he followed the stairs up to the first level. A few minutes later she watched the cellar keeper stand and walk toward her. He yanked the lid off with a tool.

"Oh my. What funny ale." He peered at her.

"Thanks, Zelin."

"A pleasure, Anna." He grinned toothily at her.

"Anna! You made it." Violet exclaimed as she ran into the room. "I was so scared when he chased you!" She threw her arms around Anna.

The cellar keeper smiled happily at them.

"Now. What can I get you ladies?"

"Where's the flour, sir?" Violet asked.

"Ah, here for flowers, miss? Well, I am afraid you will have to wait for some sweet young man for that."

Violet giggled. "No, flour for cooking."

"Oh, that. Right. In the fifth room down, call if you two need a hand."

"Thank you." Anna and Violet replied.

They hurried to the fifth room. Cloth bags labeled flour sat on a shelf five feet up, while bags of sugar lined the lower walls. Anna eyed them.

"How shall we get them down?"

"Should be able to pull it down and drop it on the floor, the bags are sewn shut, after all. Least that's how Mara and I did it. Or we could call on Zelin."

"True." Anna tugged on a bag. "It is heavy!"

Violet grinned. "Really? It is fifty pounds."

Anna laughed. "So, it is. Why don't you give me a hand?"

Violet's grin broadened. She held out her left hand and tugged on it with her right. She made an apologetic face.

"Sorry, it won't come off."

Anna rolled her eyes. "I think all the excitement has gotten into your head."

She gave the bag a hard tug. It slid frontward halfway.

"I nearly have it. Help me!"

Violet stepped toward her. Anna pulled again. Little was the distance, but it upset the bag. The bag tipped forward. Only it didn't fall. Everything turned white. The bag emptied about half its contents over them. They coughed as they breathed flour. Slowly the flour settled, and they could see each other again.

"So... the bags are sewn shut, eh?"

Violet shrugged then started laughing. "You have a pile of flour on your head."

Anna brushed it off. "Well, at least I am not the only one."

Violet could not stop laughing but swiped at her head with her hand. Flour coated the air again briefly. Anna joined in the laugh.

"Now, now. What happened here? Perhaps, ladies in distress viciously attacked by the terrible Flour of Laugh, horrid knight of the age?"

Anna and Violet turned simultaneously to see Zelin standing in the doorway.

"Sorry about the mess." Anna gasped between breaths.

"It wasn't sealed." Violet added. "But we can help sweep it up, if you like?"

"No, no. I need some excitement in my exile." He winked at them. "Otherwise, I go sampling too much wine, you know." He waltzed to the shelf. He pulled a bag down. "Here ye are, ladies. Off you go. Sure the cook is wanting you back."

"Thanks, Zelin." They repeated each other. Carrying the bag between them, they returned to the kitchen.

"So this is the Stonecliff range." Talus commented on the sheer cliffs rising before them. The sun setting behind them created a beautiful picture, but also one that one could only stare at for so long.

"Indeed, it is." Kalrick glanced. "And there is the outpost, we should barely make it with the light of day."

"And I am glad of that." Eirin added glancing back at them.

"Look," Talus grinned. "His Majesty speaks."

"Hey," Eirin protested. "I have had a lot on my mind."

"Still want to spar when we get there? Or would you rather wait until morning?"

Eirin grinned at him. One of his first real grins of the day, Talus thought.

"Well... You will be more tired tonight, so I think tonight will do. Though I doubt I could ever meet with anything but defeat at the hands of an Elerin."

Talus shrugged. "Even the best can fall by a move they have never seen. And I am far from the best."

"Time keeps its secrets." Eirin smiled. "But you never know, perhaps I will find a move unknown to Elerinkind."

"Perhaps." Talus grinned. This would be fun. He had not sparred since he left Belon. Hmm, nine whole days. Hopefully, he would not be rusty.

Eirin nodded. "A race? The gate is within sight. Mind we stop outside of six hundred cat's tails. I, for one, have no desire to become a pincushion by mistake."

"A race!" Kalrick shouted to the men. "Stop outside of six hundred cat's tails of the gate! One... two... three... go!"

The horses took off. Talus urged his horse on, faster and faster, until he feared he would fly off Altros. Talus swallowed and tightened his grip. The others moved ahead. However, Talus was preoccupied by remaining on the horse. In front of him, the other men began pulling their mounts to a stop. Talus grabbed the rein and jerked them toward him. Too hard. Altros reared, catching him off guard. He flew. Somehow he hit the ground in a roll and came to his feet. The arm that had hit the ground throbbed. Talus touched it. Bruising already. Well... at least it was his left arm, so it should not affect the match with Eirin. He touched it again. Ouch. Why? He moved it. Well, nothing broken, he could still wriggle his fingers.

"Talus! You alright?" Eirin questioned worriedly as he rode up. The others were close behind him.

Talus grinned up at him. "A little bruised, but not so hurt I cannot spar."

Eirin smiled, relieved. "So, it seems. Still, get a healer to look at you, once inside."

"Yes, my lord." Talus nodded.

"And remind me, we need to work on your horseman skills." Eirin raised his voice. "Matt, hold my standard up. Men, form up. We approach the gate."

Kalrick guided Altros to Talus.

"Here you are. You scared the life out of me. I am glad you are okay."

"Thanks." Talus remounted. "I am glad too."

They rode to join the king in the front of the column. They moved slowly towards the gate as professionally and nonthreatening as possible. Nearing, a voice called out from the Alcasan outpost.

"Hail, Eirin, king of Alcasa! Welcome to Norfort."

"Hail, faithful guards of Norfort. We seek shelter this night. Will you have us?" Eirin cried out.

The gates opened and they rode in. The place held a barrack, forge, armory, mess hall, and a small farming village. A man, the captain by insignia, stood in front of the gate to greet them.

"Your Majesty, we are honored by your presence with us."

"The honor is ours, Captain Artrick. Pray tell, what is supper tonight? We, weary travelers, are starved."

"I believe, Your Majesty, the cook has prepared chicken with mashed potatoes and green beans, but if you find another dish more desirable, we will do our best to create it." The captain bowed.

Eirin paused. "Ah, captain, chicken sounds delightful tonight."

The man smiled. "Then supper will be served in a half an hour, if you are ready. If you follow me, I will show you to your accommodations." He turned toward two other men. "Sanim, Gordon, take the king's horses to the stables and find his men some rooms."

The company dismounted. Talus slung his things over his back, while the pages gathered the king's, Lord Henry's, and Kalrick's belongings. Talus saw Eirin fall in beside the captain.

"Continuing to expand, captain? I don't remember the stone walls last visit, I was certain they were wood." Eirin asked approvingly.

"Indeed they were, my lord. My men dragged stone from the quarry seven miles west. They are thirty cat's tails as of now, but I intend to make them fifty with sixty-six cat's tail towers." It was obvious the captain found great joy in his work. He glanced at the king. "Will these plans be met with your approval, my lord?"

"Definitely, Captain Artrick. I am pleased with your ambition. How are you financing this? I don't remember seeing a request for money?"

"The village stone workers are cutting and fitting the block in exchange for meat, and the men and officers are performing the manual labor."

"The officers as well?" Eirin asked in surprise.

"Yes, my lord. It is better for morale if each man's superior works as hard as possible. And it gets things done faster."

"If I ever go to war, I will be glad of this place and I may call you out of oblivion."

"Thank you, my lord."

"Anything else?" Eirin smiled.

"Well, my lord, I guess I am training the villagers." The captain sounded uncertain. And no wonder, Talus thought, most kings kept their peasants in ignorance to prevent successful revolts.

"What is your purpose in this move? I am not opposed, so long as the people are loyal."

"With the men and older lads, it nearly doubles my force. Then if the walls and the men fail, many of the children and young maidens will make the village costly to an assailant. Is this acceptable, my lord?"

"Yes, indeed. If a time of war arose, could they successfully hold this fort on their own?"

Captain Artrick considered the question and nodded. "As of now, I would leave Lieutenant Josay in command, but I hope to select a man to act as lieutenant of the civilian force soon."

The captain pushed the door to the command barrack open. He came to the fourth door on the left.

"Your room, Your Majesty."

"Thank you, Captain."

He indicated the door across to the right.

"Lord Henry."

After the king's uncle had entered his room with his page, the captain strode to the sixth pair of rooms. The captain paused and inquired of Kalrick.

"My lord, what happened to Lentus?"

Kalrick sighed. "This is Talus, son of Valnis. Lentus... disappeared."

Talus watched his friend's face. Kalrick knew more than that, he guessed. What really happened? And why would Kalrick know? Or was Talus imagining all of it?

The captain either missed Kalrick's reluctance or determined not to press.

"My lord Talus, a pleasure to meet you. This will be your room." He swept his hand to the left door.

"Thanks, Captain Artrick. The pleasure is mine."

Talus entered his room, rubbing the dirt off his bare feet on the rug. As he closed the door he heard.

"Hey, Kal, how's it been?"

Apparently, the captain and Kalrick were good friends. Talus shut the door and examined his room. A bed, a desk, a closet, and a couch furnished the chamber. He pulled out his Garian vocabulary and grammar books. No point wasting time given for a purpose.

Talus studied until dinner. It was cheerful and hearty. The food was excellent, to the point the king inquired where the captain had found such a cook. A young man from the village was the reply.

Talus savored the last bite of his mashed potatoes, swallowing slowly.

"Ready to lose, Elerin?" The king grinned at him from up the table.

Talus paused and answered with terrible slowness.

"No..., I never intend to lose to anyone. Would you, my lord, care to?"

"Oh no." Eirin appeared horrified. "I plan to win."

"Indeed." Talus grinned.

The king turned to Captain Artrick. "Would you have a pair of blunt blades we could use?"

The captain smiled. "That I would. Because of the Elerin's race's legendary skill, would you prefer a private match?"

"No need for it to be strictly so. As you say, the Elerins' skill is legendary. If I can but hold my own for five minutes, t'would be enough to avoid shame."

"As you wish, my lord. If you will follow me?" The captain stood and led them to an open yard lit by lanterns. He unlocked a shed holding blunt and wooden weapons. Talus and Eirin passed over the wooden blades and began testing the weight and balance of the blunt Fumanic steel blades. Once both selected blades that suited them, they returned to the yard. Talus grinned.

"Prepared, Your Majesty?"

"More than you." Eirin matched his grin. "Captain, will you officiate things?"

"I am honored, my lord. Combatants ready?"

Both men gave a decisive, "Yes."

"On guard." The captain shouted. "Begin."

They cautiously circled. While Talus guessed Eirin was about his equal or less, it was dangerous to assume. So they circled, trading empty blows. Suddenly, the king struck hard and fast. Talus gave a step then blocked, allowing most of the strikes to angle off his sword as he sought a non-lethal opening. The Elerin lunged, knocking the king's blade aside. Eirin sidestepped and brought his sword toward the Elerin's back. Talus parried backhandedly and brought his sword toward Eirin's stomach. The king jumped back. Talus followed up with a flurry of light blows, forcing him back. Eirin avoided most of the blows. Without warning, the Elerin thrust toward Eirin's chest. The king blocked desperately, sending the blow to one side so Talus met no resistance. Talus kept his balance, glad Jornus had done that same block so many times. The Elerin arced his blade up in a circle toward Eirin's neck, using some of the speed the impact of Eirin' blade had given. The king ducked and stabbed toward Talus' stomach. Talus sidestepped and swept Eirin's blade left, leaving Eirin's right shoulder open. Eirin reversed the direction of his blade movement and caught Talus' blade right as it came in contact with his shoulder. The pure strength behind the king's blow shocked Talus. He stepped back, giving with his sword slightly to absorb the crushing impact. Eirin pushed his advantage with several heavy light-speed swings. Talus avoided most of them by dancing sideways or backwards.

Talus let Eirin continue this for many minutes, biding his time, looking for a perfect opening in this heavy-handed affair. Eirin swiped toward stomach level. Talus sensed this was the opportunity for which he was looking. He stepped back, then sprang forward, smashing his blade into Eirin's near the hilt. The impact threw Eirin off balance and his sword was made useless for the split-second Talus needed. Talus placed his blade on Eirin's neck.

Eirin dropped his sword and Talus pulled his away. The king bowed.

"It was an honor to fight you, sir Elerin. The legends understated nothing. The victory is yours."

Talus saluted. "Thank you, Your Majesty. The honor was mine. Seems you can challenge even a legend."

Eirin smiled.

"If you find time, perhaps you can work with Matt occasionally?" He asked quietly.

"Sure, Your Majesty."

"Thanks. Problem with being the king's page; you learn more administration work at times than the abilities of knighthood." Eirin turned to the spectators. "Anyone else like to test his skill against the Elerin?"

So many said "aye," that Eirin suggested a line with an almost mischievous glance at Talus. Talus grinned as he realized he would be fighting until around midnight.

<<<<<<<<<<<<<>>>>>>>>>>>>

"The kitchen staff is growing slow and lazy these days." The lady the cook had asked Anna to serve breakfast complained. "What took you so long, you stupid girl? One could die of old age, waiting for scum like you."

Anna kept her head down. She set the plates of warm blueberry syrup laden pancakes before the lady and knight, both still dressed in their bed clothes.

Her head snapped sideways with the impact of the woman's hand. Anna staggered.

"Are you deaf?!! What took you so long, kitchen maggot?"

"I am sorry, my lady. I was trying not to spill your breakfast tea in your pancakes."

The knight stood and slammed her into the wall. Anna's back screamed its pain, but she was too terrified to move.

"You dare talk back to my wife, dirty rat?" He growled softly in her face.

Anna's eyes went wide. "I, I di...di...didn't mean too."

He threw her to the floor. She landed on her side and curled instinctively into a ball. She could hear his breath as he crouched down beside her.

Pain exploded in her exposed ribs as he drove his fist into them. She sucked in her breath, then gasped as her broken ribs demanded stillness. Tears fell. She tried to breathe lightly. Why? Why was this happening?

"Get up, girl. Do your duty and get out before I kill you."

Anna stumbled to her feet clutching her side. Through blurry vision she emptied the platter and walked to the door. Outside she left the platter leaning against the wall, to alert whoever came by for them to gather the dishes from this room. She set out as briskly as she dared without hurting herself.

Four days had passed and the king of Alcasa was expected tonight. That meant a feast was in order and that meant extra work, which was why the cook wanted her back as soon as possible. Vaguely she plotted how to accomplish the most with the least pain. Her mother's voice echoed in her mind. "Remember, Anna, whatever happens endurance brings the greatest rewards." It was one of the last things she had said before Anna had been taken.

A hand latched onto her shoulder and her thoughts scattered. A smooth voice spoke into her ear.

"What causes the hurry, pretty maiden?"

Heart beating wildly, Anna half turned and stared up into the deep green, desirous eyes of King Hissin. Anna dropped her gaze.

"The feast, my lord. Can I get you anything?" Anna answered, praying her voice sounded normal.

"Yes." He drew out the word. "I want you, my dear. Will you step into this room with me?" Silk lined his voice.

"I'm sorry, my lord. I would rather not. I should be going." She backed away, but the king's grip tightened.

"Don't be scared, my pretty. I am the king; the cook will understand." His was still smooth, but harder.

"I do not dare go with you, my lord. Please let me go."

"No, dear. This is the will of your king."

He pulled her toward the door. Theos, please help her. The way out was certain death, but this....

"It is not the will of the God."

The king smiled patronizingly, but impatiently.

"Your parents lied to you. This is the will of the gods. It pleases them."

Anna swallowed then looked up confidently into the king's eyes.

"But not the will of the God, Theos. My lord, must you go on hating your wife's faith?"

"Fool! Her faith could not save her. I begged Him for her life. But she died. You believe an ignorant and dead faith! Say Alton is your god and I will spare you for your beauty."

"I cannot, my lord. Theos is my God." *Thank you, Theos, for strengthening me so I would not deny you,* she prayed silently. She smiled.

"GUARDS!!!" The king roared.

King Hissin lifted her by the neck of her dress and flung her at the approaching guards. She landed on her broken ribs and a cry escaped her lips. The guards snickered, dragging her to her feet. The king spoke, his voice colder than ice.

"Tie her to the post. She burns at dawn tomorrow."

Chapter 14 With King Hissin

Talus stared at the buildings in awe. As the second oldest city in Alvar, Ketlin's beauty and lines outdid any city Talus had yet seen. Its architecture was built by the Talrins in the age of their glory. The giants specialized in graceful solid stonework. No Talrins, however, were seen on its streets now. The city's place of pain in their race's darkest years saw to their rejection of it. It cost the city. Decay marred the scene: chips in the walls, missing jewel stones in the designs. It saddened Talus.

He turned a corner and started. Someone had built a red and black building among the calm, quiet, white and green ones. The house glared at him, laughing at his shock. Talus looked away, reminded of the king they were visiting. He shuddered.

Talus followed the king through the wide streets. A beggar grabbed onto his horse.

"Penny for the poor? Please, my lord."

Talus tried not to stare. The man was clothed in rags so full of holes, he was little better than naked. This man made the impoverished in Elnola look rich. Talus dug into his saddle bags and withdrew the last of his travel jerky.

"Here, eat it slowly and it might last sometime."

"Thanky, thank ye very much, my lord." He hopped away clutching his new treasure with dirty hands.

Talus looked away to see Kalrick grinning at him.

"You know, you must be the only person in the whole city who cares enough to help men like that."

"It is only temporary help for the man. He needs to find an occupation."

Kalrick shrugged with a rueful smile.

"That is his occupation."

Talus glanced at him. "Sad. Can't this city employ its own people?"

"At the castle, maybe. Most would rather die first."

"Wow."

"Welcome to the world, Talus. Only Elerins and Kazofs, to my knowledge, have no truly poor."

Talus sighed.

"Ah. Look up, Talus. The castle of Ketlin."

The gate opened in a low half circle. Two towers rose above it; red banners with the black and silver dragon flapped in the wind. The castle wall had been constructed in a circle, each tower forming a wide smooth bump. The keep with its eight minor towers and one master tower reared up beyond the wall into the sky.

"King Hissin could hold this place for weeks." Talus murmured.

"Amazing, eh?"

Talus nodded.

They passed under the gate. Inside, a stout servant greeted them in Garian.

"Your Majesty, welcome to Ketlin. My lord offers my service to show you to your rooms if you would care to freshen up." The man addressed King Eirin.

Suddenly Talus realized Eirin was watching him. Right. He translated. The king nodded.

"An excellent plan. Will you have our horses looked after as well?"

"Of course, of course, my lord." He nodded his head on hearing the translation. The servant distributed the company to their rooms, leaving Talus last. After thanking the man for his aid, he stepped inside, leaving a bewildered servant outside.

Hopefully, King Eirin would take his time freshening up. Talus dropped his pack on the floor and stretched his sore shoulders. Moving to a basin, he poured a little water into it from a pitcher. He pulled his jerkin and shirt off and splashed water on his face and neck. He redressed in a clean shirt and the same jerkin. Heading back into the hall, he started for Eirin's room which the servant had briefly pointed out. Hopefully he could find it again. He tripped over something and almost fell. He frowned and looked back. Nothing lay on the floor.

Oh. Right. The boots. Talus once again studied his confined feet. That morning, Eirin had insisted he wear them. His toes felt so trapped, regardless that they were actually too large. Talus sighed and concentrated on not tripping and not clomping. These things were loud.

Talus stopped at the door two down. He laughed. Well, he could find Eirin's suite. Walking to the other rooms must have confused him. He knocked on the king's door and Matt let him in. Both King Eirin and King Hissin were sitting in Eirin's sitting room. King Hissin's deep green eyes glared at him.

"Well, the new translator is always early, it would seem."

Eirin guessed the gist of what the older king had said by the sarcastic tone. Talus' natural grin faded slightly, becoming a little forced. Talus saluted.

"Palgat. A enikin tan U aiferth tan A liqus nunosth."

Hissin's glare darkened. Eirin decided he had better break in.

"What was that, Talus?"

"Oh, sorry. I said, 'Forgive me. I thought you would prefer I not smell like a horse.'"

Eirin kept his expression neutral, though he wanted to grimace.

"Talus, I would like to remain on good terms with the king. Please be more respectful. Because of the king's upbringing, it would be better if you only use civilities of your own accord."

Talus saluted slowly.

"I will, my lord. I'm sorry."

Talus' gaze caught on the window. He glanced at the two kings and stepped over to it. Eirin watched him and Talus noticed a puzzled frown appear on his face. Hissin spoke impatiently.

"Venth framin. Ta fasmihalin oigoth."

Talus turned from the window, his brows still furrowed, and translated.

"Come, brother-king. Let us go to the Lesser Hall."

"Certainly, *framin*."

Before Talus could speak, Hissin stood and strode for the door. Poor Matt barely got it open for Hissin, earning a fierce glare. Eirin touched the boy's shoulder.

"Thanks." Eirin murmured.

He followed the other king.

Talus nodded to Matt and fell in behind the two kings. The scene from the window dominated his thoughts. A human girl tied to an iron stake surrounded by sticks. What had caused such circumstances? Who was she? What was the crime demanding this punishment? Wait, the sticks. Talus felt sick. Was it true? Did King Hissin really burn people?

After butchering a translation for King Eirin, Talus pushed the matter aside. He had to focus. The kings were speaking of primarily boring subjects: productivity, welfare, and crime rates in their countries. At one point to Talus' surprise, King Hissin asked gently how much the death of Eirin's father still affected him.

Ahead of them, Talus heard giggling. Two girls began across the hall the kings were following. King Hissin sped up. The girls looked up and ceased giggling. They ran. Too slow.

King Hissin grabbed the closest by her dark red braid. He snatched her off the ground by her neck. Talus watched frozen as the girl's eyes bulged. King Hissin drew her near to his face.

"I do *not* tolerate servants in my way." King Hissin growled menacingly.

Before Talus registered what was happening, King Hissin thrust his knife into the girl's heart and twisted. The girl coughed up blood; it dribbled off her chin, falling on his hand. The girl looked up at her king.

"I forgive you. Theos save you."

She slumped in death.

"Stupid girl!"

King Hissin flung her body away like poison. She landed crumpled at the feet of her friend. Heedless of the surroundings, the girl knelt.

"Mara?" She stared up at her king. "Why? *Why?* Why would you kill her just because she was one step too slow?!"

King Hissin brandished his wet knife.

"Dare you question me?" He inquired too softly.

He started forward. The girl took one last horrified look and fled, gulping sobs that finally broke free. How would she handle that? How could life go on after witnessing that? How could King Hissin kill like that? So senselessly? How could anyone be so cruel? So uncaring?

For a second, Talus wondered how one could forgive a man like Hissin. He did not want it. He did not deserve it. Talus stopped the thought. Of course, he did not deserve it. No one ever deserved forgiveness. It was a shining gift in the darkness of sin.

Eirin's voice filtered into his thoughts.

"Why did you do that?" He finally questioned, stricken.

King Hissin smiled with a father-like expression, on hearing the Garian version of the question.

"You must keep the underlings in fear, or they will rebel."

Talus translated.

King Eirin nodded slowly, his face unreadable.

They proceeded in silence. Presently they came to two large doors. The guards had seen them coming, so the doors were opened ceremoniously with time to spare. Inside was a large room with a raised dais at the far end. If this was the Lesser Hall, how big was the Greater Hall? Two cushioned chairs occupied the dais with a stiff wood chair off to the left. The wooden chair must be for him, Talus thought. The thought amused him for an unknown reason. Well, at least he would not fall asleep.

As they approached the end of the room, the doors behind them busted open. A stout man in a white apron strode in, his eyes flaming. He shrugged off the guards who tried in vain to stop him.

"Your Majesty, this cannot go on! In the last three weeks, you and your knights have killed more than half my staff! This cannot go on!"

"Do you dare-" King Hissin started angrily.

"The girl on the stake, then the one at lunch, and now this innocent child! And another eight killed by your men. All today. Do you know the number of aching hearts? Do you care nothing for your people? Remember Helena's dying wish? 'Don't cease to care for the lesser when I am gone'?"

King Hissin closed the distance and hit the cook across his face. The cook's head snapped around painfully.

"Insolent fool! I forget nothing! I know an aching heart! My wife is dead, and I am alone forever. You forgot your place, cook. And you will pay." King Hissin glared. "Guards, take this man outside. Twenty lashes should thin the insolent fat off his bones." The king took a step closer and grabbed the cook's beard. "You will learn to honor your king!"

King Hissin stepped back, and the guards took the cook's arms. He didn't resist them this time. The cook spoke softly.

"Ha igit semp regum. Honosemp Ham, marege."

Talus watched King Hissin's face soften at the language. The king looked past the cook to the guards and back to cook.

"Henry," the cook looked up. Hissin continued. "Difamicitan. Guards, I don't wish for blood in my supper, ten will serve the same purpose."

"Thank you, my lord." The cook said softly.

King Hissin nodded and stared after them long past their departure.

Eirin sat to Hissin's right in the great dining hall. Across from Eirin was Sir Lithron, Hissin's chief adviser. Talus, Lord Henry, and Kalrick filled the chairs to Eirin's right. An eerie silence reigned in the darkly lit hall. No one was permitted to speak at the table save Hissin and Eirin. Well, Hissin allowed Talus as well. Eirin smiled a little at the thought. Wouldn't be much of a conversation without Talus.

The doors to the kitchens opened, releasing a flood of servants with platters. The cook approached the kings. He placed a cup and plate before Hissin and then Eirin. The cook's face was an image of unfeeling stone. However, pain marred his moments and deepened his eyes. Red lines inscribed on his sleeves and back showed where blood had soaked into his shirt. Eirin watched Hissin take all this in, then met the cook's eyes. Something showed in Hissin's face which Eirin had never seen there before: regret. The cook held his gaze for a minute before returning to the kitchen. Hissin looked back to the table and noted Eirin watching.

"Ta et kaagacamicin san citecran. Ta clumenth kan cunilum san cunucas ixor."

Talus translated quietly. "We were best friends as children. We remained close until the war and the death of my wife."

"I see, framin." Eirin replied softly. Thirty-one years had passed since the war and thirty-two since his wife's death. Hissin's expression grew far away, memories criss-crossing his face.

Eirin picked up his fork, glancing at his companions. Talus raised his head and unfolded his hands from praying, reaching for his silverware. Eirin wanted to choke. His gaze flitted across Hissin and his knights. None of them seemed to have noticed. He would have to talk Talus out of that before breakfast the next day. Not that he had ever succeeded with Lentus....

He hated the fact he missed him. Lentus had been a powerful influence in his life, even if he had avoided paying attention. Still, that didn't change that he missed him. Guilt pricked uncomfortably, the last time he had been angry at Lentus, somehow the anger had.... His sense of guilt grew stronger. He wanted to gag. He hated guilt too.

He looked back to Talus, in time to see him select a piece of cheese stuffed celery. He handed it to Lord Henry, who gave it to Kalrick.

Poor Kalrick stared horror struck at the stick. He looked helplessly from Talus to Lord Henry, who were both grinning like apes. Kalrick missed the cheese stuffing inside as he brought it to his mouth. He bit down slowly. His eyes bulged as he encountered something soft.

He screamed, throwing the piece across the room, narrowly missing the knight across from him. Every head in the room shot up. Kalrick smiled sheepishly. Talus and Lord Henry tried to constrain themselves for Kalrick. However, Kalrick noticed their trying-not-to-laugh faces and laughed as well. The others gave up and laughed with him. A sound long absent brought a ray of light into the shadowed hall. Finally, Talus picked up a celery stick and snapped it, revealing the cheese inside. Kalrick smiled ruefully.

"You two are awful."

Eirin felt his heart constrict and watched as Lord Henry paled. No one was supposed to talk. Kalrick looked up at Eirin the moment he realized he had spoken. Eirin glanced at Hissin, half hoping he had not noticed. A hope quickly squashed.

"Bukin usidomin, Eirin!" Hissin growled, with barely contained anger.

Eirin saw Talus wince. Talus spoke quietly, with what Eirin doubted was a strict translation.

"King Hissin would wish you to remind... Kalrick of the table rule."

Eirin studied Talus a minute, until Talus looked down.

"I can tell you later if you like."

Eirin shook his head and addressed Kalrick.

"My lord Kalrick, will you come here?"

He wished he did not have to do this but, well, it would make this conversation appear the most real to Hissin. Kalrick rose stiffly but obeyed. Eirin wished for Kalrick's sake the whole table wasn't watching.

Kalrick stopped behind Talus' chair and bowed.

"My lord."

Eirin kept his face stern, a hint of worry flashed across Kalrick's face. Eirin was careful to keep his tone serious.

"Hissin made that rule so he could talk and hear the reply clearly. As he was not talking, strictly speaking, there was no reason for you not to. Don't worry, I am not upset." A hint of a smile appeared on Kalrick's face. "But I will be if you dare smile." Eirin threatened. Kalrick wiped the expression away and looked fearful. "Better." Now Eirin desperately wanted to smile. "Most of the time 'strictly speaking' is not good advice, so I will ask you to be more respectful of King Hissin's rules in future. I realize it was a mistake. You had better reply and go sit down, before I start laughing at your mockery of fear."

Kalrick stared at the ground.

"As you wish, my king."

He bowed again and returned to his seat.

Eirin looked at Hissin.

"You will have to forgive him; it is only his second time here."

Talus translated. Hissin nodded slowly, but a crafty spark lit in his eye. Eirin sensed this would not be the end.

Chapter 15 The Choice

The last rays of the setting sun had vanished. Garia was cast into darkness.

Anna wriggled. Her hands were tied on either side of the pole, which was a cat's tail in diameter. Now that it was dark, she could move without attracting the guards. She hoped.

She lifted her left leg tentatively and shook it out. She repeated with her right leg. Almost. Her left leg refused to take her whole weight. She fell violently forward. The ropes dug painfully into her already sore wrists. She cried out.

A guard materialized out of the darkness.

"Stupid Follower! Did you fall over?" He jeered.

Her arms screamed with pain, but her leg refused to take the pressure to hold her up. She closed her eyes and whispered.

"Please give me strength. Help me." Desperation had filtered into the last words of her prayer, making them louder than she intended.

The guard snickered.

"You want help?"

Anna looked up at him. The day in full sun had evaporated her strength.

He met her gaze.

"Well, okay. Just don't tell no one."

Anna gave him a smile.

"I won't. Thanks."

He shrugged.

"No problem."

He grabbed her upper arms and hauled her to her feet. He leaned her against the post.

"Steady now?"

Anna nodded.

"Yep, and thanks for just helping me."

He shook his head.

"Some people are animals. Don't fall over again."

He turned abruptly and disappeared into the darkness.

"Thank you, Theos." She whispered.

Her mind drifted. The sky was overcast with the promise of rain. What if it rained at dawn? How would they make a fire with soaked wood and soaked girl?

What would it be like to burn? Images of flames of the now countless burnings she had witnessed flashed through her mind. Every one a Follower. Every one had vanished as the fire leapt up. Some had sung praises to Theos until death took them. For a terrifying second, she imagined the kitchen fires surrounding her, closing in. The heat burned into her face.

She shivered, shaking the image from her brain. Theos would handle the morning. Joy filled her heart. If this was indeed His plan, she would meet her Savior through the flames. What would it be like?

She enjoyed blissful thoughts as the clouds overhead grew dark with rain and the night turned cold.

Eirin was beginning to believe Hissin had forgotten about the incident at supper. Nearly an hour had passed and Hissin had made no mention of Kalrick, straight up or hidden.

Every lull that formed in the conversation made Eirin uneasy. What could he say? Hissin appeared deep in thought; habitual politeness kicked in and Eirin said nothing. Not that he could really think of anything anyway.

Eirin watched Talus stand up again and pace to the window. He was restless tonight. He must have wandered every square cat's tail available. Perhaps after he said goodnight to Hissin, he could find out what was up.

Hissin's voice drew him from his considerations. Talus turned from the window where he had been studying the darkness. Eirin marked the grimace that crossed his face before his features took on the blank smile-less expression he had worn most of the night. He translated.

"Framin, I have met lords like your lord Kalrick before. Beware. They are rebellious under the cloak of loyalty. They forget because they have no reason to remember. They will even forget their duty and leave you in danger."

For a second, Eirin remembered the howl of the wolves and Kalrick's voice crying, "It's hopeless." Mentally, Eirin shoved the doubt away. Talus continued Hissin's words.

"You purge every hint of rebelliousness and forgetfulness with the lash and with the executioner's blade. Else you will lose control!"

The very idea of Kalrick with either made him sick.

"I thank you for your concern, framin. However, I can vouch for Lord Kalrick, he is like a brother to me, and no one is more loyal."

On hearing the translation, Hissin's expression copied the kind one uses with a foolish child.

"Fatucumevon. U nahabth nafartan, framin."

Talus avoided Eirin's gaze.

"Pretend loyalty. You do not have brothers, brother-king."

Eirin was sick of this conversation. Would it be impolite to walk out? Probably, Eirin decided, disappointed.

"Perhaps not." He replied. "But I have men I can trust. Lord Kalrick once begged me to kill him because he thought he had broken faith."

Eirin would have smiled in lighter circumstances as he listened to Talus reduplicate his emotion into the Garian words.

Hissin answered smoothly.

"U orgenivir noifidth. Eirin, listh am, u tiwisev ulisth. Nefidth nivir. Month usaniregim bablash; can u adoth, civir nijoith jan inesiem."

Eirin waited, but Talus did not speak for an eternity. When he finally did, it was slow.

"You cannot trust forgetful men. Eirin, listen to me, you have listened to lies. Trust no one. Establish your reign in blood; until you do, no one will obey you when it is important."

Eirin nodded slowly then covered a fake yawn. He rose and bowed.

"I thank you for the advice, framin. I will remember it. However, I fear the day's ride is catching up with me. So, I bid you goodnight."

After Talus translated, Hissin stood.

"Gacunoct, framin. A ut ijuvth usaniregim onomouth. Netimth, simi es."

Talus looked away and repeated.

"Goodnight, framin. I will help you establish your kingship. Fear not, it is easy."

Eirin and Hissin bowed, while Talus saluted. As he led the way down the hall, Eirin forced himself to come to terms with Hissin's parting statement. As much as he admired Hissin for the prosperity and progress the king had brought to Garia, some things like his thirst for blood unnerved him.

<<<<<<<<<<<<>>>>>>>>>>>>

Talus followed King Eirin to the door. What kind of conversation was that? He was shaken by the translations he made. What kind of scars made King Hissin who he was?

Eirin stopped at his door and turned to Talus.

101

"Talus, will you tell Kalrick about that? And warn him, while I would never purpose to harm him, I may well be tricked. Please tell him to be extra careful. When you are done, return here."

Concern lingered in the king's eyes. Talus saluted silently. Not the stiff salute he had given Hissin, but a respected slower salute in which he bowed his head deeper.

Talus hurried down the hall to Kalrick's chambers. He knocked and, instead of the page, Kalrick answered the door.

"Oh, Talus, come in." Kalrick appeared tired. From his face, Talus guessed emotional stress.

Kalrick led Talus through his entry to his sitting room. He collapsed across a couch.

"Please be seated." He waved vaguely at the surrounding furniture.

Talus claimed a soft chair on Kalrick's left. Kalrick shifted.

"King Eirin sent you?"

Talus looked up, amazed.

"Yes, how did you know?" Talus continued more soberly. "King Hissin wants your blood, whether lifeblood or blood of shame. King Eirin wishes you to be extremely careful. He is worried he could be manipulated into hurting you."

Kalrick nodded slowly, then his brow furrowed. "Blood of shame?"

Talus frowned, confused. Oh, right. Must be an Elerin idiom created from that culture.

"Sorry, blood from a whipping."

Kalrick winced.

"I would take it if King Hissin was threatening Eirin. But I would rather avoid it." Kalrick shivered. "Tell Eirin I am terribly sorry I got him into this mess."

"I will. And Kalrick?" Talus added, troubled.

Kalrick twisted to look up at Talus.

"I am sorry I played that trick. Honestly it was not nice, and I should have considered the possible results." Why had he not? If Kalrick was beaten... Talus felt sick.

Kalrick sat up and met Talus' gaze.

"Hey, I never held anything against you. It was funny even for me. Perhaps I should have just rolled my eyes. The past is the past and we cannot change it. We must live on. So 'should haves' are useless and mean we have been thinking about it over-much." Kalrick shrugged.

"Aye, you are right." Talus nodded slowly.

Silence deepened as each fell into his own thoughts.

Talus breathed out slowly and resolved to trust Theos with whatever happened to Kalrick. A question from earlier snagged in his mind.

"Kalrick?"

"Aye?" Kalrick murmured.

"In the courtyard, a girl is bound to a post. Do you know anything about it?"

Deep pain marred Kalrick's features.

"I... um... I think... she will be burned in the morning."

"Why?" Talus begged for some justification of this possibility.

"I don't know for certain, but... last time I was here they... he burned a man for his faith."

"Faith?"

Kalrick nodded sadly.

"My beliefs and your beliefs. He was a Follower of Iasos. In this country, people are killed for believing in Theos weekly, if not daily."

"It's true, then? King Hissin does that?"

Kalrick nodded, his voice coming as barely more than a whisper.

"After his wife was killed, he tried to wipe out everything that reminded him of her, not that he could do much until he won the war. Once he did, he slowly outlawed following Iasos, her favorite color, bright yellow, and he stopped being nice to servants because she had always been so."

"So, is that why King Hissin wishes you hurt?"

Puzzlement appeared on Kalrick's face, until he connected the comment to outlawing following Iasos.

"Perhaps so. I know he hates our influence on Eirin. Thus, what happened to Lentus."

Talus nodded and asked. "What exactly happened to Lentus?"

"Um... I don't know... completely. So, back to the girl, I expect she will burn at dawn."

Talus wondered why Kalrick refused to tell him what he knew of Lentus. Was he ashamed of something? Or protecting someone? Like Eirin? Talus had to let it slide.

Burn. Why was it even allowed?

"But can't we do something? Surely someone could convince Hissin not to?"

Kalrick shook his head.

"No one will stand up to King Hissin, not even Eirin."

"Why? He is a lord of men, but not invincible or omniscient."

"Forget it, Talus. King Hissin orders death and they die. No hope is left."

Talus stood, considering.

"There is always hope, Lord Kalrick. Even here. I should probably return to the king. Will you excuse me?"

Kalrick grinned at him. He rose and bowed.

"Of course. Don't do anything too foolish. Theos bless your night."

"And yours." Talus saluted.

As he followed the hall, he spotted a guard coming toward him. Talus was disgusted by the fear in the man's eyes when he stopped him.

"Sir," Talus asked. "Why is a girl bound to a post in the courtyard?"

Confusion emanated from the man at the address of 'sir', but he answered readily.

"My lord, she is convicted of treason for denying the gods in favor of her God, Theos."

Talus carefully controlled his features. Kalrick was right.

"What will happen to her?"

The guard trembled.

"She will be burned."

"Of course. Forgive my ignorance. Thank you, I will not take any more of your time."

Talus saluted and left the poor soldier dumbstruck by mere courtesy.

Treason? Why would believing in Theos be treason? Or believing anything else? Actions flowing from some beliefs might be treasonous, but what action was treasonous for believing in Theos? Oh, right. Denying the gods. Or more correctly, reminding King Hissin of his lost wife.

Talus shook his head and knocked on Eirin's door. Inside he heard the king's voice say, "Wait, Matt, I'll get it." Interesting how neither Eirin or Kalrick let their pages get their doors. The door opened quickly, revealing the king. A smile broke across his face.

"Talus! There you are. Please come in."

Talus followed him inside.

Eirin flopped easily into a chair.

"Have a seat, Talus. How was Kalrick?"

"He regrets burying you in this mess with King Hissin. He looked tired. And I delivered your message."

Eirin sighed. "Things happened, but we will live on. 'Tis sad though."

Talus fiddled with his fingers for a moment, before refocusing on Eirin.

"My lord?"

"Yes?"

Talus hesitated. How would the king take this?

"My lord, a girl is tied to a post in the courtyard." Eirin's smile disappeared, and Talus forced himself to go on. "Apparently she is charged with the horrible crime of believing in Theos rather than King Hissin's gods. Somehow this crime is treason, and the poor girl will be burned for it."

"Why would you care, Talus? She is just some peasant who doesn't know when to obey her king."

Talus hoped that was not a hint, getting the feeling he was treading on dangerous sand.

"She is an innocent girl, my lord. I am sworn to protect the innocent. Also, I am just as guilty as this girl."

"You believe like the Belon lord and at this point I do not care what you believe in my court. However, the girl should have realized that her king knows what's best for her."

"How is making this land run with blood and fire what is best for it?" Talus' frustration leaked into the question.

King Eirin stood and stepped over to him, his eyes slick with anger.

"Talus! You will not question me like that!"

Talus stood and bowed his head. His emotions were running loose and had made his tone less than respectful. Talus drew a breath and looked up to Eirin.

"Forgive me, my lord, for allowing that tone to escape me."

Eirin's eyes flashed.

"And don't forget you are sworn to obey me, that trumps whatever you *think* is right!"

Great, now Eirin was upset.

"My lord?"

Eirin drew in a breath trying to calm himself.

"What?"

"My lord, I beg you to allow me to keep both vows. Let me rescue the girl tonight and hide her nearby, then when we return to Alcasa we can take her with us."

"Ridiculous! I will not have such a scheme found by Hissin! You realized this could cause very difficult diplomatic matters! I refuse to allow it! I refuse to go behind his back like that. If the girl chooses to disobey her king, she deserves to die!"

"My lord, if the matter comes out, I will take the blame and you can dismiss me to Belon for disciplinary action to pacify King Hissin. I will do everything I can to make it look like she escaped by herself. No one will know, my lord."

"I certainly would or more! But you will not. The girl disobeyed her king and as we have established this deserves death."

"My lord, if Kalrick told Matt to do one thing and you ordered Matt to do another thing, who should he obey?"

"Me, of course."

"Exactly. And the girl, should she obey her king or her God?"

King Eirin spluttered but found no good answer.

"I am done with this conversation! You may go to bed!"

Talus rose disappointed. He saluted and turned for the door. His hand rested on the knob, when Eirin added.

"Go straight to your room and remain there until morning. I will not have you rescuing traitors!"

Talus grimaced at the door. He emptied his face of expression and twisted back toward the king. He saluted and left.

His brain swam with thoughts. He wondered what was right. Was he to save the girl from death and disobey the king? Or did he just think that was right like Eirin had said? Was his vow to protect the innocent more important than his vow to obey the king? Or vice versa? How could he know? Dare he guess?

Talus reached his room. One thing could be, must be, done.

He knelt in the dark by his bed and poured all the questions out to his Maker who knew the right choice. Time passed; Talus stood and moved to the window. He stared into the black courtyard until he found the girl, then he lifted his eyes into the dark sky.

"I choose to protect the innocent even if it costs me my life. I will take the girl to Belon then return to King Eirin. Theos willing."

Chapter 16 Trust

Vaguely, Talus wondered if Eirin would kill him when he returned. Talus pushed the thought aside. It was not relevant now. Tomorrow was tomorrow's problem.

However, the thought produced a second thought that he dared not acknowledge. What would his people think? While he doubted the Belon lord or his father would turn away a young girl, what would if they did not approve of his choice? He pushed those thoughts aside also.

To leave tonight, what did he need to do? Talus opened his pack. He still had hard flatbread and a few dried mangoes. Hmm, it would be best to have some meat and more fruit. They needed to get out of Garia as quickly as possible. Until they were across the border, they could be caught and killed. Talus swallowed. What was he getting himself into?

He could get food from the kitchen, leaving money for it. That raised the question if that was right. He didn't see any other way. Was it really honest?

Talus left the thought to fester for a bit; perhaps time would simplify it.

He should write notes to the kings. Eirin deserved an explanation for his... disobedience. The word made Talus uncomfortable, but it could not be helped. King Hissin had to understand Eirin, and the others did not know that he was leaving. Talus imagined Eirin's rage in the morning and briefly wondered if he should not try his first idea and return to face it. He shook his head. Eirin would never allow the girl to travel with them now.

He finished the letters in an hour and a half. Now what? He had an hour left until midnight, the time he guessed the kitchen staff would head to bed.

He flopped on the bed and closed his gritty eyes. He sat up again quickly. If he did that, he would fall asleep without finishing his plans. Plans. He should make a plan, plot their escape. He grinned to himself and fished around in his pack. Ah, his detailed map of Garia. He removed it from its cylinder. He spread it on the floor and lay down on his stomach to examine it.

Time passed. Options were made and discarded. Finally, Talus decided on his course. He grinned. No one would expect it. That should buy them some time. Eventually someone would guess, but Theos willing, they would be safe from pursuit by then. North and Storm Bay.

Now back to the kitchen question. Money replaced the value of the food, so that would suggest it was not theft. However, was it honest without the proper communication? Not that he could afford communication. Finally, he elected to write a note to the cook. This and the fact no lying was done would leave it in the hands of Theos.

He wrote a quick note adding an apology for any inconvenience in meals. He packed a small bag with the money and the note. He removed his boots and placed them by Eirin's note. No point in clomping around.

He slipped out his door and followed the halls in the direction of the kitchen. His heart raced but he forced himself to walk calmly. The halls were in perfect darkness. Using his racial ability to see in the dark, he avoided guards with candles, neglecting one himself.

Following the kitchen door from the dining room, he moved carefully into the kitchen. He searched for several minutes until he found the cupboards with small amounts of cellar item. He reached for the first door and froze as he heard voices.

"Henry, please, can I just talk to you?"

"Why, my lord? You only talk to servants to kill them."

"Henry, please for the friendship we once had, let me talk to you friend to friend, not lord to cook."

The cook did not answer, so King Hissin continued.

"Henry, I do not have friends I can trust, most would stab me and steal the throne as soon as speak with me."

Still the cook did not answer. Desperation grew in the king's voice.

"Henry, please. I am sorry I hurt you. I am just asking you to accept me even with everything you dislike. Could I do something?"

The cook shook his head and held out his hand.

"No, my friendship is only and always a gift, Hissin."

King Hissin grasped his hand. "Thanks."

"Why did you search me out? After thirty-one years." The cook questioned.

"I guess at night in the darkness, loneliness surfaces, and I realized Eirin has something special I didn't. And, well, after this afternoon, I missed you."

"I have missed having you around, though, you keep me hopping with girls and lads who have seen death in its ugliest form."

"Would you be happier if I tried not to kill people as much?"

"Thanks, my lord-"

"Hissin." The king corrected.

The cook smiled. "Yes, so will the children whose lives are unknowingly spared. Hissin?"

"Yes?"

"What about the girl on the stake?"

"No, She is too public, and she must die regardless. Henry, please understand. I have no choice anymore. If I show weakness I will die. Besides," His face darkened. "She deserves it."

Well, Talus thought, his plan still must go on. After the cook's question he had thought maybe he could stay and serve Eirin. But, no.

The cook nodded slowly and looked away.

"You were close to her." Hissin guessed.

He stepped closer and awkwardly put his hand on the other man's shoulder. The cook looked up.

"She knows where she is going. Hissin, Helena wouldn't want you to grieve forever."

"I know! I... just can't help it anymore." The king turned away with a shrug. "I loved her. Nothing can fill the void. I hate everything that reminds me of her!"

The cook grasped Hissin's forearm. In the dim light, Talus realized Hissin was crying. The king wiped at his eyes.

"I am sorry. I'll see you tomorrow night?"

"Of course, Hissin. Sleep well."

The king hurried from the room. The cook finished a few things then took the candle and exited, leaving the room in perfect darkness.

Talus opened and closed a cupboard. It closed with a small thud right as the cook reentered the kitchen. Talus froze, praying he had not heard.

"Now where did I leave that?" The cook's voice came to Talus with the sound of him rummaging through a drawer.

"Ah, here we are."

Suddenly footsteps turned towards him. Without a second thought, he opened a large ground level cupboard and ducked inside. After closing the door gently, he silently wriggled behind a mostly full bag of sugar.

"A bit of sugar will enhance the chamomile, I think."

The door opened. Talus forced himself to not move, to barely breathe. The cook left the candle on the counter above. He opened the bag and dumped a spoonful of sugar into a steaming cup.

"Sugar, yes, perfect. Now to bed." The cook closed the cupboard and Talus breathed in silently.

Talus waited almost ten minutes before his nerves calmed and he climbed out of the cupboard. *You know, the cook probably would have been one of the safer people to be caught by,* Talus thought, grimly amused.

In another five minutes, Talus found all the items he required. He placed the bag of coins and money in the cupboard. Now, back to his room.

He made it back safely to his room without incident. He had just over two hours until the current guards would be the most tired and unobservant. That should be three bells and if the pattern continued, the guard would change again at four. He set a mental alarm and curled on his bed to sleep.

<<<<<<<<<<<<<>>>>>>>>>>>>>

Anna shifted. This post had absolutely no comfortable positions. She leaned on her left arm to ease the cramps forming in her arms, stretching her right painfully.

She sighed. Three bells had just rung, only two and a half hours left until dawn. Would she be as strong as Violet's brother and the countless other martyrs? She prayed for strength.

This would be terrible for her friends. She imagined their faces in the taunting crowd. How would they handle it? A tear trickled down her cheek. She wished they would not have to see this.

She would never see her family again. Ever, not in Alvar. She wished... she didn't know what she wished. She missed them unbearably. Would they ever know what had happened to her? She wanted them to know, yet she didn't.

She shook her head. She ought to use these last hours to pray for her friends and family.

A hand covered her mouth. Her eyes popped open. Two eyes glowed gently out of the darkness at her. Startled, she backed the little distance towards the pole. 'Who' formed on her lips. The figure whispered softly first.

"I am rescuing you. Don't move while I untie you."

Anna felt the ropes binding her feet move this way and that. She stared into the blackness where he must be kneeling. After a minute she felt the restraints fall away. She lifted one leg barely, wary of falling over again. Her other leg didn't give way. Carefully, she wiggled both around until they seemed awake and functional once again.

Who was this guy? And why was he helping her? Then it hit her. It might not be her time to die.

He moved behind her. How did he make so little noise? She cracked sticks by just shifting her weight. She felt the ropes binding her hand tugged. After a couple minutes, cold metal tickled her wrists. One at a time, her hands were freed.

She pulled her hands to herself and rubbed her wrists.

"This way." The whisper came from the dark. "How well can you see?"

"Nothing at all." She breathed.

"Right. Step lightly towards me."

She proceeded cautiously. The guy steadied her whenever she lost her balance. Finally, she reached the edge of the sticks. The stone was cool under her bare feet. Several steps later, he spoke again.

"Stairs."

Using her feet, she guessed the distance of each step.

As she climbed, thoughts plagued her. Who was he? What was he? No one she had ever seen had glowing eyes. Why was he helping her? However, overshadowing the other questions, another loomed. Could she trust him? With her life? With her purity? With herself?

Talus glanced back. The girl was awfully quiet, not that conversation would be good at this point. He should have thought of the fact she could not see in the dark. That certainly would complicate things. Once they were on the wall and no longer in its shadow, hopefully she would be able to see. At least a little.

They gained the top, it still amazed Talus how few guards had been stationed on the wall. He crouched. He turned to the girl, motioning for her to do likewise. No need to risk a casual observer noting them.

"See anything?"

"A little."

"Good. So, I was thinking if you tied this rope around your waist, you could walk down the wall. When you are about six cat's tails over the moat, push off the wall into a swing. You will probably need to hit the wall a couple times before you are completely across the moat, at that point I will give you the slack. The landing might be a bit hard. Sound good to you?"

She nodded slowly. Talus slung the rope he had made from his bed sheets off his shoulder. After a minute, the girl replied quietly.

"Sounds like it would work. But... can I ask you something?"

"Sure." Talus met her eyes.

"Can I trust you? How do I know you won't strand me on the rope or drown me in the moat? I am grateful you are rescuing me, but why?"

"Nothing I can say will make you trust me. If it helps, I also believe in Theos and His Son, Iasos. I believe rescuing you is the right thing to do. And... if I wanted to kill you or strand you, I would have left you on the post."

The girl nodded, considering.

Talus offered an end of the rope. She took it, then paused.

"What's your name?"

"Talus, son of Valnis, why? Er, what's yours?"

"Anna. Talus, could I leave a long tail in the rope like this?" She drew about four cat's tails through her fingers. "Then I could tie it under my thighs and sort of sit on it."

Talus grinned. She could think intelligently.

"Good idea."

While she tied herself up, Talus crawled to a flagpole and bound the other end of the rope to it securely. He moved back to Anna.

"So," She asked. "I just jump over the wall?"

"Aye. Wait! Let me get a hold on the rope."

"Right, sorry." Talus could see fear lingering in her pupils. She continued. "Got it?"

"Aye." As she climbed over the parapet, he added. "Theos bless you."

She smiled before dropping out of sight.

Talus gave her a minute to prepare the rope positions, then allowed the slack to slip slowly through his fingers.

<<<<<<<<<<<<<>>>>>>>>>>>>

Anna adjusted the ropes into a suitable sitting position. She placed her feet on the wall. The first slack caught her off guard and she dropped, leaving her feet above her. Thankfully, however, the rope was descending slowly. She picked a pace to match. How far was the ground?

She risked a glance down. The wall slid away beneath her into the moat, still fifty feet away. She pushed away the uncertainty of height. She resolved not to look down.

She winced as her foot scraped a rough stone. Every following step emulated throbbing pain. Anna wondered if it was bleeding.

Suddenly Anna wondered how she was to tell Talus when she was ready to swing. She heard a faint shout from the city. Her heart leapt into her throat. Had she been spotted?

<<<<<<<<<<<<<>>>>>>>>>>>>

Talus could have growled if there was not the possibility of sentries. How was he to know when she reached the designated height? The only problem with a plan is you can never think of everything, as Jornus liked to say.

112

Talus risked a peek over the wall. She bounced off slightly. Perfect. She pushed off the wall for real. She crossed half the moat. She hit the wall like a spring and hurled outward. Maybe, now? Too late, one more swing. Talus felt his knuckles whiten. The timing had to be perfect. She swung out almost all the way. Now! Talus released the rope.

He watched her smash into the ground. She laid still in a crumpled heap. Panic rose in Talus. Was she hurt?

However, after a minute, she stood slowly and untied herself. She stepped away from the rope. Talus yanked it quickly to avoid dropping it into the moat. They would need it again for the city wall.

Talus coiled the rope and stuck it in his pack. He removed almost all of his weapons, stowing his knives and blades in the pack. He hurled the pack and, separately, his bow off the wall. He breathed out a silent sigh of relief. Both had escaped the moat. He climbed over the parapet, hanging from his hands while he searched out toeholds with his feet. Once certain of the grips, he transferred most of his weight to his toes and moved his left hand down. Then left foot. Then right hand. Right foot. Left hand.

Talus quickened the pattern. What if someone noticed him slithering down the wall? His heart raced. His feet slipped. His left-hand fingers were the only hindrances from falling some fifty feet on the water below. He breathed out slowly, forcing his mind to be calm. Carefully he placed each limb back on the surface of the wall. Never wise to hurry on an unknown wall, Jornus liked to say. *Forget the risk of being spotted,* Talus told himself, *focus on climbing.*

After a couple minutes, Talus slid into the moat. Cold water greeted him. He pushed off the safety of the wall. The shadows of the deep lurked around him, begging to swallow him. How could he swim silently and not drown before he reached the other side? Terror built inside him; swimming was his weak point. Time slowed. Cold seeped into his heart. He would never make it.

No! No despair. He could do it, he had to. Focus on the bank.

It grew nearer. Finally, he clamored wearily from its shadows and lay exhausted on the bank.

Talus sensed rather than saw Anna crouch beside him. He rolled over and looked up at her. "Are you alright?"

Anna giggled slightly. "You know I was about to ask you that. But I am fine, only a little bruised. You?"

"I am good now; I just don't swim well."

Talus stood and walked to his pack. His bow leaned against it.

"Thought you might not want to hunt around for it." Anna spoke from behind him.

He glanced at her. "Thanks."

He dug into his pack and strapped on his knives. He paused.

"What weapons can you use?"

Anna shrugged awkwardly.

"Um... I can use a bow to some extent and... carrots are terrified of me with a knife." She added quickly.

Talus grinned and threaded three knives on a belt with his quiver. He handed them to her.

"Here you are. In case we happen across any carrots."

Talus strung the bow and gave it to her. She hung it over her shoulder. Quickly, he strapped on his short swords, his two handed blade, and his remaining knives. He knelt and dried his leg knife. He dumped the water from its sheath. Slinging his pack over his shoulder, he asked.

"Ready?"

Anna nodded.

Talus glanced around. "Let's get out of here."

Talus slipped into the shadows of the alley, checking that Anna was following.

No light filtered into the alleys Talus chose, so Anna could barely see. What if she lost him? Her mouth dried. Images of what might happen to a lone lost girl flooded her. Her heart stuttered and quickened her pace.

A yelp of pain escaped her as her shin slammed into a board. Immediately, weak hands fastened around her ankle.

"Mine, mine, food!" A harsh voice cried. "Soft flesh, food."

Anna hastily ripped her leg from their clutches. She stepped back, tripping over another low shelter. More hands grabbed at her. She screamed and rolled. The rotted roof refused to support her. She fell through, sought and fought over. Sharp teeth sunk into her arm. Was this how she would die?

Hands pulled at her hair. Hands and teeth ripped at the flesh on her arms and legs.

A strong hand gripped her shoulder and drew her from their clawing grasp. Talus put his other hand on her forearm and set her on her feet behind him, away from the seeking hands.

"Are you hurt?" He asked.

"Only my arm." She whispered in a small voice. Tears of horror and relief clogged her throat and tears fell ruthlessly from her eyes.

"I am sorry, I forgot you cannot see. I will remember in the future." Talus promised, haunted.

"Forgiven." Anna doubted the word pierced her congestion from the tears.

Anna thought, however, Talus nodded and turned back towards the hands.

"How many are you?"

"Eight!"

"Eleven!"

"Nine hundred!"

"Sixty-two!"

"Seven!"

The responses shrieked.

"Nevermind. All of you crawl to the entrance of your dens."

"Why? Don't hurt us!"

"I won't."

Sounds of scraping and sliding filled the night.

"Everyone out?" Talus asked.

Somewhere behind the sheet of terror, Anna wondered what Talus was doing. As horrible as they were, Anna prayed Talus would not hurt them.

Dimly, Anna watched Talus drop his pack on the ground and dig some packets out.

"Alright," He addressed the hands. "I am going to give you a little food. Anyone who takes from his neighbor forfeits his own food as well. Understand?"

"Understand." Called the excited voices.

Anna smiled as she viewed Talus walk around and stop five times.

Munching echoed softly in the alley.

"One more thing." Talus sounded stern. "No more scaring and eating innocent girls, it is detestable and utterly below you. Understood?"

A chorus of quiet, dejected, "Yes sir," answered. One voice added, "Sorry, miss."

"Good. Have a restful night."

"Wait! No!" Like a million snakes, they dragged themselves and latched on to both Talus and Anna.

"Please! Please don't leave us! Please take us with you!" They implored. They were so pitiful. Anna's heart constricted. If they stayed here, they would die, but if they came along, they would endanger them.

"We travel a hard road; you don't want to come."

"Please! Please! We will do anything!" They begged.

Talus said nothing for a long while. Finally, he turned to Anna.

"Would you be comfortable with this?"

"They will die if we don't, they might live if we do." Anna had no idea why she agreed, the terror filled seconds haunted her, but these people were desperate.

"Okay." Talus allowed. The people cheered. "But some rules must be obeyed. Keep your hands off anyone and anything, unless you are helping each other. And

115

until I say, stay absolutely silent." He paused. "Good." Anna guessed they must have nodded. Talus continued. "Now let's see you stand."

Heavy breathing resounded in the darkness as five figures laboriously forced themselves to stand.

"Right. Single file, put your hands on the shoulders of the one in front of you. Good. Follow me."

The going was slow, but that perhaps could be blamed on the overcast sky and deep shadow as much as the newcomers.

As she watched Talus guide them around multiple piles of junk and makeshift homes, her earlier questions resurfaced. What was Talus? He was too short for a Talrin, and they could not see in the dark anyways. That was the only other race she had met before. Maybe a Kazof or Fumin or Elerin? She knew too little about the other races to know.

Talus turned back to her and breathed, "'top," dropping the 's' for silence's sake.

He put his hand on the beginning of the line, bringing them to a stop.

The city wall rose before them. Anna noted two guards with torches at the foot of the stairs leading up the wall. How would they ever get past them?

Anna guessed Talus had noticed them. Talus whispered to her.

"Stay here."

He drew a knife and disappeared around the corner. Anna's heart froze. What would he do? Surely the same man who had been kind to the starved humans behind her would not kill these guards?

<<<<<<<<<<<<<>>>>>>>>>>>>

Talus slipped through the shadows along the wall. Once he was far enough from the guards not to attract notice, he darted a glance up and down the clearing between the wall and the city. The coast was clear. Then again, most sensible people were asleep.

Yeah. Sensible. Not him. Disobey his king. Rescue a condemned girl. Allow starving people to join him. Quite a night's work. First, he had to get them all out safely.

He dashed silently across the clearing. Once back in the shadows, he breathed out silently. He followed the wall until the parapet was barely over his head. Talus closed his eyes. If this didn't work half the guard would be on him in seconds.

With a quick prayer, he swung himself on the parapet. He dropped lightly on all fours on the stairs. He froze as one guard asked.

"Hear something?"

"Just your stomach growling, you great oaf. Nothing to be heard out here!" The other snarled.

"Fine, try talking to a bear." The first muttered.

They returned to sullen silence. Talus stood painfully slow and stepped toward them.

In one smooth motion, Talus smashed the knob of his knife into the head of the first. Before the other even registered the movement, he whirled and slammed the hilt against the second man. Both crumpled to the ground. Gently, Talus placed his fingers on their necks one at a time. He sighed, relieved. Both still lived.

He set them in sitting positions. The stone steps really did not look comfortable to lay on. He checked the coast again, then beckoned to Anna and the others.

Anna reached him well before the others. Talus noted a desperate fear in her eyes.

"You.... You didn't kill them, did you?" Anna stammered.

"What?" Talus blurted in surprise. "No. Thankfully, they are just unconscious. Why? Did you think I would?" The idea pained him, but then again they had only just met.

"I... well... just when you pulled out the knife... I assumed... never mind."

Talus saluted softly. "I am an Elerin. We do not kill unless absolute necessity drives us. Death is a tragedy, no matter how or why. But I am sorry, I should have told you."

"No, I... it's just that so many men I have seen.... They just kill on a whim. I have watched so much death, it's so horrible."

"Hey, unless in defense of ourselves, I will try to ensure that you see no more." Poor girl, but in Garia life was cheap. Still, why place killing before the eyes of those around oneself?

Chapter 17 Being There

The stairs seemed to go up endlessly. If Anna's legs were beginning to feel leaden, she could not even imagine how the others were managing. However, somehow they plodded on silently. Ahead of her Talus glided to the top, crouching behind the parapet. He held up his hand as they approached. Thankfully, just enough light passed through the clouds to make the motion visible.

She knelt beside Talus. He glanced at her and whispered, dropping all s sounds for quiet's sake.

"Two guard' 'tand in our path. I am going to 'ay, 'goodnight' to them. On'e they are napping, tie your'elf up and walk down to the bridge. Two hard tug' when you get there, then untie and tug twi'e more. Take cover acro' the bridge, don't break unle' one of them can't get up. If we are di'covered, drop in the river and find an overhang to 'helter under."

"Got it. What would happen to you?"

"I'll be 'ent back to Belon in di'gra'e."

Anna winced inwardly. "Oh, I'm 'orry. 'hould I tell the other' the plan'?"

Talus nodded. "Thank you."

He disappeared beyond the parapet. Anna swiveled to the others and re-verbalized the plan. Anna's ears caught two almost simultaneous thuds. She peeked on to the battlements.

Talus had removed the rope from his pack and left it on the floor. He was currently repositioning the fallen guards. Staying below the edge of the parapet, she tied the rope around her in a sitting position. She was careful to go slow enough to allow the others to see how it was done.

Talus took the other end and bound it to the inner parapet. Anna glanced over the wall. No gate guards, at least not visible. As she descended, she whispered a prayer that there were none. She reached the bottom and no guards presented themselves.

She followed the prescribed method. She hurried across the bridge and hid herself in the foliage beyond.

<<<<<<<<<<<<<<<>>>>>>>>>>>>>

Talus pulled the rope up and turned to the others.

"Alright, anyone who would like to go first?" Talus asked.

A black-haired boy probably a little younger than him stepped up.

"I would." He glanced at the others. "Everyone good up here with Adventurer Talus?"

How did a street kid know his race, let alone his title? And why would the youngest of the party ask a question of comfort like that?

Most nodded, but an elderly woman gasped.

"Jacqin."

The boy put his hand on her shoulder.

"I'll be fine, Grammy."

He held out his hand for the rope, and while he did manage, Talus noted the rope was heavy and difficult for him to move. Once done, Jacqin looked up to him.

"So I climb over the wall and you lower me down?"

Well, sort of. Then again, they were light. So might as well conserve their energy.

"Aye. Did Anna tell you what to do when you reach the bridge?"

"Two hard tugs, untie yourself, and two more tugs."

"Good; off you go."

Jacqin pulled himself onto the wall. Talus met his eyes and watched exhaustion mix with determination. The boy nodded then dropped off the wall.

Once he had given the signal twice Talus drew back the rope and lowered the rest down. Time dragged forever, as he convinced Jacqin's grandmother and a young man in his twenties, Elian, to overcome their fear of falling. In the end, Talus finally pushed him slowly off the parapet, with his helpless permission. Talus could always remember the terror in his eyes, but to his credit the fellow never screamed.

The last one down and safely across the drawbridge. Talus coiled the rope, and, nothing being particularly fragile, he dropped his pack down off the wall.

"Hey, you!"

Talus turned to a sergeant who had just come up the steps to do rounds.

"Pleasant night, is it not?" Talus asked. His heart tightened uncomfortably.

Talus saw his eyes stray to the downed guards. Rage flared on his face. Talus hit him with his knife hilt before he could utter a word.

It was too late, the sergeant's original call had alerted the other sentries. As the man crumpled to the ground, they yelled and charged. Talus swung himself over the wall and climbed dangerously fast, his mind replaying lectures from Jornus in the past against the action.

His fingers slipped and he fell the last ten cat's tails. He rolled to his feet. The sound of the gates opening met his ears. He grabbed his pack and dashed from the bridge. He paused where he had seen the others disappear.

"Anyone around?"

Anna's and Jacqin's heads appeared. Talus held up his hands to keep them in one place.

"I have been spotted. Once my pursuers have passed, head upstream and get in the river carefully when it is safe. Stay undercover. Now hide!"

The gates were hurled open. Talus ran downriver. He risked a backward glance. They were on foot. Good. Talus focused on running. He had to make the Covered Ford long before the men behind him. He pushed his muscles faster, much more depended on this race against time than any other he had ever run. As he rounded the bend to the Covered Ford, he stole a glance back. The men were too close! Panic threatened and he strained to gain more speed. He entered the blackness of the Covered Ford, which was technically a covered bridge, not that Talus had spare thought for technicalities.

On the other side, with a desperate glance at the surroundings, he tossed his pack into the roadside bushes and dropped under the bridge. He naturally wanted to hold his breath but resisted since the river would destroy any sounds he made. He drew air slowly, trying to breathe calmly.

He listened to the feet stomp and run into one another above. Finally, the sounds faded. Talus let a sigh of relief whisper through his lips. Safe.

"Wait! Look! Footprints lead under the bridge!" A voice called.

Talus' heart collided with his ribs. He had to get out of here!

Stay calm, he told himself. A log bounced gently, stuck in the rocks. Without a second thought, he slid into the river. He grabbed the branch stubs on the underside. He shoved off with his feet.

Immediately the current snatched him. Horrifying speed threatened to drown him. The branch whirled as it smashed into floating branches and looming rocks. Shouts from shore alerted him that he had been spotted. A second later, an arrow slammed into his log where his head had been moments before.

He hit a rock body on. He might have groaned if he was less concentrated on staying alive. Water washed into his mouth. He choked, coughing. No more shouts were to be heard. Then again, they probably figured the river was a death sentence. Maybe it was.

Ahead, he spotted a low branch over the water. Do or die, he thought grimly. It rushed toward him. He reached up with one hand. The moment his fingers closed firmly around it, he released the log. He caught the branch with his other hand. The current pulled at him. One hand over the other, he forced his way towards land. His legs were being sucked from him. The current was so strong. Land was so far away.

No! Focus on the goal. Land *was* closer. He *could* make it.

He swung his feet on to the bank. He was safe. Thank you, Theos!

He lay still unable to even comprehend the thought of motion. The world fuzzed with exhaustion.

Anna, the others! He had told them to wait in the river! What if- he pushed the doubts away. Theos, protect them. Hopefully, they would realize the very strength of the river and remain on the bank.

Talus stood. Regardless, they had a good way to go before the sun rose in about an hour. He looked upriver. The bridge was out of sight. How far downriver was he?

Well, standing around wouldn't solve anything. Talus set off at the solid pace he could maintain for hours. Not that he had hours. Ten minutes passed ere he found the bridge. Cautiously he crossed and reclaimed his pack. Once back on the gate side, he cut into the country. Large bushes dotted the terrain. After he had passed the drawbridge, he weaved down to the bank. The going became far slower, as now he either crouched or slid on his stomach.

"Talus!" Anna's voice whispered.

He moved inland. Once hidden from watching eyes by Hatillin bushes, he stood.

"Fancy meeting you here. Where are the others?"

"Sleeping. Sorry we are not in the river, the current is quite strong, and I did not think the others could handle it, being half starved."

"Tell me about it. I jumped in the river to avoid company. We should be going."

Anna nodded and Talus followed her to a valley of giant bushes. She called softly down.

"Time to wake up."

Jacqin and the others crawled out, rubbing the sleep from their eyes. The sight reminded Talus how tired he was. He covered a yawn. He refocused on the task at hand. They had a half hour until sunrise and almost an hour until full light. They needed to go a long distance yet. Determination hardened.

"Right, since you are rested, I need all of you to push hard. We have a lot of ground to cover in the next hour before we find shelter for the day."

As he spoke, the promised rain started. They stared at each other. Finally, Jacqin commented.

"At least the rain will wash our scent off the ground."

Talus gave him an intense look. How did a street kid know that?

"True." Talus agreed, nonetheless. "Let's get moving."

Anna rolled over and opened her eyes. It was the fifth day of their journey. This would be their first day by daylight. Anna felt sick. While traveling at night, she had been almost comfortable. The guards had taken all but her shift before tying her up. She could not travel like this in the daylight. She shivered, the feeling of near nakedness haunting her. Maybe Talus would have some clothes she could borrow. Instantly, guilt pressed. The others from the street undoubtedly wore less than she even with just her shift. Finally, Anna determined to ask Talus, since she could not consciously wander around in nothing but her shift.

She carefully wrapped herself in a blanket Talus had given her. He only had two, so she and Jacqin's grandmother, Mrs. Lilliam, were given them while the guys had gone without. Anna slid out from under her bush, blinking in the morning light. A gentle breeze pushed her hair back. She spotted Talus, crouched examining something. He looked up as she approached.

"Good morning, Anna." He smiled, then held out his hand, motioning to the blanket. "Want me to take that?"

Anna's face instantly developed a cherry red.

"I... I...." She stuttered. She forced herself just to say it. It was so weird to say it to a guy.

"I am only wearing a shift." She blurted.

Talus' brows furrowed in puzzlement. He did not know what that meant, Anna guessed.

"Kinda just my undergarments." She added.

Talus nodded slowly.

"I, uh, don't have any female clothes. But if you are comfortable, you can have some of my spares."

"Thanks. I realize the rest probably don't have much clothes either though."

Talus paused. "No, not really, but they are used to being exposed. In four more days, we should reach Storm Bay. Then I can restock the food and we can use the hides to give all proper attire."

"Where will we go from Storm Bay?"

Talus pointed to the map before him.

"We go around the point then across the plains to Darqin and hope we meet a Kazof."

Talus opened his pack and dug around inside. However, Anna's mind was still on the Kazofs.

"What are they like?" She asked in variable awe, everything she had heard made them sound enchanting and wondrous and mysterious.

Talus paused.

"Big, gentle, animal tamers, kind. Though some still carry hurt from four hundred years ago."

"What happened?" Anna asked, wanting to know but dreading the response.

"The races of Talrins, Fumins, and some humans enslaved them and when they resisted, war broke out. Far too much blood was shed. Many of the Kazof can still remember that time. They have become reclusive and distrustful of other races, the scars of loved ones who died before old age runs too deep."

Anna could not understand what she felt, but sympathy and horror won out.

Talus silently handed her a pair of knee length pants, a shirt, and his spare jerkin.

She took them and changed. She could give Lilliam her shift to wear under her dress for now.

These were so odd, how did people stand these strange divided skirts? She shrugged; at least she felt covered.

She rejoined Talus. He looked up.

"How is it?"

"You guys dress weird."

Talus smiled like he was trying not to laugh.

"Everything is weird if you are not used to it. Though personally, humans in general dress weird."

Anna shrugged and they both laughed.

<<<<<<<<<<<<<<<<>>>>>>>>>>>>>>>

Lord Henry stood. His voice held one last heartfelt appeal.

"Please, Eirin, let it go. If for no one else's sake, do it for your page."

Before Eirin could think of another angry response, Lord Henry left the room. His features were shadowed by great sadness.

For his page? For his page, indeed! Matt had nothing to do with this. This was all Talus' fault. That little... that little.... No word strong enough came to mind. Or none his mother would have approved of.

A sudden ache distracted him from his anger. She had died when he was twelve. What would she think of him now? He shook the question off. He had a right to be angry. Talus had abandoned him! Leaving him with no means to communicate with Hissin. How dare he? He could not help it, anger was his right. That.... Insults again failed to surface. And he was not acting like a child who had not gotten his way, as his uncle had accused. Unbidden, his father rose in his mind, and the uncomfortable feeling he would have said the same.

Someone knocked on the outer door.

"Matt, get the door." Eirin muttered.

Matt never heard.

The person knocked again.

"MATT!!!" Eirin yelled.

The boy jumped to his feet and shrunk back, fear lighting in his eyes.

"My lord?" His voice shook.

However, Eirin stared for a second. Since when had Matt been this easily frightened? Everything he had said and done to the boy in the last few days bombarded him. He closed his eyes. He never should have let Matt become the recipient of his anger. His uncle was right. He had to do something for the sake of his page.

He stood and took a step forward. Matt stepped backward and Eirin stopped.

"Matt, I'm sorry. I should not have raised my voice." He winced as he studied his page. "Or any of the things I have said and done recently. Can you forgive me?"

Matt stared at him and nodded slowly. "I forgive you, my lord."

Eirin wished Matt had left the title off. He did not feel like he should be anyone's lord, let alone a people's king.

"Um... do you want to run down to the kitchen or something? I am sure you could convince the cook to feed you." Eirin offered awkwardly. He felt like the statement should be accompanied by a smile, yet the smile refused to come.

"Sure, whatever, my lord." Matt replied.

The person at the door knocked again.

Matt moved toward the door. Eirin could not let him get that door; whoever it was could well be mad by now. Eirin overtook him in the entry room. He put his hand on the boy's shoulder. Matt tensed and Eirin hastily dropped his hand.

"Let me get it." Eirin said softly.

He pulled the door open. It was Kalrick. At first, he was relieved. Then he felt sick. How much had Kalrick overheard?

"Kalrick." Again Eirin could not smile.

Kalrick studied him.

"What's wrong?"

How about everything? Kalrick had gotten into that mess with Hissin. Then Talus.... He pushed the thought away. Now Lord Henry was upset with him, and Matt was scared of him.

Not that he could throw all that at Kalrick at once.

"Will you come in?" He asked.

Kalrick nodded. Eirin led him to the sitting room. He paused and turned to Matt.

"Matt, if you like, you could inquire if Lord Kalrick can spare John and the two of you can hang out."

An almost full smile lit Matt's face.

"Do you mind, Lord Kalrick?"

"No, of course. Go have fun."

Matt glanced at Eirin, before hurrying out the door.

"Well?" Kalrick asked as the door gave an excited slam.

Eirin flopped on the couch.

"I am a fool, Kal. I let my anger get the best of me and I took it out on Matt. Now he trembles when I speak, tenses when I touch him, backs when I move towards him. He's terrified of me! And it's my fault. I feel awful. How can I go back to the way things were?"

"Hey, you know now. Things don't have to stay this way. You know you can never go back. But you can put this behind you. Be kind. Be extra careful with your words and tones. Remember, even though you have hurt him, Matt looks up to you. Praise is more than gold. Time will repair your relationship. And Eirin, you are not a fool, even though you act like one sometimes."

Eirin winced, but his mind quickly returned to Matt.

"How long will it take?"

Kalrick met his eyes. "Be patient, Eirin." A smile flickered across his face. "I don't know everything."

A tired smile finally found his features.

"What would I do without you, Kal?"

Kalrick's always present grin surfaced. Eirin's smile lessened. Talus was always grinning too. The difference was Kalrick begged for death when he trespassed out of fear, Talus had deliberately disobeyed him.

<<<<<<<<<<<<<>>>>>>>>>>>>

"Ho and hey, my friends!"

The Talrin who had caught up to them greeted.

"A ho and hey yourself, friend." Talus returned, hiding his discomfort. He had not wanted to meet anyone between Ketlin and Storm Bay.

The Talrin crossed his wrists over his chest.

"I am Lithos Saxorum."

Talus saluted.

"I am Tal and these are my friends. How may we help you?"

"No way. No way. Just saw we are heading the same way. And safety is found in numbers." The gray skinned giant quoted.

Talus sighed inwardly. Of course.

"Welcome then, as long as our paths coincide."

The giant spoke happily among the Garians, most of whom also knew Talrin. Talus wished he had studied that language, as several conversations followed in that tongue.

The day grew long, and evening shadows lengthened. Finally, Talus resigned himself. They would have to camp with the giant's knowledge. Not that there truly was any reason not to, besides his own reluctance.

Talus called a halt and dropped his pack. Two days had passed. The day after tomorrow, they would reach Storm Bay. Hopefully the Talrin would leave them by then.

"Jacqin, if you will come with me to gather wood for a fire. Anna, Mrs. Lilliam, perhaps you will prepare the food? Faelin, Sonnen, and Elian, will you clear a spot for the fire?"

As they nodded, Talus began to turn away. Lithos stopped him.

"Anything I could do?"

Talus paused, then looked at the small wood they had entered.

"Feel free to help with the fire, or if you will, perhaps you could find us some logs for benches?"

"Certainly." The giant smiled. "Does a man good to have something to do."

Talus smiled back. At least he was friendly and helpful. Actually, he was starting to like him so long as he left them tomorrow.

Jacqin followed him on to the opposite part of the forest as Lithos chose. Jacqin remained quiet for a long time. Finally, Talus asked.

"Something on your mind?"

Jacqin shrugged. "Just the Talrin."

Talus paused; the other young man looked uncertain.

"What about? If you don't mind the asking?" Talus questioned.

"It's just... he seems too friendly, and he knew Anna's name without being told. And I... think I gave him too much information about us. He kept asking questions. I tried to be careful, because I know the trouble you and Anna are in. I am really sorry."

He knew Anna's name. Talus felt sick.

He put his hand on Jacqin's shoulder.

"Few people would have picked up on that. Thank you for telling me. It more than makes up for whatever harm you unknowingly did."

"Still, I should have been more careful." Talus could see the frustration in his eyes.

"Don't worry about it. I forgive you. Though I am sure it was not just your fault. Now what does he know?"

"What race is Talus? I don't believe I have met his kind before."

Lithos asked Anna as he placed the fourth and final log around the fire pit. No fire yet though. Talus and Jacqin were sure taking their time.

"He is an Elerin. Seems I am to meet all the different races on this journey."

"Oh?"

Anna grinned. "We are going to go around the point and meet Kazofs too."

"Really? Wow. I have only heard of that musical, mysterious race. You are a privileged young woman, indeed. This must be some gallivanting for fun?"

"Something like that." Talus' voice broke in. His expression was clouded, and he was not smiling. She wondered what was up.

They built a fire and ate supper. As the sun set, Anna curled in a blanket and closed her eyes. Sleep quickly buried her in dreams.

She woke suddenly. The moons illuminated the clearing.

"Talus, Talus." Jacqin's voice carried to where Anna lay.

"Yes?"

"He left."

"Quick." The urgency in Talus' voice was unmistakable. "Get everyone up, we must leave now."

Talus knelt beside her to wake her.

"What's happening?"

"Lithos is Hissin's spy. We have to get out of here."

Anna nodded, frightened. "He knows too much about our plans."

Talus sighed. "I know."

Anna stood and Talus took her blanket and stowed it in his pack.

Within three minutes, they were again scurrying north. An hour passed and their pace slowed.

"There. I see them!" A shout echoed behind them, yipping accompanying it.

Talus suddenly turned back to them, his eyes glowing in the darkness.

"All of you, run. Jacqin, if I never rejoin you, get to Alcasa. You should find work there. Now move!" Talus whispered, intensity thickening.

Anna ran. The others all clustered around her. The barking grew louder. A screech indicated Talus had made his presence known. Yells and screams of pain filled the air. They diminished as the distance grew. A sudden silence fell.

Anna glanced around. The only sounds were their own. No animals sang across the bush covered plains. What if there were more pursuers than just the ones Talus had fought? Every bush flickered with danger. Whenever the pace slowed in the slightest, Jacqin would urge them faster. Slowly the three moons set, leaving them in complete darkness. After several falls, Jacqin suggested a quick walk.

Uncertainty shadowed their breathing. Who else was around? What if they unknowingly stumbled by an outpost and were caught? Fear tightened Anna's throat. She shook the idea away. She was only frightening herself. The first light of dawn crept over the mountains to the east, sending its cheery promises to the weary runners.

Finally, Sonnen, a man probably in his thirties, asked, winded.

"Jacqin?"

"Yes?"

"When can we stop?"

The silence lasted a long time before Jacqin answered.

"I would rather wait until Talus catches up. How are you all holding up?"

No one replied.

"Right, I see. Five-minute break by that stream." Jacqin pointed to water bouncing down a hill maybe a half mile distant.

The thought of water spurred them on, and they stopped by the pool at the bottom of a chain of mini falls within four minutes.

The water slid down her throat. So refreshing. Anna drank as fast as she could carry water to her mouth.

"Thirsty, eh?" Questioned a voice behind them.

They jumped to their feet. Anna nocked an arrow as she spun to face the newcomer.

"Nice to see you can nock that fast, Anna, but with your permission, I would like to remain arrow-less."

"Talus!" Six people exclaimed.

"Who else would I be?"

"One of the hunters, I guess." Jacqin stared at the ground.

"That would be possible. I am glad you all are on your toes."

Anna watched Jacqin look back up to Talus. Talus gave him a smile then dropped his pack to the ground.

"Anyone ready for breakfast?"

Anna gripped the ledge of the cliff that confronted her. She put her left foot in a cleft about knee height. She pulled herself onto the ridge. She sat up and stilled.

To her right, a deep blue-black line of cliffs glistened as it ran into the sea. Before her, green grass rolled down to the blue rock of the shore, waves crashing gently. Out to sea, white ice sparkled in the sunlight.

Beside her Talus sucked in his breath.

"Well, you have a pretty country for sure, but it is so cold."

It was cold. The thought registered and she shivered.

"Thanks."

Talus shrugged mischievously.

"Must be the ice on the horizon. Look at it on the bright side, it will be colder at night." Anna smiled sweetly.

Talus shivered harder.

"Maybe it will snow." Anna added. At Talus' look of horror, she shook her head. "No, it is too early for snow even up here."

The others joined them, and silence lingered as they admired the view.

"So... what's next? The Stonecliff Range goes into the sea." Anna questioned.

"I thought we would sail around the point."

"We are sailing?" Anna asked at the same moment Jacqin asked. "Where's the boat?"

"Yep!" Talus grinned. He pointed to a grove of trees by the shoreline. "Down there I think."

"Where?" Anna asked.

"The clump of trees." Talus pointed.

Sonnen grinned. "Why do I think we are building something?"

Talus grinned back to him. "A raft, and it should go pretty quickly with the lot of you to help."

Grins surfaced in happy companionship all around.

"You ever wonder why we are standing here, wasting daylight?" Elian asked.

Chapter 18 Storm Bay

Talus woke the next morning cold and stiff. He shivered. His eyes slid closed. It was still warm in Belon in early fall. Why was it so cold up here? He rolled over and sat up. The fire was, of course, dead. The rest still lay asleep. Well, might as well greet them with a warm fire.

He wandered around, gathering sticks. After a few minutes, he returned to the dead fire. He arranged some dried leaves under the sticks and lit it with his flint and tinder. A baby fire leapt up, eating first the small twigs, but gradually it ate larger chunks of wood. Eventually, Talus was forced to leave his nice, not so little, fire in search of more food. When he returned, the fire was so happy to see him, it leapt and crackled, throwing sparks in the air. Talus huddled as close as possible, enjoying the warmth, although wary of its spark hurling habits.

Talus drifted into thoughts of hunting, skinning, and raft building. Anna rolled over and sat up, the first to wake. She blinked the sleep from her eyes.

"Good morning, Talus."

Talus jumped, as well as one can while sitting. He lifted his eyes from the enchanting depths of the fire.

"Oh, Anna. Good morning, though not a warm one."

Anna giggled.

"What did you do, make a cold fire? Because I think that close to the fire you must be quite comfortable."

Talus half grinned, shrugging as if it was unimportant.

"Suppose I am." Talus paused, thinking. "Anna, how long do you suppose drying meat takes?"

Anna shrugged. "A day or two in good sun, but it is too humid up here. If we got a good smoker, things might go better."

Talus nodded. "Okay. Can you do it?"

Anna nodded. "Aye, I... did it with my family."

Anna looked away from Talus.

Talus wished he could have taken her to see her family. How could he help her? What was acceptable in human society? If she was one of his friends from Belon, he would hug her, but Kalrick said that was different here. Finally, he put his hand on her shoulder.

She turned toward him. The glisten of tears vividly played on her face, bringing out intense color. Talus pushed the thought away. The pain was clear, the hurt burning.

"It has been so long." Her voice broke. She dropped her head into her hands. "I'm sorry."

Would she even see them again? Well, Theos can do anything. Wait, Learner field trips.

"Anna?"

"What?" She whispered.

"Anna, hope remains. Theos willing, you will see them again. You won't always stay in Belon. You can plan it and visit Garia and your parents. King Hissin won't hunt you forever."

A glimmer of hope sparkled in her eyes.

"Really?"

Talus nodded encouragingly. "Theos willing."

Anna wiped her tears away.

"Sorry, I didn't mean to become a soppy girl. I guess it's just so hard sometimes."

"Hey, I don't mind. Everyone is soppy now and then. No shame is found in honest tears."

Anna smiled. "Thanks. So... what's for breakfast? Wait, let me guess. Dried fruit, dried meat, and flatbread!"

"Why would you think that?" Talus smiled as he watched Anna push her tears behind her.

Anna shrugged.

"So would you mind if Faelin borrowed your bow to hunt today, Jacqin told me he is a dead shot." Talus asked.

"Sure, it's yours after all." Anna replied.

Talus shook his head. "No, you can keep the weapons I gave you."

"Oh. Thanks." Anna sounded a little shocked.

"What do you need for smoking meat?" Talus asked.

"A hollow log, something to cover it, and an axe to make wood chips."

"Right, well." Talus dug into his bag. "Here's a hatchet. Jacqin, Sonnen, and Elian can help the heavy work. And I expect Lilliam can help with the preparation. And... perhaps, since you are chopping wood anyways, you could keep the fire alive?"

Anna laughed. "You have a one-track mind, don't you?"

Talus shrugged. How could he help wanting to stay warm?

"Let's get the others up and get to work."

<<<<<<<<<<<<>>>>>>>>>>>>

Faelin turned suddenly on the hill he had bounded up and motioned to Talus. Talus ran up to him.

"What is it?"

Faelin said nothing but pointed out to sea.

Talus shaded his eyes.

"Is that a mast?" Talus asked, wording the question to accept a yes or no reply. He had found in the last several days that Faelin never spoke.

Faelin nodded, his face dark.

Talus' stomach sickened. "Garian?"

A grave nod.

"Thanks for telling me."

Faelin nodded.

Could they never escape? Talus thought. Hunted on every turn. He drew a deep breath. All he had to do was maneuver them on a little raft across a twenty-three mile stretch of water with an enemy ship within sight, nothing to it.

Actually, a plan like that had quite a bit to it. He glanced to Faelin.

"See if you can find more blue deer tracks. I'll be down in a second."

Faelin nodded, and Talus turned back to the ship. Difficulties tightened his stomach. Talus drew a slow breath and admitted the reason he had sent Faelin away.

"My King, you see the dangers hemming us in. Give me the strategies needed. Protect us, Father, as only you can. Your will be done. In Iasos' name, let it be so."

"Good to see your faith, Talus."

Talus jumped to his feet and spun around. Faelin still stood in the square cat's tail of grass he had the minute before.

"You speak?"

Faelin nodded, amused.

Talus shook his head.

"Sorry, dumb question."

Faelin nodded again, but his eyes sparkled.

"Sometimes, too little to please Jacqin, but he puts up with me for his father's sake."

"Who is Jacqin?"

Faelin rolled his eyes.

"Not my tale to tell. But the rest of us have had our share of planning and battle if you ever need help."

"Sorry and thanks. I will keep the rest of you in the plotting." Talus added. "Now what say we catch another little blue-black deer?"

Faelin nodded.

"You know I know you can speak now, right?"

Faelin nodded.

Talus sighed helplessly.

"Least I know you won't scare the prey by chattering."

Faelin nodded.

"Exactly whose idea was it to build this thing so far from the water?" Anna groaned.

Talus glanced at her but had no spare breath to reply. Anna, Sonnen, Elian, and he pushed and shoved the raft down to the shore. Thick fog covered the Great Broken Sea. Talus had woken in the small hours of the morning to Faelin shaking him. It was not yet three bells as close as Talus could guess.

They reached the water, waiting tensely to see if it floated. It did, but there was no cheer. Nerves strained to fraying.

"Talus!" A voice hissed softly behind him.

Talus whirled around. He swallowed, forcing himself to calm down. Re-sheathing his dagger, he stepped toward Jacqin, who had been scouting with Faelin.

"Soldiers. Mile out and closing."

Talus grinned grimly. "Thanks to Theos, they were too slow. Find Faelin; we leave the moment you return."

Lilliam hurried past with the last of the things. All five of the others were now dressed in animal hides. Between that and a week of constant food, they looked no longer like skeletons, but like people.

Talus turned refocusing on the raft. Crude oars, his pack and the new bag, Sonnen, Lilliam, Anna, and Elian all sat on board. Talus stared out into the mist.

What if Hissin's men had surrounded them? Out on the water as well as on land? An image played in his mind.

They rowed. Suddenly the prow of a great ship materialized from the fog. They could not turn. Logs splintered; rope snapped in the collision.

"Hey ho." A sailor yelled. "We have 'em."

A cruel laughter ripped the air. "Kill all but the girl, she's still firewood."

"Talus?" Jacqin asked.

Talus shook the pictures away. No point in scaring himself more than necessary.

"Good. There you two are. Let's board."

He encompassed them all, speaking softly.

"We do not know what is out there or who they could be. Try to avoid splashing your oars. If you see anything, whisper, do not shout."

Silent nods bounced around the raft.

They moved out into the white shadows. Time passed in a tense quiet. Talus' heart stopped every time someone splashed coming out of or going into the water. Faint voices drifted to him on the right.

"Awful fog, this. Could slip right along the length of the ship and we should never know."

"Don't tell Old Froglegs, I don't care nothing about the un-imprisoned prisoners so long as we get out of the bay ere the storm that follows these fogs picks up."

"Won't hear nothing from me, coming storm, you think, eh?"

"Never said 'think,' I was born an' bred on this sea. It will storm and it will kill anything in the bay! This ain't called Storm Bay for nothing."

Thankfully, the voices faded until the grim pale darkness returned. "It will storm, and it will kill anything on the bay." What had he done? How long would the fog last? Had he condemned all of them to their deaths?

"Theos willing, we will be fine." Faelin's low whisper reached him. Talus looked up to see Faelin regarding him with his average stone expression.

Talus nodded and gave him a smile.

Splash.

"You hear something?" A shout forced its way toward the mist, this time from the left and a little ahead. Talus' heart clogged his throat. Slowly, painfully, he whispered.

"Hard on the right for a moment."

Every ear stretched.

"What?"

"I was certain I heard a splash."

"Probably the cook makin' breakfast."

"That's what you think. What if it's the prey? Imagine the gold."

"Stupid, the gold goes to the captain. Fat belly does nothing but order us about and he'll get the money. You won't see a shiny coin of it, greeney."

"Still, wouldn't it be right? King's orders, captain's orders. And they're dangerous criminals."

"Right is what keeps you alive and happy, boy. Nothing else."

"But me parents said-"

"Rules are good for children, keeps them out from under people's toes. This is the world, boy, right is what you want it to be."

"Alright. So you don't wanta investigate?"

"Nope-"

Splash.

Talus glanced around. Sonnen's eyes had gone wide. He met Talus' gaze and winced.

"See?" The voices continued.

"What do you want? To be killed? Criminals are out there. They'll kill ya."

"Wait, you said criminals are out there?" A new voice bellowed. "I'll take your skins off with the cat if you don't get out there. Now!"

"Boat, boy, quick!"

Talus forced himself to stay calm.

"Right hard. Left back. Extra caution."

When the little craft had made about a ninety degree turn, Talus whispered for the left to go hard forward.

The craft moved silently away.

"Coming." Lilliam called softly.

If it was just the two he could handle them, but if there were more....

"Anna, Lilliam, swap. Anna, pick them off best you can."

The water fled by. A scream shattered the pressing demands of the fog.

A second followed it. Men shouted. More screams.

"Almost on us." Anna called frantically.

"Anna, take my paddle. Jacqin, Faelin stow yours on the raft."

Talus met Anna's eyes long enough to see the shock and horror of taking human life. He swallowed, remembering the dread and uncertain shadow.

"You did what you had to. Well done."

Anna glanced back at him but said nothing.

Talus drew his twin blades. Jacqin had his broadsword and Faelin his fighting knives. They stationed themselves on the back of the raft not a moment too late. The sailors in the boat stopped rowing and drew their weapons the moment they bumped against the raft. A peculiar thing happened as they leapt to their feet. The crafts separated. The sailors groaned as the distance quickly became too great for even jumping. Talus heard a tense laugh from Jacqin.

Talus felt something brush his cheek.

Wind.

At first it touched so gently it tickled, but it accelerated until it could knock him from his feet. It whisked the fog away, allowing them to see the darkness was not night but heavy clouds. The wind grew and the fog vanished within two minutes. The sailors yelled and screamed at each other to get back to the ship.

"Move! Row! I'll take the cat before this storm!"

Talus spared them only a glance to see them away.

Though the still rising winds, he called to Jacqin and Faelin.

"Oars! We have..." Talus stared out across the swelling waves, "I guess, five miles to land."

The grim nod Faelin gave him confirmed his suspicion that this was a die or live run.

The sky grew darker. The waves rose before them. The raft tossed across the sea. The water splashed up.

Anna screamed. The deep yanked her oar. She flew toward the sea.

Talus dove forward, grabbing her ankle as the rest of her disappeared into the sea. Elian and Faelin caught Talus as the hungry depths threatened him as well. Jacqin and Sonnen pulled Anna from the sea by her feet. Anna didn't move.

It began to rain.

"Anna?" Talus asked even though he knew the storm would drown him out.

Faelin deftly flipped her over and thudded her back. Anna coughed. A heavy breath escaped Talus. She still lived.

"Talus!" Faelin's scream echoed over the wind and waves.

Talus glanced back. A ship bared down on them.

No way to move.

A second lingered as the ship loomed high in the sky above them.

Chapter 19 Stranded

The ship crashed upon them with speed unimaginable. Logs splintered and cracked as the waves hurled the ship into the raft. Talus dragged Anna to him. Pieces of the raft flew through the air. They hit the sea. Shadows danced around him. Cold engulfed him, but Anna was warm against his chest. He had to get to the surface. Talus spotted a half log. He grabbed it with one arm, the other holding Anna. The log strong-armed its way to the surface. Talus snatched a quick breath before a wave buried them once more. Talus grew desperate, when would they reach the open air again? He needed to breathe.

They were going to die. This was it. What a foolish idea. He rescued her just to kill her and the others. Each of their faces passed before his memory. Would they all soon be dead? Was he even supposed to have saved them?

Yes. Somehow there must be a way through this. If not, better things awaited.

Talus resurfaced; the stone cliffs leveled with the sea. A desperate plan formed in his waterlogged brain. The water swamped them. They hit resistance. The cliffs. Anna slammed against them first, absorbing much of the impact, too much. Something warm washed over the arm holding Anna.

Talus rolled himself onto the log, thankful the upwards pressure prevented a flip. They broke into the rain.

At the crest, Talus stood, hurling Anna toward the cliff top. The log rolled and Talus went under.

Talus grabbed onto the cliff as the waves smashed him against it. His fingers and toes locked into holds on the wild surface. The water washed back. Threatening to pull Talus off, to send him spiraling into the shadowed depth of death.

Long years of strengthening did their work and Talus' clutch was unbroken. Talus climbed. He had only precious seconds before the next waves. *Theos, help me.* He cried, though the fevered thought never left his lips.

Spray washed thickly around him, but the waves hammered only the cliffs below him. He was free!

He could not believe the saturated air was so thick with water. So much moisture. He needed air. His arms weakened. He would never make it. Exhaustion plagued him. He would never make it. His grip lost strength.

His fingers reached a hold with no end. He felt above; where was the wall? The top, this was the top. He clawed his way onto the ledge and rolled from the side. The waves crashed behind him, lulling him to sleep.

<<<<<<<<<<<<<>>>>>>>>>>>>>

Talus opened his eyes. The sun beat down on him, pleasantly warming him. He closed his eyes again, enjoying the comfort.

Anna! Talus hurriedly sat up. Instantly, he regretted it. His head spun. Every muscle in his body was stiff. He sucked in his breath, coming slowly to terms with the pain.

After a minute, Talus took in his surroundings. He gasped.

Anna laid in a pool of blood.

He leapt to his feet, forgetting his pain. He dropped to his knees by her side. Immediately, he detected a faint rise and fall of her chest. He let go a sigh of relief.

How did this happen? Where did all the blood come from?

The cliff. She must have ripped or broken something. Her right arm. It lay at the edge, a trickle flowing into the pool from where white bone had protruded from the opening.

Talus stared at it. What was he to do? He had read about arm setting in his studies but had never done it or seen it done. Could he even do something like that?

He could not leave Anna in this state, however. He had to try; even something was better than nothing. Hmm, he needed straight poles and cloth. Sticks would do as poles.

He looked around. Barren blue rock stretched for miles. Empty described this place.

Could he just wrap it? All he had was his twins and a couple knives.

Wait, was Anna still wearing the bow, and more importantly, the arrows? He moved to Anna's head, reaching tentatively among her hair. After a second, he found his query: an arrow. Talus quickly removed the head and the fletching. He snapped the arrow in two. Yes! He had poles. Now for a wrap.

He hesitated less than a second before removing his jerkin and pulling off his shirt. Carefully, he plotted the most profitable use of the material. He slit stripes from the bottom leaving the shoulders for a sling.

Returning to her side, he gently moved her arm a little farther from the pool. She groaned softly. He grasped her arm carefully above and below the breakage. He drew a steadying breath. He firmly pulled the wrist and the elbow apart and aligned the break. Blood poured from the hole the bone had punctured through her skin. Hmm, if he had a needle, it would be best to stitch it. No needle. The best he could do was wrap it tightly and pray Anna didn't lose too much blood before they reached the Kazofs.

After stuffing a wat of cloth against the wound, he placed the arrow pieces on either side of her arm. He tied the middle of the longest strip of cloth just below her elbow and around the pole ends. One at a time, he wrapped the tails in circles down her arm. At her thumb, he tied the tails together. He wrapped a second strip over this in the same fashion.

Several knots, a shirt sleeve, and a few strips of material later, Talus had her arm securely in a sling. He picked her up gently and carried her east across the cliffs. It might be slightly disconcerting to wake next to a pool of blood.

He carefully laid her on the blue stone. He set off to explore the immediate vicinity, primarily in search of water.

<<<<<<<<<<<<>>>>>>>>>>>

Thirsty. Water. Cruel thought.

The sun had climbed to its highest, destroying the last shade provided by the cliffs. Talus' quest for water had run dry.

He never left Anna alone for an extended period of time. He did not know why exactly, but he did not want her waking to her broken arm alone. Thus, as his quest led him farther east, he returned to move her eastwards.

He stared down into the near-transparent bright dark blue of the stone. It had been pretty earlier, but now... it reminded him of water. The water he could not find. He wished he could see something not blue, but the color in many shades surrounded him in the sky, sea, and stone.

His throat hurt. Surely a mountain stream flowed along these cliffs somewhere. For two hours, his quest yielded no fruit. Fruit. Fruit had liquid. He was beginning to hope Anna would not wake yet. Not until he found water, as much as he desperately wanted her to open her eyes and say she was alright, well, for having a broken arm.

He stared up at the cliffs, searching for something. Anything. Even a trickle.

A lack of blue distracted him. Just over a thousand cat's tails away, the cliffs ended. His current altitude enabled him to see across the plains to a fringing line of darker green that was the Darqin Forest. Talus began to run, hoping for a better view.

Halfway there, his foot snagged on an edge. Talus tripped forward. He snapped his eyes shut and threw his hands out. The first thing his hand hit felt nothing like stone. It was wet. Water!

His face submerged the same instant his hand connected with the stream bed. Talus scrambled to his knees, the world beyond forgotten.

He stared at it. Water! It was really water! Talus cupped his hands, bringing the water to his parched throat.

It was probably a good thing Talus had no cup; else he would have taken the water far too fast.

After a couple moments, thoughts other than water entered his brain. He needed to slow down. He grinned at the world. His thirst quenched; everything had regained a happier tint.

"Thank you, Theos." He whispered.

So where did this stream come from? Talus looked up, glad to see it running from a hole in the cliff side. It bounced down, longing to smile to the world. His grin widened. Why not? No reason not to smile.

He jumped to his feet. He might as well bring Anna here. Once he reached her, he slid his arms under her knees and back. As he lifted, a flicker of movement presented itself. He stilled. Anna blinked. Talus grinned even harder. She looked at him. Slowly a smile formed over her features.

"Seems the storm passed. You think any of the others survived?"

Talus swallowed at the pain, unsuccessfully. His vision blurred a little.

"Unless the ship picked them up, I doubt it."

He watched helplessly as tears formed in her eyes.

"All of them? Gone?" She gasped

She turned, burying her head in Talus. He carried her to the cliffs rising over their ledge. He sat down and hugged her gently, allowing his own pain to flood over silently.

Anna stiffened. She looked up; terror filled her eyes.

"My fingers. Talus, I cannot feel my fingers!"

Talus let her lean against the wall, twisting to face her.

"No, you broke your arm, but Theos willing, you will heal quickly."

Anna nodded slowly. Talus wondered how she was handling waking to find their friends dead and her arm broken.

Finally, she spoke in a low voice.

"I'll miss them." She paused, swallowing, before continuing. "I have always wondered what breaking a bone feels like. Wait, did you set my arm?"

Talus smiled slightly and shrugged. "Couldn't just leave you to bleed to death."

A smile vaguely resurfaced. "Thanks, I suppose not. So, what's next? Please say it involves finding water." She begged.

Talus shook his head. "It doesn't involve finding water...." Her face fell. "Since water is already discovered."

Anna released a sigh of relief. She jumped to her feet.

"Where is i-it?" She staggered, clutching her head was her good hand. Talus leapt up, placing a steadying hand on her arm. After a minute, she looked up. Her eyes swam, suggesting she had a headache.

"You would think I ran into a cliff recently."

"Really? Wait, you were still conscious?"

"To that point, then I remember nothing after that. But regardless, the water?"

Talus nodded. "Think you can walk?"

Anna didn't respond but took a tentative step forward then another.

"Aye, I reckon so."

"Hurt anywhere else?" Talus inquired.

"Bruised, and I have this nice little headache. Other than that, no."

"Such being the case, water is this way." Talus motioned east.

"So if that was not the case, water would be that way?" Anna made an attempt to smile mischievously, as she pointed west.

Talus shook his head, keeping a perfectly serious face as he replied.

"Any case, water is that direction."

"Any case? Really? What if there was a drought? Would there be water then?"

Talus crossed his arms. "I thought you were thirsty."

"Right." Anna hurried east, intent on finding the water.

<<<<<<<<<<<<<>>>>>>>>>>>>

Her thirst quenched; hunger invaded her senses. A day and a half had passed since that rushed meal just after midnight. She turned from the stream, aiming to ask Talus. Suddenly, it hit her. All of the food was in the packs, which were at the bottom of the sea. Her stomach growled. She caught Talus' sympathetic smile.

"Sorry, we have to climb down before we can find anything for lunch." Talus explained.

"Okay." Anna walked to the edge and crouched. A wave of dizziness hit her as the ground beckoned to her from over two hundred cat's tails below. Anna backed away hastily.

"We have to climb down that?"

Talus nodded.

"How?" Anna asked.

"Well, if you are comfortable with it, I'll climb, and you can piggyback."

Anna was startled.

"Can you climb with me on your back?"

141

"I have no idea, so I thought we would test the hypothesis on the smaller cliffs up here and climb down on a theory." Talus gestured first to the cliffs above them from which the stream flowed, and then to the cliff leading down.

"Well," Anna paused, studying the cliff above. "I am alright with it. Guess we might as well get on with it ere we starve."

"Good point. If you will mount me, we shall give this a try."

"A horse now, are we?" Anna asked, as she wrapped her good arm over Talus' shoulder and around his chest, tucking her broken arm in front of her. She twisted her legs to leave Talus completely free to move. She shut her eyes, better just not to know.

Talus stepped forward, adjusting to the weight change. When he reached the wall, he suggested back to the already deathly still Anna.

"Keep still just like you are doing. Going to climb now."

Her reply was muffled, leaving Talus without the slightest idea what she said. From the tone he guessed it was affirmative.

He quickly found holds and pulled himself up. Anna's extra weight pulled at him, drawing him away from the wall. He stayed low until he was accustomed to the pull.

He ventured higher, grabbing an eighth inch hold. The hand slipped and refused to hoist him. So, he needed larger holds. He tried a fourth inch. Good, he could climb with it.

After several minutes messing around, testing everything he could think of, he returned to the ground and stretched his fingers. Talus spoke back to Anna.

"Ready for the final stretch?"

"Sure." She sounded petrified.

"We will be fine, Theos willing. I haven't fallen off a wall since I was seven."

She did not answer.

Talus sat down on the edge and studied it. Normally he would flip on his stomach to begin climbing but he could not do that, not with Anna's feet around his waist.

Presently, he noted a four-inch ledge two and a half cat's tails below him. With a whispered prayer of thanks, he slipped fractionally forward until his bare toes rested on the ledge. He stood and carefully turned to face the wall. He looked out across the stone one last time, the most dangerous part behind them. Now, the climb awaited.

He followed the ledge until it narrowed enough he could comfortably climb over it.

About halfway down his arms began to burn, but right at that point the cliff smoothed out, leaving him with handholds he would have avoided even by himself.

However, he had no choice, so he ignored the burns and kept his mind on the task at the tips of his fingers.

Time blurred together. Talus repeatedly told his mind not to numb, forcing himself to examine all options. Talus stepped down. His foot slipped. He caught himself with the remaining three limbs still attached to the wall, but not before his foot hit something soft. Sand. Talus stepped off the cliff completely. He grinned, a tired grin but still definitely a grin.

"Anna! We are down!"

She dropped off him and opened her eyes, landing slumped in the sand.

"I am exhausted, and I did not even do anything. How are you?"

"Glad to be down. My arms and legs and fingers will be sore for a couple days, I would guess." Talus paused. "Anna, I just thought of something, we have no means of making a fire which means, unless you are keen on raw flesh, we can't eat meat."

Anna nodded slowly, trying to avoid showing too much disappointment. While she had helped prepare a few raw dishes at the castle, they had none of the proper fixings. And the idea of eating blood turned her stomach.

"Maybe after we get really desperate. Does grass taste good?"

"It might soon." Talus furrowed his brow in thought. "Anna, in Belon as part of my training, I learned about edible mosses and swamp plants. Did you learn anything similar in Garia? Many of the plants here are bound to be in Garia also."

Anna frowned and looked out across the meadows, hoping to spot something familiar. Else she would have to tell Talus that Rocklin was in southern Garia and less than likely to share vegetation. Her eyes latched on a tall thin purple flowered plant a little distance from them. She grinned at Talus and ran eagerly to it.

She crouched next to it, plucking the small leaves that separated the flowers from the long, larger leaves.

Talus caught up to her. He knelt beside her, motioning to the plant.

"What is it?"

Anna smiled happily. "Breakfast. We Garians called it purplette after its flowers, but the Alcasans call it fireweed. They have an interesting story behind the name. However, no one ever told me the whole tale, but I am guessing it had to do with fire."

"An intelligent guess, I reckon. So how do we eat it? I'm starving almost literally."

"Only the young leaves are good for food. With that restriction you may eat anything."

"Really?" Talus raised his eyebrows.

King Eirin tugged on his second boot and stood. He gave his page a smile.

"Matt, after you get something to eat, will you pack our things? I want to leave as soon as breakfast is over."

"We are finally leaving, my lord?" A partly concealed grin appeared on Matt's face. They had made good progress in the last week. Eirin carefully kept his face neutral.

"What? Do you not wish to stay?"

Matt shook his head violently.

"Nope. Perhaps, I had better see what is left in my pack for breakfast."

Matt took a step toward his stuff.

Unlike in Alcasa, Garian pages didn't serve their lords at table. Consequently, the Alcasan pages stayed in their rooms and ate during meals or joined the staff later to eat.

Eirin glared playfully at him.

"Are you trying to get rid of me?"

Matt's eyes widened innocently.

"Would I do a thing like that?"

"Hmm... I will have to think that through over breakfast. But you did say you wanted to leave...."

Matt shrugged, grinning.

Eirin shook his head and opened the door leading to the hall. Lord Henry was standing outside his door. Seeing Eirin, he bowed. "Ah, my lord."

Eirin bowed gracefully in return.

"Were you waiting for me, uncle?"

"No, I was waiting for Matt who doesn't go to breakfast." Heavy sarcasm dripped from his tone.

Eirin grinned as they began the walk to the Greater Hall.

"Funny. You know I am supposed to ask obvious questions, it is part of politeness."

"Obviously."

Whatever had put his uncle in this mood? Wait... Eirin's grin went a little crooked.

"My page was quite pleased when I told him we were leaving today. Think anyone else is pleased?"

"Pleased? Tis hardly *polite* to be pleased to leave your host who feeds, sleeps, and protects you."

"Is that so? Then I travel with a number of impolite people...." Eirin glanced at Lord Henry, but the man kept his eyes on the road ahead.

Eirin couldn't prevent the sly grin that slipped on to his face. They continued in companionable silence until the door was before them. Lord Henry glanced at Eirin, no longer smiling.

"One more silent meal."

"Hey." Eirin protested. "It was not that bad when Lentus was here."

"I suppose. Talus was not here long enough to determine good or bad."

"Nope." Eirin hastened to the table, for once thankful for the silence that would keep his uncle quiet. Lord Henry thought he had let go of his anger a week ago. He had not. He had buried it. No matter what, no reason why, Talus had no right to abandon him!

Chapter 20 Kazofs of Darqin

The sun was dropping behind the tree line far too quickly for Talus' comfort. The day had passed in grief. Through the silent meadows, sorrow for their lost friends had fully taken hold. Neither had made their pain known, yet the very birds uttered no sound in the passing hurt. The crunch of the grass stalks under foot mourned with them.

That had been the day. The forest towered above them. A deep green lingered in its leaves, but hints of gold and red were interwoven in the branches, warning of autumn. Talus and Anna came to an unspoken stop before its wall of color. While the forest itself did not appear frightening, the grandiose majesty of the forest or, perhaps, the tales of horror that had whispered in their childhood from this land made it seem so.

A long silent moment passed, before Talus spoke softly.

"Are you ready? It truly is beautiful."

"Yes." Anna breathed. She looked up at Talus, hidden strokes of fear showed in her eyes. "Do you think we will meet any of its creatures?"

In his mind, a huge shadow arched through the air, knocking the king again from his saddle. The image changed, a sea of dark wolves stared into his head, waiting. Talus blinked the scenes away.

"Let's hope not." His voice came out hoarse.

They stood still for another minute, until Talus realized that Anna was waiting for him to move first. He glanced at her. They were so small against the magnificence of Darqin. Yet what awaited them inside? Fear remained on her face. He was tempted to take her hand....

What? Talus shook his head clear. Where in all Alvar had that thought come from?

"We should probably be moving." Talus remarked distantly.

Darkness had fallen on the forest. Silence reigned. Her foot landed on a twig. Snap! She jumped, her heart in her mouth. *You just broke a stick. It's fine,* she told herself. At least, this time she had not screamed.

A wind whispered through the leaves. They rustled. She wished she could see. In the distance something creaked.

Talus stopped ahead of her. His light blue-green eyes glowed dimly in the shadows. His voice came soft, but unquestionable.

"Anna, we need to travel in the trees. Ready for another piggy-back ride?"

She did not trust herself to speak past the clog of uncertainty in her throat. She nodded and climbed onto Talus. Were they in danger? Why else would Talus want to climb a tree? Her good arm tightened to almost a death grip on Talus' chest.

Talus' amused voice filtered into her fear.

"Calm down, Anna. Nothing will happen to us outside of Theos' will. And I'm sure you are a veteran at facing death at this point."

Leaning her head against Talus' shoulder, she let herself be comforted by the reminder that Theos has a plan. Through verses she memorized from the Logos and Talus' words, her heart was refocused on the Someone stronger than the creatures of Darqin.

A starling thought struck her: in Belon, possession of the Logos would not carry the death penalty! What would it be like to read it? So many more attributes of Theos, thoughts, concepts, and tales almost within her grasp. She whispered to Talus.

"Will I be able to get the Logos in Belon?"

"What? Yes. How come?" Talus answered, puzzled.

"I have never read it. All I know is what my parents and shepherd taught me. It's illegal in Garia."

"Oh, guess that makes sense, considering. I will look into finding a Garian copy when we reach Elnola."

Anna wriggled. What would it really be like?

"However," Talus added. "You have to stay still, or we will never arrive at the city."

"Sorry." She forced herself still, though hopes and excitement raced through her blood.

Three minutes later, Talus dragged them up into a two cat's tails wide branch about thirty-three cat's tails above the ground. He crouched.

"Are you comfortable with this height?"

Anna nodded. "Aye. I used to climb trees all the time... at home. Note, they were a bit smaller." She climbed off Talus and leaned on the trunk.

A wolf howled.

"So... now what?" She asked.

Talus glanced at her. "You asked that a lot."

Anna started to protest before Talus added.

"It really depends on how well you can see."

"Not particularly well, but I might be able to make do."

"I see. In that case, we are going to sit here while I attempt to remember the Zofish word for 'help.'"

"Zofish?"

"Language of the Kazofs." Talus answered distractedly.

"Oh, of course."

Anna slid her back down the trunk to a sitting position. She drew her knees to her chest, now that they were not moving the breeze squirmed its way to her skin with icy promises.

Talus was thinking, which, unintentionally, made him singularly nonfunctional for conversation. She needed a way to distract herself from the cold. A shadow shifted below her. Well, might as well count wolves or the shadows that could possibly be wolves. She shivered, wondering how big they truly were.

Suddenly Talus leapt to his feet. The glimmer of shadowed moonlight reflected off his twin blades as he drew them.

He murmured. "Anna, we have company."

On a branch maybe fifteen cat's tails out beyond Talus, an enormous catlike shape crouched, waiting. For a horrifying minute, its eyes met hers. Flaming wild green seemed to search into her heart.

A broken cry slipped from Talus' lips. It was like a song, a song begging for aid and full of pain and weakness.

"Ahh... achazi."

Anna was certain she must have imagined it, but something akin to amusement lit in the cat's green eyes for a moment. Then it was gone.

The black panther pounced. Its claws snatched the air as Talus leapt back. Talus began to swing one sword high at the cat's neck, the other toward its chest. The swords never made contact.

A deep majestic voice rolled softly through the trees. It was a song of peace, though the words were foreign. It melted hostility. It soothed heartaches.

The wild light left the great cat's eyes. It leapt from the branch across the forest floor with a delighted meow resembling a house cat who wishes to be cuddled.

Anna and Talus watched in silent wonder as the cat approached the huge man, whom Anna guessed to be a little over twelve cat's tails. Blue stone embedded in his sleeveless over-robe illuminated the forest with a gentle glow. His silver-gray hair fell to his chest, framing a rich, smooth, and ancient face. His sea blue eyes were sharp yet gentle with memories.

Emitting deep purrs, the panther rubbed up to the Kazof, its back just shorter than his chest. He stroked its head and neck, and, at its insistence, smoothed the fur under its chin, causing the very forest to shake with the strength of the purrs.

Wolves also bound from the shadows, nearly bowling the giant over. The Kazof paused in his song to laugh. Somehow it reminded Anna of the roar of Rocklin Falls and yet of dandelions in the wind. The song resumed, as he took the time to ruffle the fur on the head of each wolf who came to him.

Beside her, Talus spoke softly. "He calls each by name."

Anna was too awed by the song and the scene before her to respond immediately. After a long moment she glanced up at him.

"What does he say?"

Talus stared into the clearing. "He speaks love to them. He soothes their cares. He examines their hurts. Like with that wolf a minute ago, he inspected its paw and told it he was glad it had healed."

"Do they answer him?"

Talus shrugged. "It is said that Kazofs can read an animal's body language as well as the tone of its cry."

Anna nodded and studied the peaceful scene. After a second, she asked. "Do they understand him?"

Talus shrugged again. "It seems so."

They lapsed into silence. The song rose and fell until all the animals but the panther had left. Then the great man turned to them.

Anna met his eyes and stilled. It was like looking into an ocean untroubled by passing time, yet somewhere in the depths a fleeting shadow lurked. The Kazof bowed his head and raised his staff in what must have been a form of greeting. Talus gave the Elerin salute. Right. She jumped hastily to her feet and curtsied.

"Ahh... Zakox, cuxe, Azifa. Kazofa, xisah Zachassos, Aka. Kizex AEka Afika." The Kazof's song again fell gently on the air.

Talus glanced at Anna. "He greets us and informs us his name is Zachasso. He wishes to know our races. If you don't mind, I will give him our names also."

She nodded. Talus began a song like the Kazof's but only tenor instead of five octaves lower.

"Ahh... Zakox, cuxa, AEzifa. Elerina, xisak Talos, Aka. Humana, xisak Annas, Aka. Kachax Asasak Achecha."

A couple things became more apparent the more she listened to this tongue. First, the vowels are all short. And, second, it seemed the consonants were pronounced with a far softer quality.

"Ahh... kak AEcoza."

Talus turned to her with a grin. "He's taking us somewhere!"

"Well…, it must be *some* place." Anna said dryly, hiding a smile.

Talus grin twisted, mixing in a grimace. However, before he could answer, Zachasso sang softly to the panther. With a single leap, it landed on the branch directly behind them. It leaned forward. Before Anna could understand its intent, it picked them both up by the backs of their shirts. Anna might have screamed if the shirt was not choking her as it jumped the three and thirty cat's tails to the forest floor. She was sure she would remember the rush of the rising ground for years after.

The cat set them carefully before the Kazof. He knelt to reach their level.

"Ahh… cuxe, Aksixha. Elochsa Axhsoca chusfex AEkishsa."

"Ahh… Aeksixma. Ksosicas, Aka." Talus replied to the unknown statement.

"What did he say?" Anna asked.

"He apologized for the rough ride. Apparently Elochsa, the panther, thinks everything has scruffs." Talus answered.

The Kazof stood slowly and beckoned to them. They followed him. Anna smiled, content. The blue light of the great man's over-robe enabled her to see. Amazing how after being deprived, one could be content simply with light and safety. Not that contentment was dependent on the situation.

Ahead Zachasso turned onto a new path. Talus, however, walked straight into a tree.

Anna stared at him. "You know, I am the one who can't see in the dark, right?"

Talus stepped back from the tree and shrugged. "Perhaps I was thinking too hard or, maybe, I did it on purpose."

Anna looked at him, confused and rather amused. "Why would one do that?"

Talus just grinned at her.

After a long second, he said. "Probably shouldn't fall too far behind." He took off after the fading light. Anna shook her head, still confused, and followed him.

Talus was concerned. While Kazofs were reputedly hospitable, they were not fond of the other races. Distrust lingered from their dark years. Somehow, he needed to convince Zachasso to help. The idea of wandering through Darqin in search of another Kazof made the possibility of being eaten uncomfortably high.

A steep hill appeared before them, but Zachasso continued straight toward it. Pushing aside long tendrils of an ivy-like plant, he opened the huge door concealed behind it. A soft yellow-blue light flowed into the forest.

The giant motioned them inside. The doorway revealed a large room. To the left, two doors led to other rooms. On his right was the main part of the room, a living-room with two enormous deep green couches and a coffee table. In the back was an open-hearth fire, cupboards and counters, and a large table.

A female Kazof, who had been seated on one of the couches, rose as they entered. Two small Zoflings playing on the floor stilled and regarded them with wide eyes.

Next to Talus, Anna murmured. "Everything is so big."

Talus grinned, then rubbed his still fur-less chin. "Suppose it's a bit larger than normal...."

Zachasso's wife came over and took his hands, leaving his staff to lean against the wall. "Dear, there you are. I was beginning to think the children would have to go to bed without you." Her song paused. "Zachasso, who are our guests?"

He kissed one of her hands then turned toward Talus and Anna. "The Elerin is Talus who can speak our tongue, and the human is Anna."

Zachasso's wife spread her hands and inclined her head. "I am honored to meet you, Talus of Belon, and your friend, Anna of the humankind."

"The honor is ours, lady Kazof." Talus saluted.

He stifled a yawn. Now that they were safe the day was catching up with him.

One of the Zoflings had come up beside him, standing almost equal in height. Talus smiled at her. She cocked her head.

"Why are you so short?" She asked.

Before Talus could answer, Zachasso cut in. "Kessicha, time you and your brother were in bed."

The Zofling's shoulders slumped. "Yes, papa."

She glanced back at Talus and Anna before trudging to her bedroom. Her brother caught up to her and whispered. "Way to go. Now we can't observe."

"I know." She replied, dejected.

Talus watched them disappear through the first door. It did not surprise him that Zachasso had sent them to bed; Kazofs believed the other races would have bad influences on their children.

Anna's stomach growled. Talus glanced at her, careful not to laugh. She appeared mortified. Zachasso smiled down at Anna, before looking at his wife.

"Surely we shall not allow our guests to go hungry?"

She shook her head. "Certainly not. Come, my friends, to the table and be satisfied."

Talus watched her collect a variation of fruits and vegetables. Right, Kazofs did not eat meat. Anna's voice broke into his analysis.

"So... Talus, are we sitting at that table? Because it's a little large."

"Aye." Talus paused, suddenly confused. "How did you know we were eating at a table?"

Anna appeared puzzled, but with a twinkle to her eye. "Well... perhaps the hand-motions and our hostess preparing food may have clued me in." She smiled sweetly.

"Right, there is that." Talus studied the chairs. Each was four cat's tails high, but a crossbar connected the legs half up. Easy climb. No problem there. Maybe Anna was referring to the fact-

"Wait, I think we can kneel on the chairs to reach the table!"

Anna hurried over to the nearest seat. She stepped up onto the bar before swinging her right leg up on the chair and scrambling into position. Talus grinned to himself, though rather contritely. He was going to offer to help, but she seemed to have managed.

Talus climbed into his seat and sat back on his feet. The female Kazof placed a platter of fruit and vegetables in front of them. Including celery. Talus swallowed, trying not to laugh. Poor Kalrick.

How were they? How upset had King Eirin been? Would Kalrick still be his friend when he returned? Was the king still mad? He could not be, right? After all, it had been a while since he had left.

"You going to eat the rest of that? Are you lost to the world?" Anna's words broke into his train of questions.

"What? No, I was thinking."

"Hmm,when you are done, I think Zachasso wants to talk to you." Anna noted.

Talus glanced towards the watching Kazof. Seemed so.

"Right, thanks." Talus picked up a few blueberries and popped them in his mouth. While being careful not to appear hurried, as that would insult the host, he finished his meal in a matter of minutes. Once he had hopped down from the chair, Zachasso beckoned him. Talus' heart gave an involuntary stutter. How was he going to convince the giant to help? What if he decided not to aid them?

Zachasso took a seat on the couch and motioned for them to do likewise. After a minute or so of polite conversation, Zachasso asked.

"When would you like to leave in the morning? It would be preferable if you would leave before the children wake."

"Your best time is our best time." Talus replied. "Anna is a fugitive from Garia for her faith in Theos and because of my connection to the Alcasan court I have no doubt she would be considered a fugitive there as well. Because of this, I am taking her to Belon. Though we are already indebted to you for your hospitality, I would make another request of you." Talus paused but the Kazof remained silent. "I would ask that you aid us by arranging to pass us hand to hand to the southern border of Darqin."

Talus held his breath. He tried to guess the answer by the man's face, but it was uncertain and shadowed. At length, Zachasso replied. "My people have not had dealings with your people since the humans and Talrins enslaved us and the Elerins and Fumins refused to aid us."

Talus furrowed his brow, that was close to three hundred years ago. Of course, Kazofs often lived to five hundred... but still, it was ancient history. "Sir, we are both too young to remember those days. Surely you can not hold the wrongs of our ancestors against us? Even if you would, will you not consider that others have suffered, still suffer. My father, Anna was scheduled to burn at dawn only a couple weeks ago."

Zachasso turned suddenly and met Talus' eyes. The intense pain radiating from the giant's eyes startled him into silence. His heart was caught in an unknown wrenching pain. Then Zachasso looked away and stood. "Those who escaped the flames of men should consider themselves blessed. My younger brother burned in those red flames. However, I will think on your plea and give you my answer in the morning. We have no guest rooms. Make yourselves comfortable here."

Zachasso hurried from the room, followed by his wife. Talus flopped onto his side on the couch. He stared out across the green cushions. Now he had to wait until morning. After a minute, he shrugged. No point in worrying about it. With a quick whispered prayer, he sat up. Anna had her head tilted slightly, looking at him funny.

Talus felt red fever come into his cheeks without any fragment of an idea why. "Um... we are sleeping in here..." he stammered. "And..." What did he want to say about the conversation? Wouldn't it be easier for her not to know? But didn't she deserve to be aware of the possibility they might be on their own in the forest again, in case it became a reality? "Zachasso has not decided if he will help us yet. So we may have to wander around and find another Kazof tomorrow."

Anna nodded slowly. "And he might help us, and we may not need to. I think you forgot to mention that." She pointed at some blankets on the back of the couches. "Those look fun to get down."

"Sure."

At that moment, the Kazof woman reappeared, her arms full of medical supplies. These she placed on the table. Turning to them, she asked Talus in Zofish. "May I see your friend's arm? It looks to be hurt."

Talus relayed the question to Anna who nodded. As she followed the Kazof to the table, she glanced back. "Enjoy the blankets!" She grinned.

Talus mocked a horrified face, before innocently adding. "Enjoy having your arm cleaned and tended."

Anna grimaced. Having achieved the desired effect, Talus turned his mind to the task at hand or, rather, overhead. He climbed onto the couch, which held one of the blankets on its back. Hmm... well, it hung down a little. He pulled himself up the soft back to the top where the blanket was sitting. Crouching behind it, he shoved it, the heavy material gave but did not move. Maybe he could pick it up? Uh, no. It was too large. What if he could get enough of it hanging down? Then the rest would fall of its own accord. Coming around to the side of the blanket, he grabbed a corner and tugged. The corner came up suddenly, lighter than anticipated. Talus stumbled backward, falling into open air.

He hit the couch four feet below, still holding the corner. Slowly, before his eyes, half the blanket unrolled itself to hang down, looming over Talus. He tugged on the corner. Bad idea. Gravity won and the dark folds jumped on him. Everything went black. Talus wriggled. The entrance could not be too far away. However, the more he squirmed, the more the blanket unfolded. Cold sweat trickled down his back. He could not escape! No! Please. There had to be a way out. He rolled around. Into empty space. A small scream passed his lips as he fell. He hit the floor on his back. He forced the panic down, trying to clear his mind enough to come to logical terms with the situation. The darkness clutching him was suffocatingly heavy. The coffee table was around here somewhere.

The material began to rise. It was moving! Upward! Talus wriggled free of the last grasps. As soon as it was clear, he leapt to his feet. He smiled, winded, up at his rescuer. The female Kazof's eyes were filled with amusement. Talus saluted. "My thanks to you, lady Kazof. It is... a horrifying experience to be buried in an overly large blanket."

She smiled softly. "Welcome back to the world of light, master Elerin." She folded the blanket longwise and laid it out on the couch. "There you are. May I suggest keeping your head clear of the fold?" She added with a twinkle in her eye.

"I will keep the idea in mind." Talus returned; his body having calmed enough to permit a grin.

She gave a musical laugh before moving to the love seat. She took the blanket off its back and spread it out. "There. Now, I'll finish tending to Anna's arm, and you two can be off to sleep." She headed briskly back to the table.

Talus crossed his arms up on the coffee table. A delicate design in the leaves on the fern in the center caught his attention. It seemed to swirl and dance. He started to pull himself up but stopped. His mom always said feet don't belong on the coffee table. That probably put climbing around on it off limits. Talus smiled distantly, remembering his father intentionally placing feet on it just for her, he said. His mother had always rolled her eyes and walked away, but Talus had caught her laughing in the kitchen right after one of the more recent episodes.

Their hostess bound up Anna's arm and, wishing them blessed sleep, returned to her room.

"Talus?" Anna asked as they settled into their makeshift beds.

"Aye?"

"What happens when we reach Belon?"

Talus drew a slow breath. "I don't know exactly. I intend to leave you at my parents. They won't turn you away even if they or the Belon lord don't agree with my actions."

"Is there a possibility they won't?"

The question forced Talus to consider the possibility. "I just don't know. I don't really want to worry about it right now."

Anna gave a nod but said no more. The night he had left, he had thought about strain relations between Alcasa and Garia, potentially. But recently he had begun to wonder if his actions would cause tension between Belon and Alcasa. Would the Belon lord agree with his actions?

Talus released a sigh. Why did everything have so many questions? Well, one thing at a time, right?

As he pulled the covers to his chin before he fell to sleep, he begged Theos to soften Zachasso's heart and aid them.

Chapter 21 Return to Belon

Talus' prayer was answered. For two weeks, they were passed hand to hand from Kazof to Kazof. Now they again stood on the border of Darqin, but it was behind them. A huge mountain of rock laid directly in front of them. To their left, carved steps circled away around the mountain, becoming visible again hundreds of cat's tails above them. Engravings etched in the stone left no space of the mountain bare, while on little ledges, it seemed gardens of flowers grew. However, it was neither their path nor right to enter the Council Rock.

In the evening, the second day after leaving Darqin, a familiar sight laid before Talus. However, it had different sorts of complications than they had yet crossed paths with. Talus turned to Anna with a forced grin.

"Now all we have to do is pray the Border Commander around is not a stickler for tradition. Because if so then I have to run to Hangnol and ask permission from the Belon lord while you hang out here for six days."

Talus watched Anna shiver. The idea of staying with strange people probably was not all that appealing.

"Well-" Anna started.

"That's a deep subject." Talus interrupted, expression blank.

Anna half glared at him. "Old joke, Talus. Where do we find this commander person? Because it's getting late."

Talus nodded and pointed up into the Oklmar trees. "I believe that is a boardwalk. It should lead us to an outpost where an Ellinp of Elerins stays for two weeks."

"Boardwalk? I thought you ran through the trees. And what's an Ellinp?"

Talus could see the confusion on her face.

"Typically, we do run from branch to branch, but sometimes when the trees are sparse, we use them for easy movement, they are also handy for people with broken arms. An Ellinp is a group of fourteen to eighteen Elerin warriors, a lieutenant, and a commander."

Anna nodded slowly, processing it all. She shrugged. "Wel-so, what are we waiting for?"

Her smile looked painful, which gave Talus the impression she was scared. For a moment the urge to take her hand returned. Talus pushed the weird idea away. He shrugged. "Nothing."

<<<<<<<<<<<<<>>>>>>>>>>>

Anna followed Talus around a corner. She paused. Was this it? The boardwalk led to a large treehouse. Another Elerin was sitting on the porch, his feet dangling over the side. His black hair was shorter than Talus' and he seemed older. The second he noticed them, he jumped to his feet. "Talus?"

Anna watched as Talus' eyes widened.

"Commander Valoris?"

The men stared at each other for a full three seconds, before hastily remembering to salute. Something of a grin appeared on the commander's face. He asked something in what Anna guessed to be Elerin.

Talus glanced noticeably at her before replying in Garian. "It's something of a long story."

"Perhaps, if you don't mind, we can hear it later? For now," Valoris' grin took on a mischievous quality. "Who's this young lady? Did you fall in love already?"

A deep cherry-red smote Talus' face. "What? Um.... No? I mean, no!" Talus drew a deep breath, and the color faded a bit. "This is Anna of Garia. Anna, Commander Valoris."

Valoris, who had looked like he was trying far too hard not to laugh, regained his composure and saluted.

"Greetings, Anna of Garia. Might I ask how you got stuck with this fellow?"

Anna paused then smiled. "He was the only one in Ketlin who could not stomach watching me burn to death."

Her light nonchalant tone gave the commander pause. Finally, he nodded. "It is good to hear, lady." He looked to Talus thoughtfully. "King Eirin may not be too far gone if he gave you permission to bring her here."

Talus looked away and Anna winced. She knew Talus feared his people would question his decision. She watched determination gather on his face, hardening his features. But time did not permit an answer.

Behind them someone yelled, "Talus!" She and Talus spun around. An Elerin slammed full into Talus, knocking him to the floor. Talus pushed the other Elerin off and jumped up.

"Congratulations, Dalus." Talus was grinning. "You are still running into things."

Dalus grinned back. "You enjoy running into things too. Like that time right before we became Adventurers...."

Talus turned importantly to Anna. "Won't you tell this ruffian I don't walk into things?"

Anna obliged, making a disapproving frown surface. "Look here, Elerin. I have never seen Talus run into anything, except trees which he always claimed to do on purpose."

Dalus stared at her until he realized what she actually said. When he did, he could not stop laughing. From a few feet away, an amused voice broke in.

"Still tree-hugging, eh, Talus?"

Talus jumped. "Wait, Jornus? What are you doing here?"

"Border guarding." This new Elerin replied all too seriously.

"Not what I meant."

"Oh really? No? Perhaps, I asked to be placed on the Alcasan border to keep an eye on an apprentice I had recently."

Talus looked away. And a hint of concern crossed the features of who must have been Talus' mentor. Jornus seemed about to speak, when Dalus broke in. He appeared very close to bouncing on his toes.

"Talus, won't you tell us why you're here?"

Talus shook his fears away and grinned. "Anna got herself into a bit of religious trouble in Garia. So, I thought I would leave her with my parents, providing the Belon lord and my father agree."

"I see. So... Talus, you finally managed to fall in love?" Grinning, Dalus unknowingly repeated Commander Valoris' question. Part of Anna wanted to giggle, but the other part felt on the edge of embarrassment.

Talus had much better control of his face color this time. He shrugged. "Na, just friends." Talus paused and looked to Valoris. "Commander, would it be permissible to take Anna into Belon without written permission at this time, which I will obtain once at Elnola? I will vouch for her."

The movement on the tree-porch stilled. Anna held her breath. These Elerins seemed like nice people, but she did not want to be stuck with them for six days. She sensed someone watching her. She looked up and found herself staring into the depths of the commander's cyan eyes. She held the penetrating gaze. An odd thought drifted across her brain. What if some of their people saw who you are and what you have done? It certainly felt like it.

After a long, short time, Valoris nodded to Talus. "Might I suggest spending the night? The two of you have a long day tomorrow."

Wait, he had just said- She grinned. Talus saluted, no less pleased. "Thanks, Commander."

After that she seemed to fade into the background, while Talus was swamped with every kind of question his old friends could contrive.

<<<<<<<<<<<<>>>>>>>>>>>>

Talus leaned against the wall next to Dalus after supper. He glanced around. Lieutenant Rhemus was talking to Anna. He had been torn all evening. He wanted to hang out with his friends, but he did not want her to be bored or lonely either.

"So, Talus. Find anyone to fix your bow problems?" Dalus asked quietly.

"No, I haven't used it in a while."

"You're saying you are rusty on being bad? You can't just not practice for a couple months! Please tell me you have kept up on the other weapons?"

Talus swallowed. The words hurt. And the only answer he had. "Had a sword-fight on a pitiful raft in a storm two weeks ago." He forced a half smile.

Dalus' eyes widened startled. "On a raft in a storm?" He repeated. "Where? How? Did you survive?"

Talus laughed. "No, I completely died." But then he stopped abruptly, people had died. Lost. Buried in a watery grave.

"Talus?" Dalus asked. "You alright?"

"In time. Some friends we made died in that storm."

"I'm so sorry." Dalus put his hand on Talus' shoulder for a moment. After a time, a smirk grew on Dalus' face. "Talus, have you ever seen Jornus shoot a bow?"

Talus thought back. "Maybe a couple times. Why?"

Dalus grinned. He shouted across the room. "Hey Jornus! Talus and I just remembered we haven't seen much of your bow skills. And considering...."

All conversation stopped in its tracks. Jornus had his back to them. He must have heard, but he made no reply. Talus glanced at Dalus. Thud! An arrow slammed into Dalus' shirt sleeve, pinning him to the wall. Talus looked back to Jornus, as his former mentor slung his bow back over his shoulder. Jornus turned to Valoris. "I apologize for the breach of protocol."

Valoris waved it off. "He asked for it."

Jornus let a hint of a smirk show. "Won't argue that, Commander."

Talus desperately wanted to laugh but was not quite certain if that would be a safe idea.

"Talus? A little help. He stuck nearly a fourth of the arrow in the wood." Dalus pleaded.

"I don't know, Dalus. I'll ask Jornus."

Talus crossed the room without waiting for a reply. "Mas- Jornus?" His former mentor turned to him.

"Yes?"

159

"Mind if I let Dalus out? If we can get the arrow out, that is. It is pretty well in there."

Jornus laughed. "Of course, Talus. You did not really need to ask permission, you know. If you can't pull it out, you might be able to push it through...."

"Oh, right. True. Who do you think would like the spy hole more, Commander Valoris or the rest of us?"

Jornus shrugged. "I think there are a number of rascals who would enjoy innocent spying."

"So you're saying us?"

Jornus shrugged. "Most Elerins I have met are mischievous."

Talus let a half scowl twist his face. "Inclusive."

"I can't pick one or the other if both parties are a liability."

Talus laughed. "Suppose so."

A knife buried itself in the floor next to Talus' foot. He stared at it. What in Alvar?

"I think someone wants to be freed." Jornus hinted.

"Oh, right." Talus scooped up Dalus' knife and headed back to him. "Sorry, got caught up in a conversation." He said upon reaching him.

"Yes, have nice chat and leave your own friend stranded by an arrow." Dalus pouted.

Talus smirked. "Why not?"

He grasped the arrow and pulled. So much for that. Stealing the pillow from the nearest bed, he set it against the end of the arrow. The pillow protecting his hand from the end of the arrow, he placed one hand there and grasped the middle with his other hand. He slammed into the pillow. And met no resistance. His outside hand smashed almost to the wall, crushing his other hand. A faint cry escaped. He drew his hand out and opened and closed his fingers. He grimaced a grin at Dalus.

"Apparently he shot almost clear through the wall."

Dalus smiled sympathetically. "Guess he's a good shot. How's the hand?"

"Never needed my right hand anyway."

"Right...." Dalus drew out the word. "Of course, you don't need your dominant hand. Who would?"

Talus smiled and removed the fletching from the arrow, releasing Dalus. He stepped away from the wall like it was liable to ensnare him with another arrow. Talus laughed.

"Scared of the wall now?"

"No." Dalus shook his head.

Talus smirked.

"Just had been leaning on it far too long. Hungry?" Dalus pointed toward the eating area, changing the subject.

"Aye, but... I still think you're scared of the wall."

Dalus gave a long-suffering sigh. "I forgot what having you around is like. You're leaving in the morning, right?"

"Aye, I see how it is." Talus stepped away, starting across the room. Dalus caught up with him at a tray of Tongath sausages and blueberry cheese.

"But I have missed you. It's weird being the only one without a partner to jest with."

"I'm sure they'll find someone else for you." Talus started, but Dalus shook his head.

"Nope, I'm gonna hang out with Jornus and keep an eye on you. Now that you're back, I can return that couch."

Talus choked, trying to laugh and swallow at the same time.

<<<<<<<<<<<<<>>>>>>>>>>>>>

The next morning, Talus and Anna had followed the boardwalk into the swamp. Talus stopped as they reached a corner that would take them in the wrong direction. He turned to Anna. "Looks like it's time for tree dancing."

"Okay." Anna nodded. "How does it work?"

"Balance." Talus grinned. "I'll try to keep some left- or right-hand branches available if you need them though."

"If?" Anna questioned.

Talus shrugged. "Follow me. Sometimes the branch may lower under your weight, so be prepared."

She nodded. Talus stepped onto the branch, following it to the trunk. He turned to see where she was. She grinned from right behind him. "I might be able to walk across a nice fat branch, you never know. It might be really hard."

"Good for you." Talus laughed at the funny tone of her voice. "Well, come on. I am sure we'll find thin branches before long."

"No particular need to rush into that though, right?" Anna asked, the playful smile having slipped some.

Talus shook his head. "No, not unless we find a line of young trees. Now, time to change trees." He studied the possible crossings around them. Immediately in front was a five cat's tail jump. Fun, but definitely out. Hmm. There. That one would do. He climbed up a couple branches, Anna following with ease. But Talus seemed to remember her saying something about climbing trees with her brother.

It was a half cat's tail step at the closest passing points of the selected branches. She managed easily. They followed the branch to the trunk and the next branch to the next branch to the next trunk and so forth.

Talus glanced back. Anna looked so determined. He stepped on air and lost his balance. Apparently, she also looked distracting.

He fell. He purposely did not grab the branch he had been on, not sure if Anna could handle the shaking. He landed on a branch some ten cat's tails down. Anna peered down at him, eyes wide.

"Are you alright?"

"Aye." Oddly, he could feel color coming to his dark tan cheeks. He shrugged and sort of grinned up at her. "Just got a reminder to watch my step."

"Okay." Anna returned her attention to walking. Talus followed the branch and met Anna at the trunk.

Anna balanced down the branch to the swamp below. She smiled to herself. In the last four days, she had gained confidence in tree walking. Now she could watch more than the branch beneath her feet. The swamp trees glowed in the sun; their leaves arrayed in red with silver lining. She had fallen into the swamp waters twice. The first time Talus had jumped in after her, only to discover she could swim far better than him. The weirdest thing was sleeping in a tree the night before last when they could not find a Tongath Hunter's cabin to stay in. Talus had strung a couple hammocks, which he had apparently gotten from Commander Valoris, between two branches with nothing but water several cat's tails below. Talus had shown her how to hang drop into the hammock. He had made it look so easy. Jump into a piece of cloth swaying in the breeze. When she tried it, she had completely missed the hammock. That was the second of her falls into the swamp water. The next time Talus had jumped into her hammock to balance it for her. Nothing had convinced her to get out until morning since she did not think she could get back in.

She looked ahead as she reached the level of the water. Gray stone rose some distance in front of her. After a second, she realized it was a wall, but the blocks used to build it seemed almost to be the size of peasant homes back in Garia. Where was the gate? Did not it make more sense to stay in the trees until they found the gate?

"So how does another piggy-back ride sound?" Talus paused. "This is the Hangnolin Wall, the last defense of the heart of Belon. This is the end of the swamp and probably the last you will see of it until you can climb on your own." Talus grinned. "Hopefully we can meet with the Belon lord around seven bells for your permission slip and then head home."

The excitement on Talus' face made Anna's heart ache for her own home. A lump formed in her throat. More than eight weeks had passed since that day when she was ripped from them. Tears clouded her vision. She drew a deep breath and pushed it all away. She did not want Talus to know, not right now. She would see them again. She had to believe that. Putting on something related to a smile, she asked.

"Hadn't we better be going?"

Talus grinned. "Was just going to ask you something similar." He had not noticed. She released a sigh. Talus continued. "So, see the log leading to the wall? It's not secured to anything. And I don't really know if this will work with you on me, so, uh, if we get wet, make for the wall."

She nodded. "Okay." Talus crouched and she put her good arm around his neck, wrapping her legs around him as he stood. She sensed Talus draw a slow breath before stepping on the log. He leaned forward slightly to balance her weight. She hardly dared to breathe. Not that she really minded the times she had fallen in the swamp in the past, but it was a pain to dry everything.

"Whew." Talus let out his breath. "That wasn't bad. Should sword-fight out here on fallen logs sometime."

Anna raised her head. "Sword-" The slight motion upset their balance. They lurched sideways. The log rolled from under Talus' feet. Anna watched his hands tear from the stone the moment before they went under.

Anna let go of Talus and pushed to the surface. Once her head found air, she coughed up the swamp water she had inhaled. A second later Talus emerged, gasping. He moved to the wall. And looked back at Anna. "We need to get out of here!"

"What's-" Anna stopped as she watched Talus place a hand on the wall. Blood already visibly oozed, though the hand had just left water.

"Talus! What happened?" Anna gasped, swimming over to the wall.

Talus shrugged, looking down. "Nothing much. Just sliced my pointing finger at the first joint." He commented as he held up his right hand. "I can still climb, I think. But we need to get out of here before a Tongath shows up."

"Shouldn't you wrap it? Otherwise, you might slip on the blood."

"Good idea." Talus dug around the pack Commander Valoris had given him with his left until he found a strip of soft soaked material. Talus closed his pack one-handedly and held up the cloth. No way he could wrap it and hold on to the wall, Anna thought. She looked around. The log would help. "Talus, what if we used the log to keep us up while I wrap your finger?"

"Sounds good." Talus replied, already swimming toward it. "We have got to hurry though." He urged.

Tongath alligators, right. Talus had told her some about them in the last few days.

Anna swam up to the log and rested her healing broken arm on it and took Talus' right hand and the piece of cloth. She twisted it up and down around the finger. Thankfully, she could move her fingers now.

163

"Tie it quick!" Talus stared past her. Anna did so though it would have been better to go around a couple more times. "On my back, now!" Talus shouted, pushing away from the log to the wall. Anna barely got her arm around Talus before he started climbing. She twisted her legs around under his bag, trying desperately not to kick the wall.

A roar bellowed behind her. She glanced down and screamed. A long mouth snapped just under Talus' foot. The brownish green creature placed a foot on the wall.

Chapter 22 Whole New World

Its jagged white teeth reached up. This time when they closed, Anna was sure Talus must have felt them touch.

"Anna." Talus spoke far more calmly than Anna would have thought possible. "Don't look at it. I need you to stay still."

"Sorry!" Anna swallowed. What if they had fallen? She rested her head on Talus' shoulder and forced herself to remain still. The creature roared repeatedly at them before silence overtook the swamp. She heard a whispered sigh escape Talus. Anna risked a glance up. They still had so far to go. Time passed. Every now and then she could make out Talus muttering to himself. "Keep going." "Almost there." "Hmm, bad place." "Is this a crack or a crevice?" Why did that matter? Anna wondered. "Don't stub the finger, need these nine." He was going slow. Eventually, Anna realized the race at the bottom must have zapped his strength.

Seconds added to seconds, minutes to minutes. Finally, Talus called out and she sensed they had stopped.

"Friend, give us a hand. My Garian friend has a broken arm."

Anna raised her head and discovered she could see over the wall. Another Elerin grinned at her. "Miss, if you will give me your good arm, I'll help you over the wall."

Not wanting to release Talus before this Elerin was holding her arm, she nodded towards her left arm. "That's my good arm."

He gripped her arm firmly and asked. "Do you mind if I touch you under your other shoulder?"

Anna shook her head. "I'll be alright."

He slipped his hand under her sling. "Okay, release your legs."

He pulled her up and set her gently on her feet. He turned back and started to ask. "Do you want-"

But Talus was on the wall. He grinned. "I'll manage." He paused. "I am Talus. This is Anna."

"Justus, son of Amus. Wait, you are the translator in Alcasa? Son of Valnis?"

"Yeah, sorry, been meeting too many new non-Elerins, I guess."

"What are you doing here? Did King Eirin try to kill you?"

Talus shook his head. "He might when I return. No, I am here to see the Belon lord."

"Oh well, then I won't keep you."

"Thanks, but do you mind if we rest a minute before heading down?" Talus asked.

"No, of course not." Justus paused. "If... if you promise not to tell. I'll send you down in the basket. It would be way easier than carrying her down."

Talus asked eagerly. "When was the last time your Commander came through?"

"About half a bell ago. So, we should be fine." He grinned.

"Sweet. How does a basket ride sound, Anna?"

Anna frowned slightly, wondering. "Is it illegal?"

Talus and Justus reddened.

"Not officially. Learners sneak rides all the time. And they do officially allow injured people to use them. Thus, if you were caught it would be perfectly permissible."

Anna nodded. It was their country and their rules. "Okay."

Talus and Justus grinned at each other like little boys.

"Right this way." Justus said. Anna followed the Elerins to a large basket attached to cables and pulleys. Talus motioned to it. "We'll hold it while you climb in."

They steadied the basket, keeping it on the wall until she sat down. They pushed it off. Her heart accelerated as they began to lower her. Distantly, like in the back of her mind, she heard Justus ask if they had any problem with a Tongath, since he had heard one some little time before they showed up. Suddenly, she realized nothing, but the basket separated her from the ground almost two hundred feet below. She drew several breaths slowly. It did not calm her. Adrenaline pulsed through her body. This was safe, right? Of course it was, the reasonable side said. Talus would not have put her on if it was not.

She looked out over the tops of short stubby trees. In the distance they gave way to plains. To her left she thought she could make out a city. She reached the ground and climbed out. She waved up, though not entirely sure if they could see her.

"You're a Garian, right?"

Anna jumped. She spun around. An elderly Elerin stood there. Would he be mad about the basket thing?

"Er, yes, sir."

"Well, well, where did my manners go? I am Thatus, son of Albanus." He saluted.

"Anna." She curtsied. What did females do in Belon? Did they curtsy too? Or salute like Talus? Suddenly, she felt scared. What didn't she know?

166

Thatus? The name sounded familiar.

"Have I heard of you before? Are you a friend of Talus, maybe?"

Thatus smiled. "Smart girl. Would that make you a friend of Talus, son of Valnis, then?"

"Yes, sir. Talus is up there." She pointed.

"I see. Then you may connect my name to Alcasa and the position your friend holds."

Anna paused. "Wait, you were the translator injured in the war!"

"Indeed. Now let's see how Talus will explain himself." He gave her another smile before a stern expression covered his face.

"Are... we in trouble?" Anna questioned tentatively.

"We. No, your arm is good reason. However, I would like to know Talus' reason."

"He cut his finger before he climbed the outside wall." Anna offered.

Thatus glanced at her. "Then he climbed. I see."

As the basket touched the ground, Talus jumped out and started to speak. "So, Anna, did-" He stopped when he noticed Thatus, his grin fading to an embarrassed smile.

"My father." Talus saluted.

"Talus, son of Valnis. So, I hear you injured your finger to such an extent you could climb up but not down."

"No, my father. I can still climb." Talus stared at the ground and Anna felt sorry for him.

"Indeed. Talus, while I am aware that in certain circumstances as translator, it may be necessary to choose which laws to obey and which to break, I was not aware it was necessary to break the basket rules." So, there were rules against this.

"I understand, my father." Talus paused, conflict appearing in his eyes. "What about vows? A choice between your Adventurer vow and your Translator vow?"

Thatus studied Talus for a long second. "Laws or vows, you must do as you are being led to do. You didn't want a straight answer, did you?" Thatus added with a smile.

"The thought crossed my mind." Talus conceded. "How would I know if I made the right choice? How do I know what I am following? What if I thought I was, but were really following myself?"

Anna had never seen Talus so uncertain. She knew Talus wondered how his people would respond and something had been bothering him since they reached Belon. Was this it? Or just the surface?

"Calm down, Talus." Thatus looked a little amused. "You seem to have a knack for asking a thousand questions at once. What did you do to reach your decision?"

"I guess I made certain I had the facts, and I prayed and thought about it."

"At that time were you confident you had made the right decision?"

"Yes." Talus' voice was sure.

"And now, are you confident yours was the right decision?"

Talus glanced at Anna and nodded. "Yes."

"Well, then you wonder why we're having this conversation. But I understand you will have doubts, kings do not take it lightly when something or someone is chosen over them. I do not know what you did. Even if you told me, I could not tell you absolutely if it was in fact the right decision or not. But I can tell you that the value of an innocent life is more than the value of staying in favor with a king."

Anna watched thoughts flit across Talus' face. Finally, he breathed out slowly. "You're right, my father."

"One more thing though, Talus. How does the value of a basket ride compare with the value of respecting the rules given?"

Talus half grimaced. "I was wondering if we would return to that. A moment of exhilaration does not compare to a rule. But why shouldn't we ride?"

"Because you are not supposed to."

"May I ask for the reason?" Talus questioned, searching.

Thatus studied him for a second. "When your mentor was a Learner, I believe, a couple of Learners were playing on these. About ten cat's tails from the ground, the bottom fell off. He survived, but our people learned from it. These were only ever built for trading goods. I assumed your mentor would have told you."

Anna felt the blood drain from her cheeks. What if it had fallen off farther up? She shivered.

"I understand, my father. And no, probably because Jornus never caught me." Talus' voice was low.

"I see, well, the baskets are checked yearly, though that does not completely remove the risk. Well, I have kept you long enough. I expect you want to see the Belon lord before supper."

"Yes, but can I ask you something?"

Thatus laughed. "Well, I suppose I could handle another question."

"I thought you lived in Elnola. Are you... just out on a walk?" Talus questioned, appearing mildly confused.

"After you were over at my house, I realized how much I missed being with young people. So, I asked to be placed out here in Kayaina near the Learners. I guess one could say it's your fault I was here to catch you." Thatus smirked.

"Being caught is a means to learn." Talus replied smiling, though more serious than Anna expected. Talus saluted. "Farewell, my father, and thank you."

The elder returned the salute. "Farewell, Talus, Anna."

"Farewell." Anna curtsied rather hastily.

Definitely time to ask Talus to explain the manners of his country to her.

<<<<<<<<<<<<<<>>>>>>>>>>>>>

The sun had disappeared in the trees behind them by the time they reached Elnola. A pinkish gray wall opened in an arch before them. Talus grinned at Anna, though in the back of his mind a little voice asked what his father and the Belon lord would think. They would have the same view as Thatus, right?

"Here we are!" Talus watched Anna take a deep breath, a timid smile crossing her features.

"I do seem to like exploring new places." She looked up at the arch now above them. "And this city appears like it might be rather less dangerous than the last city I entered."

"Ketlin? Well-"

"That's a deep subject." Anna jumped in, fully grinning.

"-that's certainly true." Talus finished then suddenly realized what it sounded like he agreed with. "Er, about Ketlin, not the well."

Anna just grinned.

Talus gestured to the city beyond the arch. "Ready to explore, then?"

"Aye." Anna's grin faded a little, causing Talus to wonder why. As they made their way to the center, Talus noticed the slightest hesitation marred her footsteps.

Darkness had fallen by the time they reached the humble castle in the middle of Elnola. Would the Belon lord even see them at this hour?

"Maybe if we can get past the Secretary." Talus muttered.

"Hmm?" Anna glanced at him.

"Just talking to myself, it seems."

"Oh."

They started across the courtyard in silence.

"Will he accept me here?" Her voice broke part way through.

Talus stopped and studied her. She dropped her head, but not before he saw the tears in the edges of her eyes and the taunt features of her face.

"Of course, but if all else fails you're a near martyr, and that I'm sure will tip any balance."

"Certain?"

"Yes, but we can always find out."

"Right." Anna forced a small smile and marched towards the doors.

She was so brave. Talus smiled. And the moonlight played so perfectly in her hair.... Wait? What?! Talus shook his head and hurried after her.

The position of translator had its perks. The moment Talus said who he was, Urasus, the secretary, disappeared to find the Belon lord.

When he appeared, he wore a grave expression. Undoubtedly, he feared the worst. After the greetings were exchanged, the Belon lord asked. "Talus, my son, what brings you so soon from Alcasa?"

"Some things happened in Garia, my lord. You know of the deeds of King Hissin? Anna, here, was a near victim to his crimes. I would presume to ask that you would allow her to remain here in Belon until such a time as she may return to her people?"

"Why did you not take her to Alcasa?"

"King Eirin would not have permitted that, my lord."

The Belon lord's eyes met his, searching. Talus held them. He probably guessed a story was behind that.

"What happened?"

"I rescued Anna despite the king's orders against it." Talus winced; he should not have said it like that. He forced himself to keep the Belon lord's gaze, resisting the overwhelming urge to look away.

"Why?" The elder's face was impassive.

"I swore to protect the innocent." Talus responded, hoping he would accept that.

"You disobeyed the king?"

Talus swallowed but managed to reply firmly. "Yes, my lord. It was a difficult decision."

The Belon lord nodded slowly. "Will you return to Alcasa?"

"I will, my lord. My place is with King Eirin now. I hope to work out any tension." Talus added.

The Belon lord considered this statement for a long moment. "Tread carefully, young Talus. The peace between Belon and Alcasa is hundreds of years old, I do not want the Elerins to be the ones to break it. I would like a full report by the end of tomorrow to accompany Anna's legalization papers." Talus swallowed, at least it would not affect her legalization. What would he think of it? What if he didn't approve? The Belon lord turned to the secretary. "Urasus, could you find three pieces of paper?"

"Coming right up, my lord." He hurried behind his desk, rummaging through drawers. "Paper, now what did I do with it?" He muttered. "Not this one, or this one. Maybe this one? No. Perhaps- No. Ah, here we are." He placed three sheets on the desk, as well as an ink well and a feather. "My lord."

"Thank you, Urasus."

The Belon lord scribbled out three admission slips, pausing only to ask the name of Anna's father.

"Ah, there." He nodded to Anna. "One for you to carry, my daughter. One to keep where you are staying. And one for the records. Talus." Talus stepped over. "If you will sign here to vouch for her, you may be on your way."

170

Talus wrote "Talus, chilris Valnie" under the Belon lord's signature on each paper.

Urasus tucked each in an envelope and the Belon lord sealed and distributed them. Talus noticed he gave Anna a gentle smile as he handed hers to her. He stepped back.

"Theos go with you, my children."

"And with you, my father." Talus answered. Anna echoed him, though the salutation still came a little awkward.

<<<<<<<<<<<<<>>>>>>>>>>>>>

Anna followed Talus through countless streets lit only by stars. The Belon lord had accepted her, but what about Talus' family? What if they did not want some human around? How would she fit in? She did not seem to know anything valued in this culture. Languages. Weapons. She had not even read the Logos, except fragments hidden in her village.

Her stomach tightened. Could one get sick from fear of the unknown? Suddenly she remembered Theos. Why had it been easier to trust Him with her future when she was bound to that pole?

"Here we are, Anna!" Talus grinned at her, stopped in front of a gate.

Anna swallowed, nodding. She forced herself to smile back. A touch of concern softened Talus' features. "It will be fine, Anna." He persuaded her. "Kellia will love having an extra sister, and Mom will enjoy having another woman around and having a bit of help entertaining Marcus."

Was Marcus a baby? That would make this better. She liked babies.

"How old is Marcus?" She asked, curiously.

"About two and a half." Talus looked a little confused. "Kellia is nine. My parents are in their late sixties, um, you know Elerins retain health longer? I have a couple older siblings, but you probably won't meet them."

Anna nodded slowly, processing that over-informative answer.

"So, uh." Talus asked after a moment. "Ready to go inside? I, for one, would like some supper."

"Sure." Anna pushed confidence into her voice.

Talus grinned and unlatched the gate, letting it swing open. Inside the mini courtyard, a path wound through the grass up to the two-story house. She followed Talus as he hurried to the door. When they reached it, Talus glanced at her and gave her another smile before knocking.

After a moment the door swung inwards. A man stared at Talus a second before recovering himself. He exclaimed something in Elerin, which Anna took to be, "Talus, what in all Alvar are you doing here?!"

Talus grinned harder, undoubtedly, enjoying his dad's, she guessed, shock. But he answered in Garian. "We two travelers are looking for a meal and beds for the night."

171

The address in Garian gave the man pause for a moment. He gave her a keen look, but simply replied. "Of course, of course. Come in. Who is your friend, Talus?"

"This is Anna of Garia. Anna, this is my father, Valnis, son of Patris."

Valnis gave her a smile. "Welcome Anna, I hope you are none the worse for hanging out with this serious son of mine?"

Anna felt some of the tension in her stomach relax. As he spoke, she got an idea. She glanced noticeably at her broken arm then at Talus.

Talus' eyes widened. "I didn't- I didn't do that on purpose."

Valnis furrowed his brow. "You broke her arm?"

Talus reddened.

"Not exactly- It just- sort of happened. We were in a storm at sea and were washed against the cliffs. I threw her at the top of the cliffs. Somewhere along the way, her arm broke." Talus spread his hands, shrugging.

Anna decided to help him out. "I was unconscious after hitting the cliffs. He might have saved my life... a second time."

"So, supper...." Talus interjected.

Valnis rubbed his chin. "Talus, I thought you knew supper is served at six bells. The time is well past nine bells."

Talus made a sad puppy face. What? No supper? Anna thought. Her stomach growled. Now she reddened. She had not been hungry until Talus mentioned it. At least she had not really thought so.

Valnis gave her an amused smile and added to Talus. "But I am sure your mom will find something."

Talus took a step forward, intent on his stomach. "May we find out?"

Valnis grinned and led them deep into the house. The living-room held two couches like the nobles had in Ketlin as well as a chair, a rocking chair, some stands and two coffee tables. A female Elerin, presumably Talus' mother, occupied the rocker. As they entered, Anna watched her eyes widen. She leapt to her feet. Pure joy filled her face. When she reached him, Talus embraced his mother. Homesickness overwhelmed Anna. She looked away, fighting to shove the tears back.

"Anna," Talus said. She turned her head, internally wincing at the concern she saw in his eyes. "This is my mother, Corra, daughter of Elidus. Mom, this is Anna of Garia."

Corra smiled softly and saluted.

"A pleasure to meet you. Are you hungry?"

Anna shrugged. "Well, yes. We never had supper so...."

"Well, well, we can't have you going hungry. I'll go to the kitchen and make something." She mothered.

"May I help you?" Anna asked. She didn't want to be stuck in this room to be reminded of her family. Besides, if she was to stay here, she might as well start helping now.

Corra studied her for a moment. Anna wondered if her eyes showed any trace of the tears hidden there.

"If you wish, dear. These men will probably find some disgusting topic to discuss anyway."

Talus and Valnis put on identical *What? Us?* expressions. Anna let herself laugh with Corra and it made the room seem a little less gray.

Chapter 23 Uncertainty

Talus grinned as he watched his father plop down on a couch and rest his feet on the coffee table.

"Don't let Mom catch you."

Valnis grinned good naturedly. "Oh, she doesn't mind."

Talus raised his eyebrows in disbelief.

A shout of "Talus!" erupted from the stairwell across the room. Kellia shot across the room, hurling herself at him.

Talus had no time to prepare. They crashed to the wooden floor in a heap. Talus broke the fall with one arm. He stared up at the enthusiastic Kellia in her nightgown. "How did you know I was here?"

She smiled happily. "I heard voices, so I investigated."

"Why... one would think you're an Elerin, they are nauseatingly curious."

Kellia's face became the perfect picture of horror. "What?! An Elerin? How could you compare me to one of that dreaded race?"

Talus reached up to tickle her, but she jumped back and retreated to a safe distance. Talus did not move for a second, hoping to lure her into a sense of ease. She took a step forward. "Are-" Talus leapt to his feet and snatched at her, but he only found wind. He chased after her.

She squealed. "You'll never catch me!"

"I will too!" Talus called, smirking.

"Won't!" Kellia scrambled across a couch and made an unexpected full turn around the rocker. Talus slid, going too fast to turn. The first second possible he reversed, racing after the child in her nightgown.

He cornered her next to the couch their father watched from. Almost. He dove in. And missed. Kellia raced in between the coffee table and couch, darting under her father's legs. Talus ran and jumped the middle of the coffee table, landing in front of her just as she stood. He scooped her up and settled on the couch. She squirmed and wriggled. How was he going to hold on to her? He hugged her tighter, cutting off as much movement as possible. But not enough to risk freeing a hand to tickle her.

"As much as I dislike interrupting your fun," Their father broke in, "a certain young lady is supposed to be in bed."

Talus let Kellia sit up. She hung her head. "Sorry, Daddy."

"I forgive you, daughter. Now, off you go; you can see your brother in the morning."

"Okay. Goodnight, Daddy, Talus." She climbed off Talus. She ran to the stairwell. She looked back and gave a wave, before disappearing upstairs.

"When did you take to jumping coffee tables?" His father grinned at him.

Talus shrugged self-consciously. "Some five minutes ago."

"Don't let your mom catch you." Valnis mimicked.

Talus barely restrained from rolling his eyes.

"So, what have you been up to?" His father asked.

The question clanged in Talus' head. His father would be the first person he would tell the full story. Would he approve? What if he didn't? Would he agree like Thatus that the value of life surpassed the value of obeying the king? What if Anna ought to have been saved some other way? A way that was obvious to all but him?

Talus swallowed and started at the beginning with lighter events. He enjoyed storytelling and he tried to let it calm him. And it did, to some extent. But the question of what his father would think still lurked.

Talus slowed as he approached his choice. He believed it was the right thing, yes? Yes. He pushed on. He forced his original confidence into the words he had spoken to the clouded darkness more than three weeks ago.

Silence echoed in the room after he finished the words. Talus drew a slow breath and looked at his father. Valnis wore a thoughtful expression.

"So you rescued Anna despite King Eirin's orders against it?"

Talus nodded, his voice frozen.

"Well, my son," Valnis smiled. "I think it is safe to say few people have considered their vows as intensely as you have."

"So, you agree I did the right thing?" Talus asked.

Valnis paused before speaking. "Rarely would I condone disobeying a superior, but I believe you were right in this case, Talus."

"The Belon lord wants a report in the morning." Talus commented.

"Talus." Valnis met his eyes. "You are a man now; you can no longer hide behind what others think of you. Listen to truth in others and learn from it, but don't shape your image of yourself from others' opinions of one deed. Pursue truth, even if it's difficult. And you're about to return to King Eirin and it is possible he will not agree with you."

175

Talus nodded. He was pretty sure he knew most of that, but the reminder was always good. And he had been wondering what others would think a lot lately. "Is it wrong to care what others think?"

Valnis shook his head, almost smiling. "No and yes. No, because of a completely different matter called reputation. Yes, because it can make you insecure."

Talus paused and asked slowly. "Do you think I am insecure?"

Valnis shook his head. "I think you are in danger of the possibility. But no, after all, you disobeyed a king to save the life of a peasant girl. But you will face times that will test you to your limits. Be strong and when you can't, lean on the One who is."

Talus saluted, wondering what his father thought he would encounter. "I will remember your words."

"Now." His father put his arms on his knees in eager expectation. "I have seen Ketlin. How did you escape?"

Anna opened her eyes. Sunlight streamed in through the window of the room Corra had found for her. The bed was warm and part of her was reluctant to leave it. But the other side was still curious. After a couple lazy seconds, the curious side won. She sat up and hopped out of bed. She frowned at the chair she had left her clothes on the night before. Where were they? She couldn't exactly go downstairs in a nightgown.

She turned, surveying the room. Wait, clothes sat on the desk. She walked over to it. A deep blue dyed knee-length dress and some pants very similar to the ones she had borrowed from Talus. No shoes or socks, of course. Not that she had worn them anywhere except in Ketlin.

She dressed and hurried downstairs, not entirely sure when breakfast was. No one was in the living-room. As she approached the door to the kitchen, she could make out singing. The words were foreign, but the melody was sweet and comforting. It felt like the sound of soaring gently, like a bird.

As she reached the doorway, a young voice interrupted the song. Corra replied to the child, who, now that she could see into the kitchen, she guessed was Marcus.

The little boy picked up his spoon and continued eating his oatmeal. Corra spotted her from a counter across the room. She smiled. "Anna, there you are. Talus is in his room working on an official report of what you are doing here." She paused. "Would you like some breakfast? I am sure my youngest, Marcus, would enjoy your company."

Marcus, himself, was staring at her, sucking on the end of his spoon. Anna smiled and made a face at him, rewarded with a giggle. Looking back to Corra, she answered. "Sure, what's for breakfast?"

"Blueberry and bacon oatmeal."

Anna nodded, intrigued by the different combination. "Sounds good."

She ate and played with Marcus. She had babysat for a couple of the younger wives in the village sometimes. Being with a little child again resurfaced those memories. Determined not to let every little thing make her sad, she distracted herself by making Marcus laugh. It took them both a long time to finish eating.

After they did, Anna covered her face with her hands. She opened them slowly. "Peek-a-boo!" Marcus giggled, but he stopped abruptly when she closed her hands. She opened them again and he laughed once more.

"Looks like you're having fun."

Anna looked up. Talus was standing on the other side of the table. Anna smiled, though wondering slightly how he had gotten that close without her noticing. "We might be."

"Just might? Hmm, that's good. So, I was wondering if you would like to stay here with Mom and Marcus or go explore the city a bit?"

It would be cool to see the city in daylight. She stood up. "Sure." She skirted the table to Talus, but paused, waving at Marcus. "See you later."

Marcus stuck out his lower lip and stared at her with big puppy eyes. Anna's heart constricted. "It's all right, I'll come back."

He stared at her, looking like he might cry.

"Go on, Anna." Corra spoke, amused, from where she was doing dishes. "Don't let him work any magic. Have a good time, you two. Shall I expect you back for lunch?"

Talus shook his head. "Probably not. We'll grab something at the market."

Must be a big city, Anna mused. She smiled at Corra before following Talus out the door. She more or less forced herself not to glance at Marcus, not wanting to see his sad face again.

"Dangerous thing having my brother around. He's stealing your heart." Talus teased, slowing to let her come up beside him.

Anna shrugged. "I like little children. Did you finish your report?"

"Yep. At some point today we'll drop it off. Hopefully it sounds official. I haven't even read anything official, least not in Elerin, since my Government and Literature classes when I was eleven." Talus sounded nonchalant, but Anna could tell it was a mask.

Anna nodded anyway. Then, following a random impulse, straightened and made the most ridiculous serious face possible. She refined her voice. "I am afraid I would not know, good sir. 'Tis not my area of expertise."

Anna caught a wisp of a grin that crossed Talus' face before it returned to perfectly calm. "No? We are a fine pair, dear lady."

177

Anna could not think of a reply, so she gave a serene nod. A couple seconds of silence followed, before they both burst out laughing. Conversation resumed for a few minutes as they left the house and crossed the yard. As they approached the gate Talus paused and Anna waited, getting the feeling Talus wanted to say something more serious. After he latched the gate again, he asked. "Anna, how... comfortable are you with my family?"

Horror at the implication tightened her stomach. "They...They are nice. Why? You're not leaving already?"

"What? No. I won't just drop you and run. For one thing, I want to see you comfortable at home and in Elerin culture before I leave."

Anna smiled, although weakly. "Thanks. When do you want to leave?"

"King Eirin was planting on visiting Vestin on the way to Aubin Castle. He should arrive eight days from now. So I would like to leave in five days to get there when he does."

"Oh." Five days? She had to figure out Elerin culture in five days. She drew a deep breath. Five days was a long time, and she only really needed to know the basics. After Talus left, his family would help her anyway, right? Besides, she had been dropped into several new situations. First Ketlin, though she had Mara, Cat, and Violet for that. Then the first few days with Talus. Now five whole days was a luxury, right?

That reminded her of something Talus kept saying. She assumed he was joking, but.... "King Eirin won't actually kill you, will he?"

"What?" Talus looked up, startled. "Um, he's not supposed to by the terms of the treaty. I don't think he would anyway."

"Okay." Anna answered. "Just wanted to make sure."

<<<<<<<<<<<<<>>>>>>>>>>>>

Four days later, Anna followed Talus up the last of the stairs onto the wall that surrounded Elnola. Talus, of course, thought stairs were a waste of time and space, but he had admitted they were nice for her.

Talus had brought her here on their first full day in the city to see the sunset. It had been stunning. The wall was high enough they could see forever out across Hangnol Isle. They had come back each of the following nights. This would be the last. Talus was leaving tomorrow.

"Did you hear back from the Belon lord yet?" Anna asked a few moments later as they leaned against the parapet.

"No." Talus shook his head. "At the moment, I'm going to take no news as good news."

He paused, but then said nothing, staring out into the setting sun. It was not much of a sunset, it was too clouded over. Actually, it would probably rain.

178

"Anna, I found a Garian copy of the Logos as promised. It's back at home. But I, uh, wanted to give you something else."

She was definitely excited, but her curiosity was just as strong. "Thank you. Oh? What is it?"

Talus handed her a dagger. It had lilies dyed into the leather sheath.

"Since lilies are your favorite and, um, so you can, well, not have any problem with any carrots you run into." He finished quickly and looked away.

He didn't fool her.

"Thank you, Talus." Almost tentatively, she put her hand on the wall next to his hand. She let them touch. He looked back suddenly. She started to pull her hand away, uncertain. Talus caught it and they stared at each other.

The sun set in the west, and it started to rain. A sort of sad, embarrassed half-smile came to Talus' face. "Should we go home?"

Anna nodded; her voice lost.

Another long minute passed before Talus released her hand and headed for the stairs.

The next morning, Anna followed Talus into the yard after he had said goodbye to his family. The last five days had gone by too quickly. Her heart felt like it was tearing, but she was determined not to cry. At least not until after he was gone. Gone. She had not realized how much she was going to miss him until now. They had spent so much time together, and she discovered last night undeniably that she, well, it did not matter now. He was leaving.

He turned and looked at her. Was he expecting her to say something? Struggling desperately to keep her voice calm, the first thing that came to mind tumbled out.

"Why do you have to leave?" Her voice broke and she looked away.

"Anna." Talus said gently.

She turned back to him.

"Are you not ready for me to go?"

"No, you can go." Why did she have to be this weak?

"Anna, I have to go back to King Eirin because I swore a vow to serve him. To not return would make me a liar. For a little while, I believed it was my duty to obey my vow to protect the innocent. Now, you are safe, and I must return. But I will miss you." She could see the pain in his face as he struggled to be strong for her.

"Why? Why must you? No one keeps their vows!" The torrent freed itself. "Not of knighthood, not of marriage, at least not in Garia."

179

"Anna, some people do not care if they make their word a lie. But we are called to speak only the truth. I must honor Theos and keep my vow. Farewell, Anna, 'til we meet again."

Talus turned away abruptly with a half wave, walking towards the gate. Anna watched him disappear through the gate, the tears streaming down her face."

AN END

BUT NOT THE END

Appendix 1- Races Profiles

Elerins

<u>Homelands</u>
Elerins primarily live in Belon Swamp, though some also live in Carna.
<u>Characteristics</u>
Elerins are typically calm, easily amused, loyal, faithful, hardworking, and rarely angry. They can climb almost anything and see in the dark. Elerins are proud to be the second-best warriors in Alvar. Life expectancy is about 120-130 years.
<u>Appearance</u>
Elerin males grow between 5ft and 5ft 8in, while females average between 4ft 6in and 5ft 2in. Their skin is a dark tan. Their hair ranges from black to a deep brown or reddish. Males normally wear it short, although some, mainly those serving as foreign translators, will grow it out to shoulder length. Females often like their hair quite long typically mid-back at shortest. As for eyes, Elerins have a range of unique blues, purples, greens, and occasionally reds. Though thinly built, Elerins are strong and agile. The defining trait that separates them from humans is their fingernails and toenails which are harder and stronger, allowing for the climbing their lifestyle often demands. Clothes are made from the skin of the Tongath Alligator's belly and sides. Males wear knee-length pants with a shirt and jerkin, females dress similarly only exchanging the shirt for a knee-length dress.
<u>Children</u>
Elerin babies are born between three and seven pounds, often as twins or even triplets. Children are rambunctious and curious, traits they may temper with adulthood but rarely lose. Elerins often have several children.

Fumins

<u>Homelands</u>

Fumins inhabit Colmea, but some also have made Carna their home.

<u>Characteristics</u>

Fumins are grave, quiet, loyal, rule-makers, fair, and just. It is rare to meet a Fumin who is outwardly cheerful. However, Fumins enjoy mind-games. They also love long walks, though their work ethic does not allow for many of these. They are the best smiths in Alvar. Despite this they use only a Sharprod, a three-and-a-half-foot iron rod with a spearhead. They use it both has a spear and javelin. Life expectancy is 40-50 years.

<u>Appearance</u>

Fumins grow to be between 4 to 4 foot 6 inches. Fumins are covered in white or light gray fur everywhere except the palm of their hands, front and sides of their fingers, and the sole of their feet. Females have lighter fur than males. Their eyes are variations of cyan, light blue, violet, and black. Males wear sleeveless bearskin robes, while females wear sleeveless bearskin dresses. Males wear a cord around their waist, while females wear a sash; both articles of clothing match the wearer's eye color. At first glance most people assume that Fumins do not have ears. This is false, they have ears just very small ones buried in fur. However, it should be noted that their hearing is sharper than a cat's. It would not do to scream next to one.

<u>Children</u>

Babies are born around 4 to 6 pounds. They mature fast, fully an adult by 12 years of age. They will then marry before sixteen. Boys are apprenticed to a master in the guild of their choice at age eight. Children are quiet and respectful, reflecting their parents' solemness.

Kazofs

Homelands

Kazofs live in Darqin Forest and stay there. No one remembers if any have ever moved, none certainly do anymore.

Characteristics

Kazofs are gentle, quiet-spoken, kind, and hospitable to all people and creatures. However, because of recent events, they are suspicious of the other races. They love the Darqin animals and are the only race not terrified of the creatures. They are even said to be able to speak to the creatures.

Appearance

Kazofs are ten to twelve feet tall with a typically thinner build. They have light brown skin with black or dark red hair. Their eyes are deep, like a bottomless ocean, and come in shades of purples, blues, or greens. Men wear a long sleeveless garment over a wool ankle-length robe. Women often wear a sort of poncho over a wool dress. Kazofs wear soft boots on their feet. Mature Kazofs carry a walking stick that doubles as a quarter-staff.

Children

Kazof babies are born about 9 to 11 pounds. Young Kazofs are considered children until 20 and youth until 28. On a Kazof's 28th birthday they leave home and move to their own home. However, they typically will not marry until 60-100 years of age.

Talrins

Talrins live in and by the Stonecliff Range. At one point they inhabited the main portion of Garia, but since their freedom, they have remained to themselves for the most part.

Characteristics
Talrins are the greatest stone-builders in all of Alvar. They tend to be diplomatic, but if cornered will rely on brute strength or natural clubs. They are confident in regard to individual ability. Talrins' active lives are sustained by periods of hibernation. As children they have four periods of seven years divided by a year of sleep. Following this are two period of thirty years, after each period they sleep for seven years. They are now in old age and go into hibernation more and more often until they die.

Appearance
Talrins have gray skin. Their hair changes from blonde in their childhood to red in their first adult period to green in their second to blue gray in old age. Their eyes are large balls of hazel gray holding flecks of color reflecting the hair of their phase. Talrins wear fur clothes and may be seen in Tongath jackets from time to time.

Children
Children are born to Talrins in their second adult phase, babies weighing about 12 pounds. In their first seven years, they are left to play and make friends. The next seven years they are taught manners, language, history, and culture of Garia. The rest of their childhood is spend learning the art of stonework.

Shadowmen

(All known facts come from the Elerins, who are the only ones with contact to these strange people.)

Homelands

The Shadowmen live in Tritha.

Characteristics

Shadowmen are the best at stealth in all Alvar. Most shun other races. Those living on the borders of Alcasa and Carna tend to pillage the villages and even castles nearby. They live in tribes; thus they also fight among themselves. They seem to live 80-90 years, if they are not killed in battle. They are usually between 5-6 feet tall. Their weapons consist of bows and spears. Some believe they can disappear at will.

Appearance

Their skin is deep tan, and their hair is a dark brown. Their eye color is dark purple, dark blue, or brown. They dress in the fur of the giant black squirrel and of the deer. Men wear a long shirt and pants. They wear nothing on their feet save dirt. Women are thought to dress the same. Men have a quiver with arrows over their back and a belt with a stone or iron knife. (Only tribes that trade with the Elerins, or raid a tribe that does, has iron.)

Children

It is thought they have 2-6 children. Boys, at least, are trained by their fathers.

Weets

<u>Homelands</u>
Weets live in Saxa.

<u>Characteristics</u>
Weets are cheery and always giggling. They almost always seem childish. They are notorious for tricks of all kinds, which is their preferred method of defense. Weets eat a dried seaweed that they make bread from. They also enjoy a sort of underwater grown fruit like a strawberry but shaped as an apple and with skin like an orange. They typically live about 20 years.

<u>Appearance</u>
Weets grow to about three to three and a half feet. They have green backs and white/yellow stomachs. They wear only a patch of cloth around their midsection. Despite reminding one of frogs, their faces are more humanish, though they have two long gills running down the back of their neck.

<u>Children</u>
Children are born quite small. They receive little education, preferring games. They are adults by 8, not that most races think Weets ever grow up.

Appendix 2- Maps

ALVAR

ALCASA

N

Great
Broken
Sea

Garia

Darqin
Forest

Hithlin Pass

Norfort

50 miles

Dunlong

Calmford

Vestin

Council Rock

Seaworth

Selthon River

Aubin

Anchor Cove

Emworth

Sea of
Kaylona

Wylong

Duoaquae

Scarlet River

Belon

Rock Stream

Hartford

Aquin

Pugnin

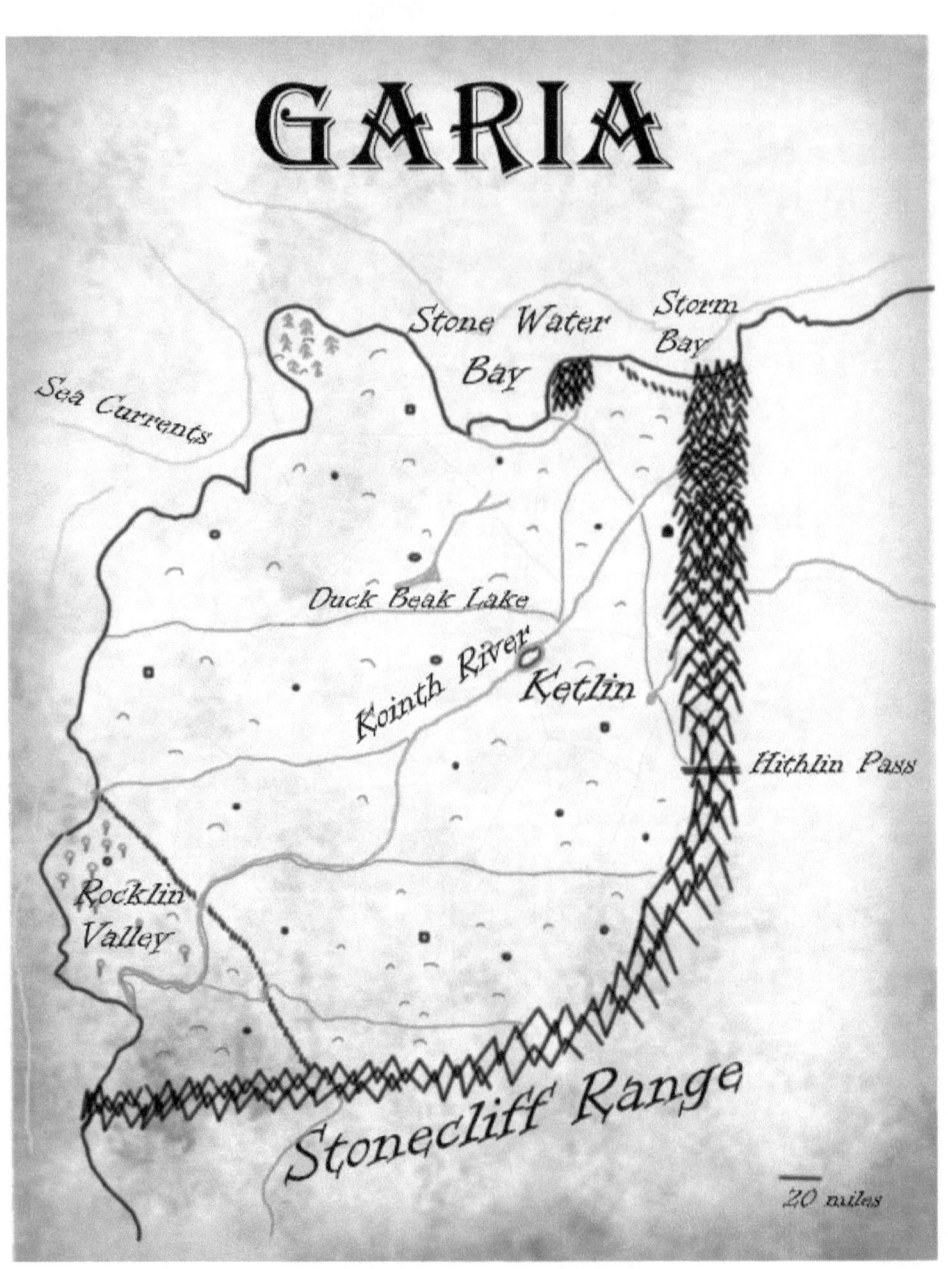

GARIA

Stone Water Bay

Storm Bay

Sea Currents

Duck Beak Lake

Kointh River

Ketlin

Hithlin Pass

Rocklin Valley

Stonecliff Range

20 miles

HANGNOL ISLE

Hangnolin Wall

Jornus' Cabin

Kayaina

Elnola

Catha Forest

Hanglen Meadows

Catha River

Hangna River

Pana River

Belon Swamp

10 miles

Market
Belon Castle
3rd Judge
2nd Judge
1st Judge

Author Bio

 M. M. Liles wrote her first short story around age eight and began *A Choice of Vows,* her first novel, around fifteen. She is now married to a loving husband and attending Cornerstone University. Megan enjoys reading, writing (obviously), painting, hiking, and solving problems. She loves cats, as might be noticed at points in her writing, but are more so visibly in the worldbuilding papers not seen by most readers yet. To find more of her writing or to receive updates on upcoming books check her website at meganmliles.wordpress.com.

Picture credit: Angelo Liles

Acknowledgements

Writing and publishing this book did not happen in a little bubble with just me, so I would like to thank a few people.

To my parents for everything they have done to get me here.

To my husband for the crazy amount of encouragement and support he has given me.

To my brother for all the fun and imagination we developed together and for his enthusiasm to read each chapter as soon as possible.

To my other first readers for their encouragement and for putting up with the quantity of errors.

To my editor for solving many of those errors

And to the One who created the greatest story and gives inspiration and perseverance.